YANKEE JUSTICE

Captain Belton turned his attention to the prisoner. He studied the young man intently. "Another belligerent Rebel who doesn't know he's been whipped," he remarked. "What unit did you serve with, Reb?"

Matt, who had been studying the captain just as closely, hesitated a moment before replying, "Twenty-second Virginia Cavalry."

"Twenty-second, eh? I guess they didn't teach you to stand up in the presence of an officer."

"Not a Yankee officer, I reckon they didn't," Matt replied.

A wry smile creased the captain's face. "Still got a few burrs, ain't you? Well, let me tell you what happens to smart young men like yourself who murder an officer of the U.S. Army. We're gonna take you back to Lexington in chains, so all the other Rebs can see you. Then we're gonna hold a trial, so that everybody knows we stand for justice. Then we're gonna hang you in the square to teach the rest of your kind a lesson."

There was no doubt in Matt's mind that a trial would be no more than a formality and the prelude to a hanging. The question before him was when to escape, for he knew he would rather a bullet in the back than a rope around the neck.

OUTLAW

Charles G. West

BERKLEY
New York

BERKLEY
An imprint of Penguin Random House LLC
penguinrandomhouse.com

Copyright © 2006 by Charles G. West
Excerpt from *The Hostile Trail* copyright © 2006 by Charles G. West
Penguin Random House supports copyright. Copyright fuels creativity, encourages
diverse voices, promotes free speech, and creates a vibrant culture. Thank you for buying
an authorized edition of this book and for complying with copyright laws by not
reproducing, scanning, or distributing any part of it in any form without permission.
You are supporting writers and allowing Penguin Random House to continue to
publish books for every reader.

BERKLEY and the BERKLEY & B colophon are registered trademarks of
Penguin Random House LLC.

ISBN: 9780593441497

Signet mass-market edition / May 2006
Berkley mass-market edition / November 2022

Printed in the United States of America
1   3   5   7   9   10   8   6   4   2

For Ronda

Chapter 1

Making his way silently up through the dark forest that covered the east slope of the ridge, a Confederate sniper stopped and dropped to one knee to listen to the sounds of the night. Above him a Union picket passed in the darkness, following the narrow path that circled the crest of the hill. He had spotted the Union soldier when still some twenty yards away from where he presently knelt, and now he paused to allow time for the unsuspecting sentry to reverse his post. On the neighboring ridge, an owl hooted softly in the darkness. Several yards to his right there was a gentle rustle of leaves as a rodent scurried to seek a hiding place, aware that he might be prominent on the owl's menu. Matt paid the rodent no attention. He was accustomed to the night sounds of the forest, and he had his own neck to worry about.

Come on, dammit, I ain't got all night, he silently urged the sentry, impatient to make his way across the ridge. Unaware of the Confederate marksman less than a few yards directly below him, the Union soldier paused to light his pipe. A dense cloud of tobacco smoke spiraled around the man's head as he pulled vigorously on his pipe, tamped the load down, and relit it. Satisfied that it was lit to stay, he began his tour again, completely unaware of the inviting mark he presented. It was this Yankee's good fortune that he was not this night's primary target. Matt had been sent to seek a more specific target. He had been told only that part of Sheridan's troops, under General George Crook, were encamped along the bluffs overlooking Cedar Creek. His orders were to infiltrate the Union picket lines, and if possible, to take out any officers he could get in his sights. It would be unlikely that he would be able to get close enough for a shot at Crook himself, but the higher the rank, the more demoralizing it would be for the Union soldiers.

While he waited for the picket to move on, Matt glanced around him in the darkness to make sure he was still undiscovered. He unconsciously reached up to stroke a small St. Christopher's medal that hung on a silver chain around his neck, a gift from his mother. His brother wore one just like it. Not really sure who St. Christopher was, both boys considered the medals to be good luck charms.

Matt Slaughter had spent a good portion of his young life in the hills and forests of the Shenandoah Valley, hunting every wild critter that dwelt there. He felt at home in the forest, alone, away from the confusion of his cavalry unit. His commanding officer, Captain Miles Francis, had recognized the wildness in the young volunteer from the central valley and was not at all surprised that the quiet young man proved to be the best marksman in Company K. Consequently, Francis was quick to use Matt's woodland skills to the regiment's advantage.

Thoughts of his service since joining the 22nd Virginia Cavalry flashed through Matt's mind as he readied himself to continue his climb up the slope. It had seemed a long time since the summer of 1863 and the formation of the 22nd. He had participated in most of the fighting in the Shenandoah Valley from the time his unit was thrown into the Third Battle of Winchester a little over a year before. It was a glorious effort, and a decisive victory for the South. But things had not gone well for the Confederate Army in the Shenandoah Valley since, for the Union troops had regrouped and come back with a vengeance. Now his regiment was engaged in little more than harassing attacks against an overpowering Union force—fighting and retreating—with the sickening knowledge that the valley was no longer theirs.

Slowly rising to his feet again, Matt paused to look around once more, the careful precaution of a man who had no one to rely on but himself. It was late October. The leaves were already changing color on the hardwoods, but in the gray predawn light, they appeared cold and lifeless. He thought of his role in this fight: marksman, sharpshooter, sniper. By any name, the term that lodged in his mind was *assassin*. At first, he looked upon his assignments as no more than soldiering. Like any other soldier in the line, he was doing his duty as ordered. But after a while, it soured on him. In an infantry or cavalry charge, an individual was simply part of one army against another army. But when *he* killed, it was a personal thing, and the thought was beginning to weigh heavily on his conscience. In his mind, there was nothing heroic about slipping silently through the forest to wait in ambush, to kill, and then to slip away again. He no longer took pride in being the best shot in the regiment. In fact, many times he felt no better than a lowdown bushwhacker. *Best get my mind back on my business,* he reprimanded himself, *before I get a Yankee miniball in my behind.*

He paused only briefly to glance in both directions when he crossed over the path the picket paced. Then he disappeared into the trees that covered the crown of the hill. Making his way down the other side, he continued until the fires of the Union camp were in sight on the bluffs above the creek. Slinging his rifle so he could free both hands to help scale the steep bluffs, he climbed up to a point high enough to be able to see into the camp. Edging a little closer, he positioned himself to look over the encampment, making note of the sentries posted about the perimeter. Satisfied that he had a clear view of the officers' tents, he next determined his route of escape, for he would not be able to retreat the way he had come. His primary means of escape, his horse, was tied to a gum tree a quarter of a mile beyond the other side of the ridge he had just crossed. After giving it a couple minutes' thought, he decided his best route would be to follow the creek to a point where the bluffs were steepest. From there, he could scramble down and cross over. Carrying nothing more than his rifle and ammunition, he was confident that he could outrun anyone giving chase. With that decision made, he settled himself in a thicket to wait for a target.

In no particular hurry now—for it would be at least an hour before daylight—he readied his weapon. One of only two issued to his company, the long, British-made Whitworth was especially suited for his purpose. With its tubular telescopic sight mounted on a hexagonal barrel, he could hit a target up to eighteen hundred yards away. And that was six or seven hundred yards more range than the Enfields carried by most of the infantry companies attached to the regiment. The Whitworth had to be loaded down the muzzle, which was not ideal in a skirmish. But for accuracy, there was no better weapon.

Now came the part he hated—*waiting*—for there was too much time to think over what he was about to do. If the opportunity presented itself, and it usually did, somebody's wife was about to become a widow. What seemed unfair about it was the simple fact that his victim would not be prepared to die. There would be no battle raging, no suicidal charge upon an enemy position, no anticipation of the possibility of the fatal shot. *Assassin.* The word kept coming back to haunt him. He hated it. It was a word without honor.

The only person with whom he had discussed the issue was Lieutenant Gunter. Gunter was a favorite among the men of K Company. A giant of a man, the jovial second lieutenant always seemed to have a word of encouragement for everyone. He had sensed the basic decency in the young soldier from Rockbridge County, and often took time to talk with Matt about his job. It was Gunter who advised Matt to think not of his targets as individuals, but to picture them only as faceless bluecoats. If further encouragement was needed, the lieutenant suggested thinking of the beautiful Shenandoah Valley, now laid waste by Sheridan's invading troops. Matt had tried to think of these things, but the word that lingered most in his mind was *assassin*.

First light finally began its gentle intrusion upon the darkened forest, creeping almost imperceptibly until the individual trees began to take shape in the morning mist. A light fog lay across the creek bottom, but was not dense enough to obscure the tents above the creek. Captain Francis had ordered him to hold his fire until first light, which should be around five o'clock. The captain would not elaborate, but Matt figured that the company was to be involved in an early morning assault upon General Crook's division. It shouldn't be long now. A thought of his brother, Owen, flashed through his mind then.

About twelve miles back down the Valley Pike, his brother was most likely stirring from his blanket. Owen always woke before first light, a habit ingrained from long years working a farm. Unlike Matt, Owen was a family man. Older by two years, he had volunteered to fight for the sole reason that the valley was his home, and he felt a strong sense of duty to defend it and his family from the Union invaders. *Poor Owen,* Matt thought, *he's got no business in this fight. He should be home with Abby and his two sons.* Both brothers thought the war would never come to the Shenandoah, but come it had, like a deadly plague of locusts, leaving the very ground gutted in its wake. Only ten days before, at Tom's Brook, Matt's unit had fought over ground less than thirty miles from his little parcel of land near the river before being forced to retreat back to Woodstock. They had been whipped badly on that day. The memory of it still smarted. The Yankees chased them twenty miles up the Valley Pike and then eight miles up the Back Road. The inglorious retreat came to be known as the Woodstock Races. He wondered now if his cabin and Owen's house had been spared when the Union troops swept through. There had been no opportunity to find out.

Suddenly his senses were brought back to the present, for the Union camp came to life as soldiers crawled out of tents and blankets. Soon fires were reborn all along the bluffs, and the sounds of a waking army filtered through the hardwoods. Matt sat motionless as a Union sergeant walked out among the trees, approaching to within ten yards of him before stopping to empty his bladder. With no thought of panic, Matt watched until the soldier finished and returned to the camp. Then he turned his attention back to concentrate on the officers' tents. In a few minutes time, a soldier appeared at the flap of the closest tent carrying a cup of coffee. *Time to go to work,* Matt told himself, forcing himself to ignore the feeling of reluctance that always came. Rising to one knee he brought his rifle up and rested the barrel in the fork of a young dogwood. Sighting through the long telescopic sight, he trained the weapon on the tent flap. Moments passed. Then a gray-whiskered face appeared and stepped outside to accept the coffee. He wore no tunic, so his rank could not be determined. But since he was the one who was served coffee, Matt guessed that he was in command.

Matt took careful aim. His intent was always to make the shot count, to kill his target as quickly as possible with minimal suffering. At a range of one hundred yards, he was confident enough to take a head shot, so he trained his sights slightly above the gray whiskers. He waited a few moments to allow his victim a sip or two of hot coffee before squeezing the trigger. The face in the telescopic sight disappeared with the sharp report of the Whitworth rifle. With no hesitation, but without unnecessary haste, Matt reloaded his weapon, ramming home another bolt, as the odd-shaped bullets were called. Although the sudden shot had caused pandemonium in the Union camp, with soldiers running for cover, Matt was not yet concerned with escape. He felt reasonably sure that his muzzle blast had not been seen, especially with the fog rising from the creek. His rifle loaded, he turned to sight on the second tent. As he expected, an officer emerged from the tent, a pistol in his hand. He took one step toward his fallen commander before collapsing on the ground, shot through the heart.

There it was, that little sick feeling Matt always experienced when he assassinated an unsuspecting victim. It made no difference that the two officers were the enemy, and would send troops forward to kill him and his comrades. In his mind, it was outright murder. As Lieutenant Gunter advised, he tried to think of the officers as barbarians, laying waste to the Shenandoah.

His job done, Matt wasted little time withdrawing from the thicket that had shielded him. There were probably two or three more officers in the camp, but he wasn't willing to risk another shot. His assignment had been to demoralize the enemy by killing the commanding officers. At this point in the war, it seemed a pointless task, but he had done it one more time, and had accepted it as his duty.

Making his way along the creek at a steady trot, he listened to the excited sounds behind him, alert to any that might indicate pursuit. He knew from experience that at first the soldiers would be seeking cover in anticipation of an attack upon their position. Not until they realized that there was no Confederate force about to descend upon them would they mount a hunting party to go after the sniper. By that time, he planned to be long gone.

He had barely crossed over to the other side of the creek when he heard the opening barrage of the battle behind him. Confused, he immediately turned and worked his way back along the bank to see for himself. "Damn!" he uttered as he spotted a wave of Confederate infantry sweeping along the bluffs, flanking the Union position. *They must have marched all night to get here,* he thought. This was what Captain Francis had hinted at the day before. From his vantage point on the creek bank, Matt could see that the Confederate attack was successful, for Crook's soldiers were already falling back in retreat. *God,* he thought, *we damn sure need a victory after Tom's Brook.*

Giving no thought toward joining in the Rebel assault, he continued to watch until the Confederate infantry succeeded in driving the Union soldiers back toward Middletown. His reasoning was simple: he was apt to get shot by one of his own comrades if he came running out of the woods to join them. He elected to withdraw and go back to retrieve his horse. He had done enough killing for one day.

When he found his company later in the morning, he was greeted by several of his friends. Still basking in the heady wine of victory, they offered good-natured derision. "Well, lookee who decided to show up," a lanky farm boy from Lexington called out.

"Damn, Slaughter," another asked, "where the hell were you? You missed a helluva party."

Matt just smiled in reply. He looked around him at the soldiers taking their leisure. "Anybody seen my brother?"

"I saw him earlier this morning," the lanky farm boy replied. "He was with Lieutenant Lowder when we charged up the bluffs. I expect he's down the line a piece." He pointed toward the lower end of the camp. Matt nodded and took his leave.

He found Owen perched on a log, drinking a cup of coffee. His brother's eyes brightened when he spotted Matt striding toward him. When Matt approached, Owen got up to greet him, extending his coffee cup. "This is the last of the coffee beans," he said.

Matt accepted the cup and took a quick swallow of the fiery-hot liquid, then handed it back. "Thanks. I didn't expect to see you today."

"We didn't expect to be here," Owen replied. "General Gordon ordered everybody out for a night march. We got here at about four o'clock this morning and waited around for about an hour before the attack."

Matt smiled, grateful that his brother had survived another skirmish. Although Owen was the elder, Matt felt a sense of responsibility to make sure his brother returned home safely to Abby and the boys. He had always felt responsible for Owen, ever since their parents had perished in a cabin fire. He sat down on the log. "Yeah, if I'd have lingered a few minutes longer this mornin', one of you boys mighta shot me. I'd just left that creek bank when I heard all hell break loose behind me."

"We heard two rifle shots not more than ten or fifteen minutes before we got the signal to advance," Owen said, nodding his head as he recalled. "Was that you? It sounded like that Whitworth, come to think of it."

"I was wishin' I had my carbine with me when I heard all the shootin'. I thought it was the Union Army coming down on me." He gave Owen a wide grin, happy with the knowledge that both he and his brother had survived yet another battle.

The men of General Early's Confederate forces were not to celebrate their victory long, for General Sheridan returned to take command of his demoralized Union troops. He mounted a counterattack at around three o'clock that afternoon, driving the men in gray back up the valley in an all-out retreat. There were several more battles fought in November, but the Confederate forces were so badly outmatched that the Shenandoah Valley was virtually lost before spring of 1865. Through it all, Matt and Owen Slaughter managed to stay alive. In a final crushing blow by Union forces near Waynesboro, backed up to the South River, their company put up a fight for as long as they had ammunition. Finally, it was every man for himself as General Early fled along with some of his aides, leaving the valley in the hands of the Union Army. Seeing what was developing, Matt grabbed Owen by the arm. "The officers have cut and run," he exclaimed. "Come on, we ain't stayin' here to get captured!" Along with droves of others, the two brothers escaped up the mountainside. The war was over for the Slaughter boys.

Chapter 2

It took four days of hard riding along mountain trails and back roads before they reached the last low ridge between them and Owen's farm. During that time, they sighted only occasional Union patrols along the main road. Still, they thought it best to avoid the Valley Pike. With no ammunition to spend, the two were unable to take advantage of any game they happened upon except an occasional squirrel or rabbit curious enough to get caught in a snare.

When at last they reached the ridge that protected his farm on the eastern side of the little valley, Owen galloped ahead to the crest, unable to contain his excitement. When Matt joined his brother at the top of the ridge, he found Owen sitting silent and disconsolate. Below them, the fields were black and scorched. The house was a pile of charred timbers around the stone fireplace, its chimney standing like a solitary grave marker. The two brothers stared dejectedly at the remains of the second Slaughter homestead burned to the ground, the first having been the cabin that had claimed the lives of their parents.

With thoughts of his parents' fate with the burning of the original cabin, it was all Owen could do to keep from choking on a sob. He looked fearfully at his brother and gasped, "Abby." Then he kicked his horse hard with his heels and drove recklessly down the slope. Matt followed, instinctively scanning the valley back and forth with his eyes, cautious in case there were Union soldiers about.

Owen was out of the saddle before his horse came fully to a halt, frantically pulling burnt timbers this way and that, searching for what he hoped he would not find. He picked up broken pieces of dishes and scraps of singed cloth, remnants of his life, now destroyed. Finding nothing whole, he finally sank to his knees defeated, tears streaming down his face.

Matt watched his brother's sorrowful return to his home, in silence to that point. Then he sought to comfort him. "We'll find Abby and the boys," he said. "We'll rebuild the house. The Yankees burned the crops, but they couldn't hurt the ground. We've still got time to plant this spring." He paused to judge if his words were enough to rally his brother. "You know, Abby most likely took the boys to my cabin. Maybe the Yankees didn't find my place."

Owen looked up hopefully. "Sure, that's probably where they are. Come on!" In the saddle again, they loped off along the river, following a narrow trail that led through a wooded gulch to a small meadow beyond. There, at the far end of the meadow, the simple log cabin remained, apparently unmolested by Union troops. The brothers galloped across the open expanse of grass.

"Ma!" Jeremy exclaimed, "Somebody's comin'."

The nine-year-old ran to fetch his mother. Abby Slaughter moved to the window. Six-year-old David clung to his mother's skirt as she peered out to see who it might be. Not certain if her eyes were deceiving her, she continued to stare at the two riders driving hard toward the cabin. In the next instant she was sure. It was Owen and Matt. Suddenly she felt as if her strength had deserted her and she almost collapsed, forcing her to hold on to the windowsill for support. There had been no news after the fighting at Cedar Creek and the Confederate retreat. The only word that had reached the tiny valley was that hundreds of men on both sides had been killed. Abby had tried to steel herself to the possibility that Owen would not be coming back. But in her heart she feared she could not survive if he had perished.

She wiped the tears from her eyes, her fearful expression replaced by one of joy as the riders approached. She ran to the door, almost knocking David to the floor in the process, hurrying to greet her husband. Owen leaped from the saddle to meet her. Matt, grinning with pleasure, dismounted and watched the joyful reunion. Abby released Owen long enough to give Matt a hug, then flew into her husband's arms again, her sons clinging to their father's legs.

"We saw the house," Owen said, "at least where the house once stood." He looked at his wife, reassuring her. "Don't you fret, honey, me and Matt'll build us a better one." Matt nodded in agreement. Owen continued. "It'll soon be time for spring plowin'. We'll have us a garden goin' in no time, and we can stay here till Matt and I can build the house back." He turned to his brother. "If that's all right with you, Matt."

Matt grinned, surprised that Owen would even bother to ask. "Of course it's all right," he said. "I'm just sorry it's so small."

Abby placed a hand on her brother-in-law's arm. "I don't know what we would have done if the Yankees had burned this cabin down. I don't know where the children and I would have gone."

He patted her hand gently. "Well, you know you're welcome to the cabin as long as you need it." He smiled at Owen. "Matter of fact, I think I'll sleep in the barn. I've spent so many nights sleepin' with my horse till I'm not sure I can stand being shut up in a cabin."

"Bless you, Matt," Abby whispered. Then realizing that the two men were probably hungry, she said, "Come on inside, and I'll fix something to eat. I've got some corn left, and a little piece of side meat. There may be enough flour to make a little gravy."

Matt and Owen exchanged glances. Then Owen spoke. "Is that all the food you've got?" When she nodded silently, he asked, "What happened to the money I buried under the corner of the corn crib?"

"Owen," she exclaimed in despair. "It's all gone—long ago." When she saw his look of disbelief, she insisted, "You've been gone for over a year. All we've had to eat for the last six months is some corn and some side meat from time to time from Reverend Parker and his wife. The only way I could get food for the children was to borrow money from Zachary Boston." She read his eyes and pleaded her case. "I had no choice. My babies were hungry. He said it was all right, and that you could just pay him back when you came home."

Owen shook his head. Zachary Boston was about as

unlikely a man to help a neighbor in need as anyone Owen could think of. *I guess the war does peculiar things to people,* he thought. *Maybe it taught an ol' skinflint like Zachary Boston to give a helping hand.* "I'm real sorry, honey. I'm sorry it's been so hard for you. But I'm home now. We'll get that place up and runnin' again."

Abby pulled a chair back from the table and sat down, suddenly overcome with a feeling of exhaustion. She had not let herself dwell on the hardship of having spent so many long months of waiting, not knowing if her husband would return to her. It had been her endeavor to never look beyond the day that was presently before her, trusting in God to take care of things. It had not been easy when weeks would pass with no word of Owen's unit, or even where the fighting was. But now she sank back against the chair, watching the two brothers eat the meager repast she had scraped together, and she knew that everything would be all right again. Owen was home.

She didn't realize that she was smiling as she gazed at the two strapping young men. Though dirty and unshaven, they looked beautiful to her. Owen was the shorter by an inch, but heavier through the chest and darker of complexion. She turned her gaze toward her brother-in-law. Matt, the fairer of the two, had always put her in mind of a mountain lion, moving with a wild grace that seemed effortless. There was something different about him. He had grown a mustache. She smiled warmly at him when he glanced up to meet her gaze. Then she looked back at her husband. It was so good to have them back, both of them. The long, empty months were finally over.

*   *   *

The next month passed quickly, with the two brothers working every day to restore the house and prepare the scorched fields for planting. Seed was supplied by Reverend Parker, who insisted that Owen could repay him by coming to services every Sunday. Matt even attended one Sunday in order to personally thank Parker for his help.

Owen's farm and Matt's small strip of land by the river were not subject to much traffic from the world outside. It was almost May when word of Lee's surrender reached the little hollow deep in the valley. The news was met with stoic regret from both Matt and Owen, but it came as no surprise. As far as they were concerned, the war had ended in March when they had retreated up that mountain along with their officers.

Some of the men at church had brought news that Union soldiers had been posted in Lexington, and the area was officially under martial law. The news was somewhat unsettling, but the brothers and their closest neighbors didn't anticipate seeing any soldiers in their isolated part of the valley. There was no time to worry about who won, anyway. Now was the time to recover what had been lost in that unfortunate struggle between North and South. All that mattered was the land. There were no plantations in the Shenandoah Valley, no slaves to be freed. Every man they knew worked the land with his own back, and the two brothers set out to reclaim Owen's farm with a determination that already showed dramatic results. By the first of June, crops were in the fields, and the house was almost completed. It was at that time that Zachary Boston made his appearance.

A lawyer by profession, Zachary Boston had never been held in high esteem by many who had dealings with him. He kept a small office in a crossroads settlement called Rocky Bottom, about eight miles from Owen's farm. When most of the men marched off to defend the valley, Boston stayed behind to take command of the Home Guard. A short, pinched man in his mid-forties, he always rode a big black Morgan stallion. Matt recognized the horse before Boston was close enough to see his face.

"Looks like we got company," Owen remarked, pausing to watch the rider approach. He dropped his hoe, and he and Matt walked to the edge of the field to meet their visitor.

"Afternoon, boys," Boston offered as he pulled up before them, the big Morgan stamping aggressively and snorting at Owen's mule. "I heard you boys had gotten back from the war."

"Boston," Owen acknowledged. "What brings you out this way?"

"Just checking on my property," Boston replied. He paused to take a long look around him. "You boys have done a helluva lot of work out here, but I can't understand why you'd trouble yourselves to work someone else's land."

"What the hell are you talkin' about?" Owen retorted. He didn't like Boston's tone.

"I'm talking about you working my property." He said it as if explaining to a child. "Didn't your wife tell you she sold me this land in exchange for supplies?"

Both brothers were stunned for a few moments. Unable to believe his ears, Owen could only stare at the smug face while he searched for words to reply. "Like hell she did," he finally blurted. "This land belongs to me. It was my father's, and now it's mine."

"I'm afraid I'm gonna have to differ with you on that," Boston insisted. "I bought it fair and square. I've got the paper with her signature on it to prove it."

Owen became frantic as he realized the spindly lawyer was deadly serious. "There's been some mistake. Abby said she signed a loan or somethin' for some food, and that's all. I aim to pay you back for that."

"Well, now, that mighta been all right if you had met the payoff deadline, but you didn't. Your wife put up the farm as collateral. It's a simple business deal. I wish I could help you, Owen, but business is business."

"Why, you low-down son of a bitch . . ." Owen started for him, but Boston, anticipating such a move, pulled his horse back and drew a revolver. Matt caught his brother by the arm, lest his anger cost him his life. Boston continued to back away, his pistol leveled at Owen. "This is my land," Owen roared. "Get your sorry ass outta here and don't come around here again because next time I'll be carrying a gun."

When a safe distance away, Boston turned his horse, and called back. "This ain't the last of it, boys. The law is on my side, and I'd advise you to get off my land."

Work effectively finished for that day, they returned to Matt's cabin. A thoroughly shaken Owen immediately questioned his wife about the so-called loan. Confused and frightened, Abby swore that there was never any mention of putting the land up to secure the loan. She maintained that it was a simple loan, supposedly out of the goodness of his heart, for a little food. She remembered that Boston had produced some papers, but she didn't take the time to read all the wording. He had told her that it wasn't necessary, anyway. Her babies were hungry, so she signed.

Owen sank down heavily at the table. He said nothing for a long moment while he thought about the devastating blow to their lives. After a long silence, he looked at his wife, whose tears were streaming down her face as she realized what her carelessness had cost. For a moment, his eyes softened. "It ain't your fault, honey. That slimy snake took advantage of you. I'll straighten this thing out. We'll go to court if we have to. He ain't gonna get away with it." He looked then at Matt. "We'll go see Judge Crawford." He glanced back at Abby. "I reckon he's still around Rocky Bottom, ain't he?" She nodded in reply, her face a picture of desperate hope.

Judge Lionel Crawford listened attentively to Owen's recounting of the underhanded deal Zachary Boston had forced upon Owen's unsuspecting wife. His comments on the situation were not good news to Owen, however. "If he's got a quit claim on the property, like he says, there may not be anything you can do about it. If the case was to come before me in my court, I'd throw the scalawag out on his ear. The problem is I've got no jurisdiction here anymore. The whole valley is under military law and Union regulators. I'm afraid I can't help you. I'm real sorry. I truly am."

"Well, I ain't givin' up my land," Owen said to Matt

as they stepped off the judge's porch. "I'll shoot the son of a bitch if he shows up again."

"Well, that would be nice, wouldn't it?" Matt scolded. "That would leave Abby and the young'uns in a fine mess when they hauled you off to jail."

"It ain't right, Matt," Owen complained.

"I know it ain't, but we still haven't heard what the Yankee regulator has to say. Maybe he'll see what a stinkin' trick it was."

"I've been expecting you, Slaughter," Captain Harvey Mathis said when Owen and Matt were shown into the office over the feed store. The entire building had been confiscated by the occupying Union troops, it being the only structure large enough to meet their requirements. "Mr. Boston said you would be showing up here hoping to get a piece of land from him."

Owen was surprised to hear that the captain knew Zachary Boston. "Yessir," he replied respectfully, after a quick exchange of glances with Matt. "That piece of land belongs to me. It's always been in my family, and he took advantage of my wife's desperation while I was away."

"While you were away at Winchester and Fisher's Hill," Mathis quickly retorted. "Boston said you boys rode with Early's troops in the campaign for this damn valley."

"Yessir," Owen replied. "We rode with General Early."

"I was at Winchester, and I was with General Sheridan when we routed your cavalry and chased you out of Waynesboro."

Owen simply stared at the gloating Union officer

for a few moments, struggling to maintain his calm. "The war's over as far as I'm concerned. This ain't got nothin' to do with the war."

"No, I suppose not." He got up from his chair. "Let me make this short, Slaughter. I've already seen the quit claim deed. It was signed and witnessed. As far as I can see, it's a legal document."

"Witnessed?" Owen exclaimed. "Witnessed by who? My wife said there wasn't anybody there but that low-down swindler. He stole my land!"

"Maybe he did," the captain replied impatiently. "It's hard to say which one of you is lying. But he's got the legal claim." He smirked as he added, "I guess you just lost another battle, Reb. You boys oughta be used to that by now."

Matt could see that Owen's short fuse was already lit. Fearing that his brother might do something foolish, he said, "Come on, Owen. There's gotta be somebody higher up we can see."

But Owen just stood there, fuming, his fists clenched. Finally he spoke. "You low-down Yankee scum. I shoulda known better than to even bother with a son of a bitchin' bluecoat."

"By God, that's gonna cost you, Reb. Your mouth just landed your sorry ass in jail." He yelled for his clerk in the next room. "Private! Take these men into custody!" His call was met with silence, for the private at the desk outside had taken advantage of an opportunity to slip downstairs to fetch a cup of coffee.

Seeing no immediate response to the officer's summons, Matt tried to defuse the incident. "Hold on, Captain. There's no call for trouble. We'll just be on our way."

"The hell you will," Mathis shot back, and drew his pistol from his holster. With the weapon leveled at Owen, he said, "Some of you Rebels just have to learn the hard way."

Owen, smoldering to that point, could contain his anger no longer. When Mathis turned his attention toward Matt, Owen lunged forward, driving his shoulder into Mathis' gut, landing both bodies on the floor. They struggled violently, each trying to gain control of the pistol. Caught as much by surprise as the officer had been, Matt moved to intercede. But before he could reach them, he heard the sharp report of a gunshot. The sudden sound reverberated in the small room like a cannon, and the two struggling bodies became still. Shocked by what had just happened, Owen slowly disengaged himself from the unmoving body of the Union officer. Mathis lay dead, killed instantly by the pistol ball that had entered beneath his chin, tearing into his brain.

"Oh, God. . . . Oh, God," was all Owen could utter at the moment, as his world came crashing down around him. "I didn't mean to kill him." He looked helplessly at his brother, his eyes pleading. "What am I gonna do?"

Hearing the sound of running footsteps downstairs, Matt quickly moved to close the door and lock it. Then he went to the single window and looked out. Just a few feet below the window was a shed roof. "Here's what you're gonna do," he ordered, taking command of the crisis. "Go out the window, and don't stop till you get home. I'll take care of things here."

Confused, Owen hesitated. "What about you? I can't leave you here!"

Matt grabbed him by the arm and pulled him toward the window. "Listen, Owen, we ain't got time to talk about it." Already, he could hear the private running up the stairs. "You've got Abby and the boys to worry about. I'll take care of this. It was an accident."

"No, Matt," Owen insisted. "It ain't right. I killed the son of a bitch."

"Dammit, just do as I say! Think of your family. They need you. I don't have any family. Hell, I can do some time in prison. Nobody's depending on me. Now, go, dammit, before they break in here."

Still feeling guilty for letting his brother take the blame, Owen nevertheless did as he was told. Matt had barely closed the window when the door was smashed open. He turned to face the clerk and a sentry who had been posted downstairs. Seconds later, an officer and two more soldiers burst into the room, weapons drawn.

Matt raised his hands. "Take it easy, boys. This was an accident." That was as much as he had an opportunity to say before the lights went out in his brain, the result of a solid blow from a rifle butt from behind.

"I believe you cracked his skull good and proper." Matt heard the voice, but he wasn't sure where it came from.

"You reckon you kilt him?" Another voice asked.

"It don't really matter," the first voice answered.

Painfully, Matt opened his eyes. The effort of raising his lids seemed to intensify the throbbing pain in his head. A third voice, this one slightly familiar, asked, "Matt, do you know where you are?"

He strained to focus on the face peering down at

him. After a moment, he recognized the tired features of Dr. Benjamin Bates. "Yeah, Doc, I know where I am," he managed.

"I believe you might have suffered a concussion," Doc Bates said. Then glancing up at the soldiers gathered around him, he added, sarcastically, "Thanks to these brave lads."

The comment brought a snicker from the two soldiers standing closest to him. The officer, a lieutenant, pushed forward to have a closer look at the prisoner. "He's damn lucky they didn't shoot him, the murdering Rebel trash. Now, I expect we'll have to give him a trial before we hang him."

Ignoring the comments, Doc Bates questioned his groggy patient. "What happened, Matt? Can you remember?"

Matt took a few moments to compose his thoughts, still waiting for the room to stop spinning around him. Bates was about to repeat the question when Matt spoke. "It was an accident, Doc. The damn fool pulled that pistol and it accidentally went off."

"Ha!" the lieutenant scoffed. "Right under his chin, too."

The captain's clerk stepped forward. "There was two of 'em in here when I went downstairs. What happened to the other one?"

The lieutenant turned to look at the clerk. "Is that right?" Then, without waiting for an answer, he turned back to face Matt. "What happened to the other one?" He repeated the question.

His mind clearing now, Matt answered. "He followed that soldier downstairs and went on home. He said there wasn't any use in arguing any more.

He wasn't even here when the damn fool shot himself."

"How come I didn't see him?" The clerk demanded.

"I don't know," Matt replied. "Maybe you were interested in somethin' else."

"Well, I guess that leaves you holding the bag, doesn't it?" The lieutenant concluded. Staring down at Matt, he said, "So Captain Mathis shot himself, did he?" He stepped over to look at the body more closely. "I guess he fell outta his chair and landed over here on the floor, and scraped the skin off of his knuckles in the process." He turned back to Matt, a wry smile on his face. "I believe a six-year-old coulda come up with a better story than that. We're gonna use some new rope to hang you, Reb." He stepped back and ordered the guards, "Get him outta here."

There was no jail in Rocky Bottom. An empty corn crib behind the feed store served the purpose temporarily. Although the door was padlocked, a man could easily break out a few slats in the wall of the crib to affect an escape. The only thing preventing such an escape was a twenty-four hour guard detail, posted with its only duty to keep an eye on the prisoner.

The lieutenant was inclined to hang the suspect without further delay. The facts of the murder were blatantly apparent to him, but standard operating procedure required that a provost marshal be summoned to rule on the case. A rider was sent to Lexington to request such action. Matt spent a chilly night, sleeping on the bare planks of his makeshift jail. Early the next morning, Owen showed up.

"Are you all right?" Owen asked upon first sight of the bandage around his brother's head.

"Yeah, it was just a little love tap," Matt replied, anxious to discourage the worried expression on Owen's face.

"I brought you some corn bread. I didn't figure the Yankees would feed you." He started to hand it through the slats, but the guard quickly stepped forward to intervene. After making sure there was nothing more than corn bread being passed to the prisoner, he permitted Matt to accept it.

"Thanks," Matt said. Then primarily for the guard's benefit, he added, "I shoulda listened to you, and left when you did, but how did I know that captain was gonna shoot himself?"

"Matt, we've gotta get you outta here," Owen whispered. "They're not going to give you no trial."

"Listen to me, Owen." Matt was deadly serious. "I'll take care of the situation here. Your responsibility is to Abby and the boys. I'm afraid you've lost your farm. That was bad luck. Don't go blamin' Abby for gettin' taken by that weasel. She was in a bad way when he cheated her. At least you've got a roof over your head. You're welcome to my cabin and my little piece of land for as long as you want it. The land ain't half the size of yours, but it's good fertile land. You can get a helluva lot more outta that land than I ever could." Owen started to protest, but Matt cut him off. "Don't worry about me. Just do like I tell you, and everything will be all right." He gave his brother a smile. "Hell, they saw it was an accident," he lied, "and said I probably wouldn't get much prison time. I'll be home before you know it."

Owen was reluctant to leave, but he eventually agreed to go and leave Matt to his own devices. "It's best this way," Matt assured his brother. "There's just one thing you could do for me, and then I don't even want you comin' back here anymore. Just see if you can find out where my horse is, and let me know. All right?"

Owen nodded and turned away. In less than an hour's time he returned with the information that Matt's horse was in a stall at Monk Weiner's livery stable. He could have guessed that. Some of the settlement's citizens had been critical of Monk's willingness to do business with the Union Army. The two brothers exchanged deep glances, the elder realizing fully what the younger was sacrificing for him and his family. "You take care of that family of yours," were Matt's parting words to his brother.

The Union provost marshall in Lexington wasted no time in investigating the death of Captain Mathis. A detail of one officer and six enlisted men arrived in Rocky Bottom before dark. The investigating officer, Captain Wilford Belton, asked to see the prisoner as soon as they arrived. He was appalled when led to the corn crib behind the feed store. "This is what you're using for a jail?" Belton asked, hardly believing his eyes.

Plainly defensive and somewhat embarrassed, Lieutenant Foley tried to explain that a suitable jail was in the not-too-distant plan, but there had been no time as yet to start the project.

"Why, hell," Belton mocked, "with a little bit of a

running start, a man could run right through the side of that corn crib."

"Yessir," Foley replied sheepishly. "But that's why we keep a guard on it twenty-four hours a day when there's a prisoner in there. Captain Mathis was planning to request some materials to start a jail."

"Well, I hope to hell so." Belton turned his attention to the prisoner then. He studied the young man seated against the side of the crib intently. "Another belligerent Rebel who doesn't know he's been whipped," he remarked aside to Foley. To Matt, he demanded, "What unit did you serve with, Reb?"

Matt, who had been studying the captain as closely as he himself had been studied, hesitated a moment before replying, "Twenty-Second Virginia Cavalry."

"Twenty-Second, eh? I guess they didn't teach you to stand up in the presence of an officer."

"Not a Yankee officer, I reckon they didn't," Matt replied.

A wry smile creased the captain's face. "Still got a few burrs, ain't you? Well, let me tell you what happens to smart young men like yourself who murder an officer of the U.S. Army. We're gonna take you back to Lexington in chains, so all the other Rebs can see you. Then we're gonna hold a trial, so that everybody knows we stand for justice. Then we're gonna hang you in the square to teach the rest of your kind a lesson." He turned abruptly on his heel, and addressed Lieutenant Foley. "You make damn sure you keep a guard on this man all night. We're starting back first thing in the morning."

"Yes, sir," Foley replied, and saluted smartly.

* * *

There was no doubt in Matt's mind that events would happen precisely in the order that Belton had stated. A trial would be no more than a formality and the prelude to a hanging. The question before him was when to attempt escape, for he knew that he would opt for a bullet in the back instead of a rope around the neck. It required little thought to decide the best chance for escape was before morning when he would be trussed in irons and turned over to the captain. Watching the sentry walk his post around the makeshift jail, Matt tried to calculate the odds of breaking through the flimsy boards of the corn crib and attacking the guard before he had time to react. He immediately rejected that plan, knowing that he would probably still be stuck in the slats when the guard shot him. It was going to have to be done slowly, loosening one slat at a time, so that at the precise time, all boards could be removed at once. It would take time, but he figured he had all night.

Under the wary eye of the first soldier posted to watch him, Matt got to his feet and moved around his wooden cage. Pretending to stretch his muscles a little, he glanced at each corner post of the crib, looking for signs of a loose slat. When he decided upon the corner that looked the weakest, he sat down against that post, and waited for the guard to lose interest in him. Once the guard shifted his attention to something else, he began to quietly push against the bottom board, exerting all the pressure he could manage. It was not an easy thing to do with his hands behind his back while still facing the guard. He had almost decided that his plan was impossible when he felt the slat give a little, enough to wedge his fingers between the board and the post. Encouraged, he tried to twist the board back and forth, staying with it until he was finally rewarded with the loosening of the two nails securing it to the post. Satisfied that he was making progress, he started on the next board up.

The guards were rotated on two-hour shifts. Their routine was predictable. At the start of their tours, they usually paced around the corn crib a few times before taking a position by the door. There they remained until boredom prompted them to take another turn or two around the caged prisoner. It was Matt's good fortune that none felt an inclination to examine the nails holding the slats on the sides. He worked steadily until he had the nails loose in two slats. Then, supposedly getting up to stretch, he moved over to the next post to begin the procedure again.

The afternoon sun faded away behind the ridge west of the tiny settlement. Working continuously in the twilight and into the dark, Matt strained against the rusty nails holding the side boards on the crib. Lucky for him, the crib had been constructed to hold ears of corn, and not Confederate prisoners. Not long after darkness fell, Lieutenant Foley made a visit to the crib. Satisfied that all was in order, he soon departed. There was no concern on his part that the prisoner had neither food nor water. The guard, evidently confident that the lieutenant wouldn't be back before morning, took advantage of the dark to make himself comfortable. With his back against the wall of the feed store, he sat down facing the crib.

As the guard rotation continued throughout the night, the diligence to duty was less in evidence as each soldier came on duty again, intent only upon completing his two-hour tour and getting back to his bed. Sometime shortly after midnight, Matt had succeeded in loosening two boards to the point where a firm shove would remove them completely. That part of his escape completed, he waited for the right moment to attempt the dangerous part of his plan. It arrived in the wee hours of the morning.

"Where the hell you been?"

"I ain't late," his relief answered. "I'm right on time." He stepped aside while the other man grabbed his rifle, and prepared to depart. "Anything goin' on?"

"Nah," the first soldier answered. "He's just settin' in his cage, sleepin'." He did not linger to make small talk. "I'm headin' for my bed," he said in leaving.

Matt sat slumped against the corner post of his cage. He pretended to be asleep when the guard took a single turn around the crib. Seeing nothing out of place, the soldier wasted little time in settling himself comfortably against the rear wall of the feed store. In a short time, Matt heard the steady drone of snoring. It was time to act. Pressing a shoulder against the loosened boards, he began to apply a firm and steady pressure. The rusty nails squeaked in quiet protest as they were backed out of the posts, followed by a soft clump when the board fell free to land in the dust. Although muffled, the sound was enough to make Matt look back quickly in the direction of the sleeping guard. He held his breath for a moment, watching, until certain the sound had not been sufficient to disturb the soldier's repose. He then returned to his task, forcing the second board from the posts. As soon as it dropped to land on top of the first slat, he squeezed his body through the opening to freedom.

Undecided at that point, he stood motionless before the sleeping guard. Should he take some violent action to silence the man forever? Maybe take his weapon? The man was sleeping like a baby. Why risk the noise that might result from an attack upon him? In a moment of compassion, he turned and slipped away in the darkness, leaving his guard in peaceful sleep.

Moving silently and quickly through the shadows, he made his way directly toward Monk Weiner's livery stable. He wasn't sure what time it was, but he estimated that there was little more than an hour before first light, and he knew he could not afford to let daylight find him still in Rocky Bottom. Encountering no one on the dark street, he hurried into the stable, and began a search from stall to stall to find his horse. In short time, he found the blue roan gelding; the horse nickered softly when it recognized his master.

Monk Weiner sat up on the cot he slept on in the back of the tack room. He blinked the sleep from his eyes, and looked around him in the semidarkness. It was too early to get up. Something had awakened him—a sound from the stalls outside the tack room perhaps. He wasn't sure. He started to lay back again, but then he was certain he heard a sound, and it didn't sound like one of the horses stamping or snorting. He decided he'd better take a look.

Pulling his boots on, Monk struck a match and lit the lantern by his cot. Passing through the doorway from the tack room, he stopped abruptly when the lantern light fell upon the man cinching up the saddle on his horse. Both men were startled, each freezing for a moment, speechless.

Monk had known Matt Slaughter since Matt was a

youngster. Just the afternoon before, he had watched when the Union soldiers escorted Matt to the corn crib behind the feed store. After the awkward silence had extended to several moments, Monk finally spoke. "Well, I thought I heard somethin', but I reckon I was wrong. I guess I'll go on back to bed." He turned around and started back to the tack room. Before leaving the stable, he remarked loudly, "I was afraid somebody might be after that little bit of money hid in that little soda cracker tin under the oat sacks by the back door." He disappeared then, and Matt heard one last uttering from inside the tack room. "On the left hand side."

There was no time to express his gratitude; already he could see the first evidence of the new day outside the stalls. Matt knew that he would never forget Monk's compassion in this moment of crisis. He led his horse out the back door of the barn, half expecting to hear an outcry from behind the feed store at any second. He hesitated for a moment when he saw a stack of feed bags just inside the left door post. Monk had offered the money, but everyone in the valley was suffering from want after Sheridan had ravaged the land. He was reluctant to take what money Monk may have acquired. Time was running out. His situation dictated a surrender to his desperation. He quickly dragged the sacks of oats aside. There, underneath a layer of hay, he found the tin box. Inside was a roll of U.S. currency, along with a stack of Confederate bills. He counted ninety-five dollars in Federal currency. Taking only what he thought he needed to buy a gun and some supplies for the trail, he replaced forty-five, and returned the box to its hiding place. Spying an empty flour sack draped over the end stall, he grabbed it and filled it with oats for his horse. Then he said a silent thanks to Monk, and stepped up into the saddle.

Although first light was rapidly approaching, the little settlement was still quiet. It wouldn't be for long, he thought. It had to be getting close to the guard change. He wheeled his horse toward the north road out of town, and left Rocky Bottom at a gallop.

Young Tommy Fletcher stopped on his way to work in the stables when he heard a rider approaching on the north road. Whoever it was seemed to be in a hurry. Curious, Tommy ran up the path from the footbridge in time to see the rider pass. "Dang," he whispered, and ran to tell Monk. Bursting into the open end of the stable, he confronted Monk coming from the tack room. "Mister Weiner!" Tommy blurted. "I just saw Matt Slaughter hightailin' it outta town on that blue roan we took in yesterday! He was burnin' up the road toward Staunton."

"Is that a fact?" Monk replied. "Are you sure it was Matt Slaughter?"

"Yessir, it was him all right. That Yankee officer said we weren't supposed to let nobody take that horse. Reckon we oughta tell him?"

Monk stroked his chin whiskers thoughtfully. "That we should, boy. That we should. But first we should make us a pot of coffee. Then, after we've had our coffee, we should report it to the captain right away."

Tommy, a bit slow for a boy his age, looked confused for a moment, but then a wide smile crept across his freckled face. "Yessir," he exclaimed, "I'll go fetch some water for the coffeepot."

Chapter 3

With only one thought foremost in his mind—to leave Virginia and the Shenandoah behind him—Matt left the north road and headed west. He had no destination, only a curiosity about the frontier beyond the Missouri River. Since he was a boy, he had heard tales about the lands west of the Missouri—the untamed wilderness of mountains that made the Appalachians look like foothills. *Maybe so,* he thought. *I'd have to see that for myself.* It was difficult to imagine any place prettier than the Shenandoah Valley. He had seen parts of West Virginia and Tennessee. The mountains there were not a great deal different in appearance than those around his home. Yet there seemed to be something special about the Shenandoah.

He pushed his horse hard that first day, making his way through the mountains on some old game trails he had discovered when deer hunting. Though he felt confident there was little likelihood he was being followed, he took some pains to disguise his trail. He was an outlaw. It was a label he never expected to be attached to him. But outlaw he was, and he had no doubt that the

Union Army would be determined to capture the man who had killed one of its officers. *Well, they're gonna have to go some to catch me*, he promised.

It was a lean camp on that first night. He had nothing to eat, and no weapon with which to hunt. He had flint and steel in his saddle bags, so a small fire was his only comfort. But thanks to Monk Weiner, he had money in his pocket, and he knew where he could supply himself with what he needed—that is, if it still remained. He had stumbled upon the little crossroads deep in the West Virginia mountains some three years before. He was on the last real hunting trip he had taken before he and Owen joined the 22nd Virginia Cavalry. *God, it seems longer than that,* he thought. So much had happened since then. He had a worried thought that maybe the little store by the crossroads had suffered the same fate as so many in the Shenandoah. It might not be there anymore.

His fears were unfounded, however. Following a busy stream leading through a hardwood hollow, he emerged from the trees to find the store still standing. Not only had it survived the war, it had evidently prospered. There was now a blacksmith shop attached to the log structure. Matt breathed a sigh of relief, for his belly was beginning to growl for something to eat.

Oscar Pratt pumped the bellows on his forge, sending a cloud of sparks swirling around his head. He glanced up from the cherry-red piece of iron he was shaping into a gate hinge when something caught his eye over by the creek. Turning his attention back to the hinge, he pulled it from the fire and hammered it a few times on the anvil before plunging it into the tub of water beside him. With that taken care of, he took a couple of steps away from the heat of the forge to see who his visitor was.

Oscar didn't recognize the rider approaching on the blue roan—a young fellow, by the look of him. The young man wasn't from around here, of that Oscar was certain. There was something odd about him, and it took Oscar a moment to realize what it was. From all appearances, he might have just been out for a little ride, for he had no weapons, no pack behind the saddle, no coat, not even a hat.

"Afternoon," Oscar greeted his guest when Matt pulled his horse to a stop before the forge. Oscar continued to stare at Matt, his curiosity aroused.

"Afternoon," Matt returned, and stepped down. "I see you've got a forge since I was last here." Although it was obvious Oscar could not place him, Matt remembered the stocky, bald little man with the snow-white beard.

Still at a loss, Oscar nodded. "Year ago this past August," he replied. He studied Matt for a few moments more. "Seems like I seen you before, young feller, but I can't recollect when."

Matt laughed. "I expect it's been close to three years. I came chasing an eight-point buck through here. Dropped him right down there by that big oak."

A light went on in Oscar's eyes. "I swear, that's right! I remember you now. From over in the Shenandoah, right?"

"That's right," Matt said, grinning. "If I remember correctly, you came running out of the store with your rifle—thought I was stealin' your mules."

Oscar threw his head back and laughed. "I swear, that's the truth. I heard that damn buck run by the door, and then here you came, and I heard a shot. Hell, I thought at first you'd shot one of my mules."

"I guess I could have waited till I got by your place before I shot, but I'd been chasing that buck for two miles. I was afraid if he got to the creek, I'd lose him for sure."

"Well, I'll be damned," Oscar exclaimed. "I shore wouldn'ta recognized you. You know, I et off'en that deer shoulder for a week." He paused to have a laugh over the memory. "What brings you over this way again? I don't reckon it's huntin', unless you've started rasslin' 'em down," he said, again noting the absence of any kind of weapon.

"That's why I came by this way. I lost all my possibles in the war. I was hopin' I could get a gun and some supplies from you."

Oscar became at once defensive. "Well, now, you know I can't keep much merchandise, what with the war and all. Things is pretty scarce."

Matt smiled. "I've got money to buy what I need."

Oscar fidgeted a moment, eyeing the faded gray trousers Matt wore. "Well, now, you know Confederate script ain't much good no more."

"Union dollars," Matt stated.

Oscar's frown relaxed at once. "In that case, maybe I can scrape up a few things. I tell you though, there ain't much left, and I ain't had a wagon in since spring."

Oscar was able to supply Matt with most of his basic requirements: salt, coffee, a coffeepot and a frying pan, a couple of blankets, and a few other essentials. As far as weapons, he could only offer a hard-used Army Colt and a box of cartridges. Matt needed a rifle. A man just wasn't much use to himself or anyone else if he didn't have a good rifle. He expressed as much to Oscar.

"I'm sorry, I can't help you there," Oscar apologized. He paused to study the young man's face. "Are you a pretty good shot with a rifle?"

"Fair, I reckon," Matt replied modestly. He didn't feel it necessary to speak of his time in the army as a sharpshooter. "I usually get meat when I go after it."

Oscar nodded knowingly. He suspected that such was the case. "Well, if you're good enough to bet on it, and you can hang around until Saturday, I can tell you where you might get yourself a rifle." Seeing Matt's immediate interest, he was quick to caution. "Mind you, I said *might*. There's a feller named Puckett over in the next hollow that's puttin' up a Henry rifle for the prize in a turkey shoot Saturday. I ain't seen the rifle myself, but a feller told me it looked like a brand-new Henry. This Puckett feller bought it offen a soldier. I don't know what he paid for it, but a brand-new Henry goes for about forty-two dollars." Noticing Matt's eyes widen with interest, he asked the unnecessary question, "Are you interested?"

"Hell, yes," Matt immediately replied, "but I don't have anything to shoot but this pistol I just bought from you, and a pistol ain't much good in a turkey shoot."

"I reckon not," Oscar said. "But I'll tell you what. If you've got enough money left to buy a chance on it, you can shoot with my rifle."

"How much is a chance?"

"Five dollars for three shots," Oscar replied.

"Five dollars? That's pretty steep. I haven't got much more than that."

"Maybe," Oscar said, "but, hell, it's for a damn-near new Henry repeater."

"I'll do it," Matt replied, after thinking about it for a moment. He would still have a little over two dollars left. It was a reasonable gamble. He had never met a man who was a better shot than himself, even without knowing what kind of rifle Oscar had.

As it turned out, Oscar had a British-made Enfield, like those the Confederate infantry had been supplied with. It was a weapon that Matt had fired many times, and one that was extremely accurate at long range. Oscar was even considerate enough to trust Matt to borrow it to go hunting while he waited for Saturday's shooting match. "I appreciate it, Oscar. I sure as hell need the meat, and it'll give me a chance to see how the rifle fires." He paused when he considered what an advantage that was. "Come to think of it, that's mighty big of you. Won't you be shootin' against me Saturday?"

Oscar laughed. "Nah, I ain't no good with a rifle. I couldn't hit the side of the barn if I was standin' inside it." So Matt took the Enfield the next morning and rode up in the mountains to hunt. In return for Oscar's hospitality, Matt shared the venison he brought back.

Early Saturday morning Matt packed up his supplies, and he and Oscar set out on a small trail that led between two mountains to the west of Oscar's store. Before leaving, Oscar pulled the door to his store shut and placed a large padlock on the hasp. Noticing that the bald little man failed to lock the padlock, Matt asked, "Ain't you gonna lock it?"

"Nah," Oscar replied as he climbed up on his mule. "That's just for show. I don't know what happened to the key for that lock." He laughed. "If I was to lock it, I'd have to take the door offa the hinges to get in." Seeing the look of amazement on Matt's face, he went on. "I don't have to worry about my neighbors, and we don't get many strangers back in these hollows. You're the first one I've seen since last fall." He laughed again. "And I'm ridin' with you. Hell, the Union Army never even found this part of the woods."

Following the narrow trail along a busy stream that cut its way through patches of rhododendron and laurel, Matt sat easy in the saddle while Oscar bounced ahead on his mule. After a ride of approximately forty-five minutes, they emerged from the trees to find themselves in a long valley. Already a sizable crowd had gathered at the north end of the valley, with more filing in from the trail on the far side. Oscar kicked his mule into a trot and made straight for the crowd.

One after another, almost everyone there called out a cordial greeting to Oscar as he and Matt rode up and dismounted. "Don't tell me you're aimin' to shoot this time," a tall, lanky man called out when Oscar stepped down.

"Hell, no," Oscar replied. "You know I ain't no shot. I just come over to watch you boys throw your money away to ol' Puckett over there."

Hearing the comment, the man called Puckett responded. "Now, Oscar, don't go discouraging these boys. Somebody's gonna win this rifle and a box of rimfire cartridges to go with it. Even if you don't win the rifle, you get to keep any turkey you hit."

"That'ud be a dang expensive turkey dinner, though," the lanky man remarked.

The playful banter continued for a few minutes, but all eyes were studying the young stranger standing beside Oscar. Finally, Puckett asked, "Who's this you brung with you, Oscar?"

Oscar turned to look at Matt. "This here's a friend of mine from over near the Shenandoah. He figures on shootin' for that fancy gun of your'n."

Puckett nodded, and extended his hand. "Pleased to meet you, Shenandoah." He then cocked his head to squint at Oscar. "You ain't brought in no crack shot to win that rifle for you, have you Oscar?"

"Well, now, you never know about that, do you?" Oscar joked. "Let's have a look at that rifle."

Puckett walked over to his horse, and drew the weapon from the saddle sling. "She's a beauty, boys," he said. "Barrel's over two feet long, forged out of a single piece of steel. Just load fifteen cartridges in the magazine and one more in the chamber, and you can shoot for the rest of the day without reloadin'." He handed it to Oscar.

"It's got some weight to it," Oscar remarked as he lifted the rifle and sighted upon a tree across the narrow valley. He handed it to Matt.

"It weighs almost nine and a half pounds," Puckett said.

Matt pulled it up to his shoulder, and aimed at the same tree. The rifle felt solid. The balance was good. He decided that it was just the rifle he needed. He passed it on to the man standing next to him. The Henry rifle went from man to man as they all admired the weapon. Suddenly a dark, fearsome-looking man with a scowling face elbowed his way between two of the men, and snatched the Henry out of the tall, lanky man's hand.

"I reckon that rifle belongs to me," he growled, holding the weapon close to him while gazing around him defiantly.

The wide smile fled from Puckett's face. "You'll have to win it fair and square, Tyler."

"I'll win it right enough," Tyler answered, cocksure. "Who the hell is gonna outshoot me?"

Matt looked the man over. A meaner-looking man he could not recall having seen. He noticed that the men Tyler had elbowed aside stepped back a couple of feet, obviously uneasy.

Tyler looked around him, grinning at the begrudging respect he commanded, his long black hair resting cape-like on the shoulders of his smoke-darkened deer-hide shirt, giving him the appearance of an evil priest of some unholy religion. Matt took the measure of the man, and having done so, answered his challenge.

"I reckon that would be me," he stated softly, counting out five dollars to Puckett.

Tyler jerked his head sharply around to see who had spoken. He took a moment to study the stranger before demanding, "And who in hell might you be?"

"I might be the man that outshoots you for that rifle," Matt replied simply, without emotion. With that said, he wasted no time to exchange stares with the belligerent Tyler, but returned to his horse to ready Oscar's Enfield. His actions served to encourage the other men to shell out their money for a chance on the rifle, feeling secure in the belief that Tyler's venom would be reserved for the young stranger.

Oscar strolled casually over to join Matt. "Tyler's a shore-nuff son of a bitch, but he's a damn good shot. I'm right sorry he showed up for this shindig. I know damn well nobody invited him." When Matt showed only casual interest in the man, Oscar went on. "He's a Kentucky man. He don't show up around here very often, and that suits most folks just fine. Him and his brother rode with a band of bushwhackers over in Missouri and Arkansas durin' the war. Called their-selves guerillas for the Confederacy, but they did more harm to Southerners than the Union Army."

Matt shot another glance in Tyler's direction. "What's he doin' around here?"

"Danged if I know," Oscar responded. "Maybe it got too hot for him in Missouri. He just showed up a couple of weeks ago."

"Well, maybe he ain't as good at shootin' turkeys as he is at bushwhacking innocent folks," Matt said to Oscar, and returned his attention to loading the rifle.

After all the contestants had paid for their chances, there were some twenty-two shooters, some having purchased two or more chances at five dollars each. It turned out that they were not actually going to shoot at turkeys. Instead, a section of a pine log about a foot and a half in diameter was placed on a stump. In the center of the log, a wooden wedge about two inches wide and about an inch thick was driven into a split. This was the target, and the winner was the man who split the most wedges with three shots. Any wedge split was worth a turkey to the shooter. At five hundred yards, there had to be a little luck involved, because it was almost impossible to even see the wedge at that distance. After hearing the rules, Matt decided that although Puckett was putting the Henry up as a prize, he didn't intend to give away many turkeys in the process.

All the betting done with, the shooting started as the first contestant crawled up to rest his rifle on a log provided for the purpose. As man after man took his three shots, it was plain to see that there weren't going to be many turkey dinners in the valley afterward. Finally one man split the wedge, and a new wedge was driven in. When it was Matt's turn, he laid down behind the log and rested Oscar's Enfield on it. His aim was directed at the center of the round trunk, thinking that the wedge was most likely driven dead center. He drew a shallow breath and held it, slowly pulling the trigger until the Enfield suddenly fired.

"Miss!" Puckett called out from his station about fifty yards from the target. "Weren't by more'n half an inch, though."

Matt reloaded and drew a bead on the target once more. He adjusted his aim to allow for the half inch, figuring that his miss had been to the right of the wedge, remembering that his shot that killed the deer had been off a hair to the right. Once again the rifle barked.

"Dead center!" Puckett shouted. "Hold your fire till I drive a new wedge in."

Matt took great care in reloading for his final shot. As he replaced the ramrod, he glanced at Tyler. The scowl on the dark face seemed even deeper. Back to the business at hand, he took dead aim a hair right of the center of the target, squeezing the trigger so slowly that the weapon surprised him when it fired.

"Dead center again!" Puckett shouted, excitedly. "That's two outta three for Shenandoah."

Matt got to his feet and walked back to stand beside Oscar. "This is a fine rifle you got here, Oscar. Shoots as true as any rifle I've ever shot." Oscar took the weapon when Matt handed it to him, beaming as proudly as if he had done the shooting himself.

One by one, the remaining contestants tried to match Matt's score, all failing to hit more that one wedge if any, until the man called Tyler stepped up to take his turn. His weapon was a model 1861 Springfield, the rifle used by both sides during the Civil War. He split the wedge with his first shot, causing the crowd of onlookers to move in closer. He smirked for Matt's benefit as he reloaded.

"Missed it," Puckett shouted after the second shot. "Not by much, though, just a tad high." As soon as he said it, he realized that he was giving unfair information on the shot's location. "I can't say by how much," he offered weakly. Tyler grinned and reloaded. His third shot split the wedge again. "Looks like we got us a tie," Puckett announced.

There were several more shooters after Tyler, but none was able to match two out of three. When the smoke lay like a shroud of mist over the little valley, and the shooting was all done, only two remained. "We're gonna have to have a shoot-off," Puckett stated. "But just so it'll be fair and square, both men will use the same rifle. They'll use the Henry, and they'll shoot at turkeys instead of a piece of wood."

"That's a little fer for that repeatin' rifle, ain't it, Puckett?" Oscar asked.

"Well, maybe," Puckett allowed. "We'll bring it in about a hundred yards." He faced the two finalists to give them the rules. "You'll each have three more shots. We'll stack about three of them logs up so you can just see them turkeys' heads above 'em. The one that hits the most turkeys wins the rifle." He then turned to the crowd. "Give us a hand, boys, and let's stack up them logs."

It was a bizarre contest. A couple of handfuls of corn were scattered behind the log barricade, and the turkeys were tied with a length of cord attached to one leg of each so they couldn't scatter. Still, it was going to be quite a trick to hit the bobbing heads of the big birds as they pecked at the corn. After a coin toss, Puckett loaded the Henry and handed it to Tyler.

The exercise proved to be exasperating, and served to infuriate Tyler. He missed with the first shot, sending the frantic birds flapping back and forth in a frenzy. Firing again, he missed on the second shot. He was ready to protest the fairness of the contest when he got meat with his last shot. Knowing it was pure luck, he grinned, and handed the rifle to Matt, confident that it would have to be luck that beat him.

Matt had hunted a few wild turkeys in his life, and he knew a little about their quirks. Knowing that the birds had a tendency to cease bobbing their heads for a second after the snap of a passing bullet startled them, he aimed at one head popping up and down. As soon as he fired and missed, he quickly cranked another round in the chamber and shifted the sights to the next turkey. As he had anticipated, the startled bird held his head still for an instant. It was all the time Matt needed. The rifle fired straight and true, snapping the turkey's head off. Without wasting a moment, Matt cocked the weapon again and nailed the second bird when it, too, froze for an instant.

Oscar whooped delightedly, and ran to pound Matt on the back. Most of the other men gathered around to offer their congratulations as well. Puckett handed him the box of cartridges that went with the prize, and said, "It looks like that rifle belongs to you, young feller. That was some shootin'."

"It was luck"—Tyler snorted in disgust—"pure damn luck, and I'd like to see you do it again."

Matt took a long look at the surly man before answering. "I'd like to put on a show for you, mister, but I don't reckon I'll waste the cartridges." He left a deeply fuming Tyler to glare at his back as he abruptly turned and led his horse over by Oscar's mule.

"Why don't you light a while around here, son?" Oscar offered. "You could stay in my barn till you fixed you a place of your own." Oscar had obviously taken a liking to the young stranger.

"Thanks just the same," Matt replied, "but I've got it in my mind to see the Rockies." He didn't feel the need to confess the urgency to remove himself from this part of the country.

"I can understand," Oscar said. "If I was a younger man, I might go with you." He thrust his hand toward Matt. "If you get back this way, you'll be welcome at my place."

"Thanks," Matt replied as he shook Oscar's hand. He stepped up into the saddle then. "You take care of yourself, Oscar," he said, and turned the roan's head toward the lower end of the valley. Several of the men signaled with a nod or a slight wave of the hand as he rode out. One stood apart from the others, his stony stare fixed upon the young stranger until Matt had ridden out of sight beyond the bend of the stream.

Chapter 4

Several good hours of daylight remained when Matt took his leave from the valley where the shooting match had taken place. Surrounded by mountains, he followed a trail that wound back and forth through narrow valleys, leading in a westerly direction. He glanced down at the one turkey he had kept, tied by the feet from his saddle horn so that it would bleed out. The bird's blood formed a long thin streak down his horse's withers that glistened when the afternoon sun reflected off of it. *I reckon I'll have an early Thanksgiving dinner,* Matt thought. His marksmanship had resulted in two turkeys. The other bird had gone home with Oscar. *I guess that's pay enough for the use of the Enfield.* He smiled when he thought of the bald little man on his mule with a dead turkey dangling on his saddle.

It had been a fortunate trail that had led him to Oscar's store, deep in the West Virginia mountains. Not only was he looking forward to a turkey dinner, but he had acquired the rifle he sorely needed. He had fought against Union troops armed with new Henry rifles at Waynesboro. *That damn Yankee rifle you loaded on Sunday and shot till Wednesday,* as the men in K Company had referred to it. While the weapon was not especially suited for long-range kills, it would do nicely for his purposes. Matt had just seen proof enough of its accuracy at four hundred yards. Thinking about the rapid fire of his new rifle, he drew it from the saddle sling he had devised and admired his prize. The Henry felt at home in his hands. He cautioned himself to be mindful of wasted shots. At ten dollars a thousand for the rimfire cartridges, a man could throw away a small fortune if he was prone to engage in frivolous target practice.

Guiding on the setting sun, he continued to make his way through the mountains until the sun dropped behind the hills before him. In an hour's time, it would be dark in the valleys and draws—time to make camp. He was resigned to making a dry camp when, luckily, he skirted a small hill and found a wide creek flowing gently through moss-covered banks. *Made to order,* he thought, glancing down at the turkey hanging from his saddle horn. *Much longer in this warm weather, and this ol' bird will be starting to get ripe.*

Selecting a spot under a water oak with roots half exposed along the bank, showing evidence of numerous past floods that had swelled the creek, Matt made his camp. He pulled the saddle off of the roan and led the horse to a patch of grass near the water's edge. He still had oats for the horse, but he decided it prudent to start training the animal to live off the land.

His horse attended to, he turned his attention to the turkey. Holding the bird up by the feet, he eyed it as if seeing it for the first time. "I wish to hell I had a kettle," he murmured. "It would be a helluva lot easier to pluck it if I could dunk it in a pot of boilin' water." He continued to stare at the bird for a few seconds more. "If wishes were horses, beggars would ride," he recited, shrugged his shoulders, and laid his supper on the ground while he made a fire.

It was almost dark when the last of the stubborn feathers gave up the fight. He tried dunking the carcass in the creek. Then he tried boiling a frying pan full of water over the fire and dousing a small area at a time. He achieved some success using the latter method, but there was a liberal amount of cursing before he held a battered and abused naked carcass up before his eyes. He decided the bird was ready for roasting when suddenly the carcass was jerked violently to one side, and raw bits of flesh flew up in his face. An instant later, he heard the sharp report of the rifle. He recognized the sound of an army Springfield.

Although caught completely unaware, his reactions were automatic. He dropped to the ground, releasing the turkey as he did, and rolled away from the fire toward his saddle and rifle. With the weapon in hand, he scolded himself for being careless as he scrambled up behind the trunk of the oak. He cranked a cartridge into the chamber of the Henry and waited, listening. With no clue from where the shot had come, he had no choice but to continue to wait, knowing that his assailant was no doubt moving to a new position. The question now was whether or not his stalker had seen where he had taken cover?

His question was answered almost immediately when a second shot rang out, ripping a sizable chunk of bark from the oak, only inches above his head.

Damn! He thought, hugging the ground as he pushed away from the tree and slid down the bank on his belly. *The son of a bitch can see in the dark!* Being reasonably sure his assailant was on the move, Matt knew he had better keep moving as well. Crouching in an attempt to keep his body as low as possible, he ran along the edge of the water, using the bank as cover. Gradually, his eyes became accustomed to the darkness, after having been staring into the fire moments before the first shot was fired. Reaching a shallow cutback in the creek bank, he stopped and crawled up close to the brink. Raising his head slowly, he surveyed his campsite, now some twenty or thirty yards behind him. There was no sign of his attacker. All was quiet; the only sound reaching his ears was the frightened stamping of his horse as it pulled against its tether.

Damn! he swore to himself, angry that he had not been able to spot the muzzle blast when the second shot was fired. His assailant could be anywhere out there in the darkness. As if to underscore the thought, a spray of sand suddenly stung his face, followed by the sharp crack of the Springfield. This time, however, he had been able to detect the muzzle blast. The stalker had moved through the trees, paralleling Matt's escape along the bank. *How in hell did he know which way I was going to run up this creek?* The thought only flashed through his mind. He didn't have time to ponder it. He had to move.

Back down near the water, he slipped on a moss-covered root, splashing his foot in the creek. A shot immediately rang out, and he heard the snap of the lead as it passed harmlessly overhead. *Now we're on equal terms*, he thought. *He's guessing, same as I.* Looking around him on the dark creek bank, he picked up a couple of clumps of dirt. In quick succession, he threw them back toward the way he had come, the first several yards away. As soon as he heard it splash down in the water, he threw the second clump a few yards farther. Then he quickly crawled up to the edge of the bank, his gaze moving back and forth through the trees. *There!* Just for one brief moment, he spotted a movement among the trees, and then it was gone, swallowed up in the deep shadows. At least he was able to tell in which direction his bushwhacker was moving. The man was obviously following the sounds of the dirt clods splashing in the creek, apparently mistaking them for the sound that a man running along the water's edge would make. Matt immediately rose up from the bank and slipped into the trees.

He was at home now, moving silently through the oaks and poplars, a few cautious steps at a time, then stopping to look and listen. Some two dozen yards ahead of him, he suddenly saw the shadowy form of a man moving toward the creek, but it disappeared before he had time to raise his rifle. Without hesitation, he moved quickly forward, his rifle ready, searching the tangle of brush and vines that obscured his vision. Once again he stopped to listen. There was no sound other than the gentle stirring of the night breeze in the leaves above him. The sobering thought struck him then: the man stalking him was as much at home in the forest as he.

On the move again, he continued toward the spot where he had caught a glimpse of his assailant. After making his way carefully through the brush, he found

himself back at the creek, only twenty-five yards
below his camp. There was no sign of the stalker.
Kneeling near the bank of the creek, he peered up and
down the creek for as far as he could see in the darkness. He realized that he was making no progress in
this deadly game of tag. As he lingered there, making
up his mind what his next move should be, a full
moon made its initial appearance above the ridge behind him. In a matter of minutes, the trees began to
emerge from the deep darkness of before and take
shape. Matt's gaze darted quickly back and forth in an
effort to spot his enemy. He was suddenly distracted
by a flicker of light, and he glanced down to discover
the reflection of the moonlight from the shiny brass receiver plate of his new rifle. His reaction was immediate. Without taking time to think, he dropped flat on
his belly and rolled over the edge of the creek bank.
The snap of the bullet over his head at almost the same
time as the sharp report of the Springfield rifle bore
grim testimony of how close he had come to going
under.

There was no time to consider what the consequence would have been had he not reacted so auto-
matically. This time, Matt had spotted the muzzle blast
of the shot. It had come from the large oak tree that he
had first taken cover behind, near his campfire. Knowing that his assailant had to reload the single-shot
Springfield, Matt sprang up from the creek bank, his
rifle blazing as he pumped round after round toward
the oak. Aware that it took only seconds to place another cartridge in the Springfield's breech and throw
the bolt, Matt sprinted to cover behind a tall poplar on
the opposite side of the fire. He dove to the ground

behind the tree just as another shot from the Springfield ripped the bark above his head. Without coming to rest, he rolled over in a continuous motion to scramble to his feet and charge the oak tree while his enemy was reloading.

Running straight for the oak, his heart pounding with the excitement of combat, he leaped over his campfire in full stride. Just as his foot hit the ground again, Tyler stepped out from behind the tree, a pistol leveled at the charging man. Matt barely had time to recognize the evil grin on the belligerent face before he felt the sharp sting of the bullet that grazed his shoulder, spinning him around and knocking him off balance. It happened so fast that he would not later remember having pulled the trigger, cocking the Henry, and pulling the trigger again before Tyler doubled over, grasping his gut.

Ready to fire again, Matt scrambled to his feet, but it was immediately apparent that there was no longer any threat from Tyler. While keeping a wary eye on the stricken man, Matt picked up the pistol Tyler had dropped and stuck it in his belt. The man's face was twisted in pain as he lay clutching his belly. Matt came to stand over him.

"You son of a bitch," Tyler spat between spasms of pain, "you gut-shot me."

"I reckon," Matt answered without emotion. He turned his attention momentarily to his bloody shoulder. After satisfying himself that the wound was superficial, he returned his gaze to settle upon the wounded man at his feet. At the moment, Matt was undecided what to do about him.

"You've kilt me, you son of a bitch. I'm hurtin' like

hell. What are you waitin' for? Go ahead and finish me off."

"I oughta, you low-down bushwhacker." Still undecided, he continued to gaze down into the scowling face. "Did you want this rifle bad enough to kill a man for it?"

"To hell with you," Tyler forced out painfully. "Go ahead and do it."

Matt had no desire to execute the man, even a man as evil as Tyler. He was satisfied that he had stopped him. If Tyler died, it was God's decision, not his. "I'm gonna put you on your horse. Maybe you'll make it home. Maybe you won't—all the same to me."

When Matt tried to pick the wounded man up, Tyler let out a loud moan, and a trickle of blood appeared at the corner of his mouth. "I'm done for," he gasped painfully, "just let me lay back." Holding him by one arm, Matt tried to ease the dying man back down. Only a flash of moonlight on the knife blade saved him. In one determined final act, Tyler suddenly struck with a long skinning knife in his other hand. Matt was quick enough to catch Tyler's wrist before the blade could reach his ribs. For a long moment, there followed a desperate struggle as they strained against each other for control of the knife. The effort proved to be the final act that drained Tyler's life away. His eyes, gleaming with hatred only seconds before, suddenly glazed, and Matt knew he was looking at a dead man. Tyler's body relaxed. Matt released his hold on the wrist and let the body drop back to the ground. With time to think now, he stepped back and marveled at the turn of events, and the fact that a man placed such low value on another man's life that he would kill him for a forty-two dollar rifle.

Taking Tyler's body by the bootheels, Matt dragged it away from his campfire and deposited it in a shallow gully. Feeling suddenly weary, he decided he would wait till morning before searching for Tyler's horse. He picked up a few dead branches on his way back to the fire to freshen the flames. A pale object stood out in the moonlight a few feet from the firelight's glow, and Matt gazed at it for a moment before realizing what it was. In the deadly game of tag, he had forgotten about the turkey. Issuing a grunt of amusement, he picked up the plucked carcass and brushed the dirt from it. A sizable portion of it had been torn away by Tyler's first shot. "Happy Thanksgivin'," Matt muttered as he drew his knife from his belt. After gutting the bird and removing the entrails, he washed it in the creek before devising a spit to roast it over the fire. While he waited for it to cook, he tended to the wound on his shoulder, satisfied that it was not serious enough to concern him.

After eating, the next thing on his mind was to try to find some way to take the shine off the brass of his new Henry. That shiny brass receiver had almost cost him his life, and he didn't intend to have it happen a second time. He knew if he had some vinegar, that might tarnish the metal. Since he didn't have vinegar, he thought that possibly grass might do the trick. So he went to work pulling up handfuls of grass and mashing it between two rocks until he had squeezed the juice from it. Then he rubbed it all over the brass. It appeared to work as long as he avoided handling the rifle too much. Unfortunately, the dull rubbed right off. *Maybe if I had some deer piss,* he thought, *the acid in it would cause the brass to tarnish.* But, of course, he had no deer urine. So he decided to use what he could produce himself. The mixture of urine and grass juice appeared to be a successful temporary solution, reducing the shiny metal to a dull finish. It would have to do until he had a chance to do some hunting and make a deerskin cover to fit around the receiver mechanism.

The morning broke cool and clear in the mountains, unusually so for this late in June. A good day to travel, Matt thought. He placed his coffeepot on the fire to boil while he went over to the gully to have a look at the late Mr. Tyler. "You're a pretty sight first thing in the mornin'," he remarked as he gazed down at the twisted snarl, frozen for eternity. He removed the dead man's gun belt and searched the body for anything useful. He took a moment to examine Tyler's pistol. It was a Navy model revolver, considerably better than the cheap pistol Matt had bought from Oscar. Then he stood back and left the corpse with some final words. "I reckon you won't be alone for long. There's plenty of buzzards in these mountains. I hope the meat don't kill 'em."

After a breakfast of cold turkey and coffee, he saddled the roan, and went in search of Tyler's horse. It didn't take long to find the animal. Starting out through the trees, Matt rode in a wide arc from the creek. The roan whinnied when it caught the scent of the other horse hobbled in a laurel thicket. Tyler's horse answered with a gentle neigh with a little grunt on the end, a characteristic common to stallions.

Matt dismounted and approached the wary stallion.

From the nervous stamping displayed, he guessed that Tyler had been no gentler with the horse than he was with humans. Holding the bridle, he stroked the horse's neck, calming the nervous animal while he looked it over. "You'll be all right," he said softly. "It might take a little time, but you'll be all right." He removed the hobbles. "I expect you'd appreciate a drink of water," he said as he stepped up on his horse and led the stallion back to the creek.

A lot of things had changed since the preceding day. He thought about it while he considered his newly acquired possessions: principally a horse, a rifle, a pistol, and some cooking utensils. Having no desire to use Tyler's frying pan and coffee kettle, he quickly discarded them. The extra horse would no doubt be useful as a pack horse, but he was undecided about keeping the saddle. Rummaging through the saddle bags, he found a small amount of Union currency and some tobacco. There was also a *Wanted* paper on some unfortunate named Ike Brister, wanted in Missouri for murder. *I wonder if Ike knew this vulture was on his trail,* Matt thought as he gazed at the sketch of a bald man with a full, bushy beard. He discarded the paper along with the personal items in Tyler's bags. The inventory complete, he was ready to continue his journey west, deciding to keep Tyler's saddle until he had an opportunity to trade it for something later on. It was an expensive saddle, hand tooled. It should be worth something.

Chapter 5

Leaving West Virginia behind him, Matt followed the sun through Kentucky, traveling roads when they were available, riding cross-country when they were not. He tried to keep some track of the days at first, but soon became bored with it. Avoiding towns and even homesteads, he made his way through mountains and valleys, hunting for his food. It was not a lonely time, for he felt very much at home in the backwoods and mountains, at peace with the solitude.

At times, he thought about his brother, and wondered how Owen fared under the new Union occupation of the valley. *Owen will do all right,* he decided. *He'll get a helluva lot more out of that little piece of land than I ever would have.* Maybe it was best that things had worked out as they had. He had never harbored a desire to be a farmer, and could never imagine himself settling down with a wife and babies. He would always have a yearning to see what lay beyond the distant hills.

With a clear conscience, he pushed on. There were no troubling thoughts of guilt over what he had left behind him. Outlaw in name only, he felt no remorse for killing the bushwhacker, figuring he had done the world a favor by ridding it of that small piece of vermin. He had been offered no choice in the matter, at any rate. If he were inclined to feel guilt, it would possibly be because of taking Tyler's possessions. His choices in that matter would have been to attempt to return them to Tyler's kin, or to leave them in the mountains. *And only a damn fool would ride off and leave them*, he concluded.

He guessed that it was late July when he topped a ridge one sunny afternoon to discover what appeared to be a small store sitting in one corner of a crossroads. He needed supplies, so he decided there was little risk in approaching. If *Wanted* papers had been sent out, he doubted they would have reached an isolated store like the one before him. Since he had no idea himself, he thought it would be a good time to find out exactly where he was.

"Afternoon," the storekeeper offered in greeting as Matt dismounted and tied his horses up to the hitching post. Standing in the doorway, the proprietor eyed the stranger openly. "Looks like you been doin' some hard ridin', young feller." He was looking at the two horses when he made the comment.

Matt followed the direction of his gaze. The horses were, in fact, showing the stress of many days without oats, his supply of feed having long since been exhausted. "I've been tryin' to wean 'em off oats and grain," he said. "But they sure ain't gettin' fat livin' off grass."

"Well, I can fix you up with some oats if you're of a mind to give 'em somethin' besides grass."

"I reckon that would be a good idea," Matt said. "I'll need some coffee and a few other things, too."

"I ain't seen you around here before," the storekeeper remarked, looking Matt up and down. "Where you headed?"

"West," was Matt's simple reply.

Nodding toward the empty saddle on Tyler's stallion, the storekeeper said, "Looks like you lost your partner." Judging by the look on Matt's face, he decided the young stranger was not inviting questions. Most of the young men from these parts, who had gone off to war, had straggled back after the surrender. He supposed this stranger was just one of the many trying to get back home. He stepped aside and said, "Come on in. My name's Porter. This here's my store." He held out his hand.

Matt shook Porter's hand, and, realizing the man was waiting to hear his name, had to think fast. Not willing to give his real name, yet not wanting to appear unfriendly, he tried to come up with a name other than the obvious Smith or Jones. Remembering then that the men back at the turkey shoot had called him Shenandoah, he gave Porter a smile. "Shenan . . ." he started, but cut the word off, realizing just in time that Shenandoah would tell the man whence he had come. "Shannon," he pronounced clearly, "my name's Shannon." He walked inside. "I'll be needin' a few things," he said as he looked around the room. He glanced back at Porter, who was still standing by the door.

"That's a fine lookin' saddle on that bay there. What is that? Spanish? The pommel ain't hardly high enough to be Spanish, though."

"I expect not," Matt replied.

"I need a new saddle," Porter said. "Maybe you might be interested in a trade. You got no use for two saddles, do ya?"

Sensing an advantage, Matt scratched his chin and gave his mustache a little tug, as if thinking hard on the matter. "I don't know, I'm mighty fond of that saddle. That's the reason I've been carryin' it along. I probably need a pack rig for that horse instead of a saddle"—he hesitated for a moment—"if I was a sensible man."

Porter immediately rose to the bait. "I can fix you up with a dandy pack rig for that horse—make you a good trade."

"I don't know. . . ." Matt winced painfully.

"'Course I'd throw in a sack of oats and a sack of coffee beans—maybe some salt and sugar."

"You drive a hard bargain," Matt replied, "but I do need the supplies."

"Done, then," Porter quickly pronounced, before the young stranger could change his mind. They shook on it.

When his possibles were securely strapped on the bay stallion that had previously transported the late Mr. Tyler, Matt prepared to take his leave. The afternoon was aging fast, and he wanted to be on his way. With a final tug at the strap on his new packs, he stood for a moment at the crossroads.

"That there's the road to St. Louis," Porter said, pointing toward the north.

Matt considered that for a few moments. St. Louis was a sizable town, or so he'd heard. He'd never been there, but he suspected a fellow might go unnoticed. On the other hand, his name and description must surely have already been telegraphed to the sheriff.

"Where's that road go?" he finally asked, nodding toward the south fork.

"Sawyer's Mill," Porter replied. "It'll give out in about fifteen miles. Feller named Sawyer had a grist mill down there by the river, but it's been shut down for a long time, before I was born. If you keep on goin' south after you cross the river, you'll be in Tennessee."

"I expect that's the way I'll go, then," Matt decided. He stopped to think for a moment. "Where am I now?"

Porter laughed. "Kentucky," he replied.

Matt thought about that for a moment. "Kentucky, huh? Well I sure didn't know that." He stepped up in the saddle then and turned the blue roan's head toward Sawyer's Mill. "Much obliged to you, Mr. Porter," he said, and gave the roan his heels.

"You take care of yourself, Shannon," Porter called after him.

The days that followed were pleasant days for Matt as he dropped down into Tennessee before setting a course west again. The hills and forests of Tennessee reminded him of Virginia. There was plenty of game to supply his food, and plenty of water and grass for the horses. He traveled as long and as far as he felt like each day, stopping to hunt and rest his horses whenever it suited him. Late August found him on the bank of the biggest river he had ever seen. He sat motionless for a long time, eyeing the wide expanse of water that separated him from Arkansas. He felt certain that he had reached the Mississippi. There could be no doubt. The question now was how to get across. Up to this point, he had not come to a river he couldn't ford or swim the horses across. This river looked to be a little too wide and deep, the current too swift. He might lose his pack horse and all his belongings if he attempted to swim it. There seemed no choice but to ride down river until he came across a ferry.

Following a wagon track that led along the bank of the river, he made his way downstream. As he continued south, he saw small farms here and there with most of the fields grown up in weeds, the result of losing all the country's menfolk to the army. Cotton fields that spread almost to the water's edge lay fallow, as dead as the occasional ruins of a house that had been burned to the ground. The scars of war would be a long time healing. He guessed that he must be approaching a town of some size. A mile farther, where the river narrowed and formed a bend, he finally found a ferry.

BRAMBLE'S FERRY, the sign read, the letters big and bold, painted on a rough pine board, FIFTY CENTS. "Fifty cents," Matt commented to the stout old man coming forward to greet him. "That's a little steep, ain't it?"

"Everythin's gone up since the war," the man responded. "It used to cost ten cents." He stood before Matt's horse, peering up at the stranger. "I reckon it all depends on how important it is to get to the other side of the river. It don't cost no more'n a shot of whiskey, and ain't nowhere near as hard on your liver."

Matt smiled. "I reckon not." He nodded his head toward the south. "Looks like a town on down the river."

The stout little man seemed surprised by the comment, astonished that anyone had to ask. "You must be new around these parts, mister. Them buildings you can see from here ain't really part of the town. Memphis is about five miles from here." He continued to gaze up at the young stranger, half expecting him to change his mind about crossing the river. "Looks like you been travelin' a spell, young feller. If you're thinkin' about a drink of likker, you don't have to ride all the way to Memphis. My brother runs a store less than a mile from here, keeps a barrel of corn likker on hand."

"Reckon not," Matt said. "I'll just take a boat ride across." He stepped down from the saddle and got fifty cents from his saddlebags. "Memphis," he said, "I reckon I'm still in Tennessee. What's that on the other side? Is that still Tennessee?"

"Mister, you are new around here, ain'tcha? That's Arkansas on the other side, different as night and day from Tennessee." He held out his hand to take the money.

"How so?" Matt asked.

"Why, hell, every way. Them's strange folks over there—not like us here in Tennessee."

"You must spend a lot of time over there," Matt commented facetiously.

"Hell, no," the man quickly replied. "I don't never stay longer'n I need to load or unload passengers." He turned then and led Matt down to a small dock where the ferry was tied. "My name's Billy Bramble," he volunteered, as he removed a single pole that served as a gate to the dock.

"Shannon," Matt replied, and led his horses aboard.

Matt remained silent for most of the ride across to the other side, answering in mostly one- or two-word replies to Billy Bramble's remarks. There was very little need for him to carry a share of the conversation, since Billy hardly paused for breath between comments.

When the boat ground ashore in the soft sand of the bank, Matt wasted no time in departing. With a brief nod of his head, he nudged Blue with his heels, and the big roan was off. "Good day to ya, Shannon," Billy called after him. *He sure ain't a talkative fellow*, he thought as he watched Matt disappear over the bluffs.

"I swear, Jack," Billy exclaimed, "I believe that's the feller crossed over on my ferry yesterday." He took a step closer to the wall where his brother had just tacked up a new *Wanted* notice. He peered at the drawing of the square-jawed young man with a full mustache.

His brother shrugged, not really believing. "Hell, what would he be doin' down in this part of the country?"

"I don't know," Billy insisted. "But I knew there was somethin' peculiar about that young feller. He weren't much for conversation, and that's a fact. He shore looked like that pitcher, though." He took a swallow of beer while he sought to remember details. "He was a Reb, too, still wearin' them gray army britches—said his name was Shannon."

"Well, accordin' to this notice, his name's Matt Slaughter, and you mighta just missed makin' five hundred dollars for yourself."

"Damn," Billy sighed, "five hundred dollars." He shook his head in amazement. "He's long gone now, even if I was of a mind to stop him. Maybe it's a good thing at that. From the look of him, and the way he held that Henry rifle, it mighta been a little more work than I'd care to take on."

*   *   *

With the Mississippi behind him, Matt felt a sense
of freedom. In his mind, the mighty river served as a
boundary for those who might pursue him, and there
was a new sense of relief. His rational mind told him
that he was still an outlaw, and was still wanted by the
army. But the Shenandoah was so far behind him now
that perhaps he was no longer important enough to
warrant the army's time and effort.

With no sense of urgency, for he had no real destination, he traveled leisurely across Arkansas, holding
always to a generally westerly course, taking time to
hunt when he wanted to. The country was pleasing to
his eye, as long as he kept to the woods, with heavily
forested hills and sparkling streams. Off to the north,
he could see the distant mountains. He felt at peace
with the world around him, his mind drifting less and
less back to Virginia and the plight of those he had left
behind.

There were things with which to concern himself,
however. Summer was rapidly slipping away, and he
would soon be in need of warm clothing. He had ac-
cumulated a sizable pack of deer hides, but had no
thread to sew a coat. At this point, he was reluctant to
stop in one place long enough to work the hides and
soften them up. He was not especially handy with a
needle and thread, and had never attempted to sew
any kind of garment. But he was determined to give it
his best effort, figuring that if other men could do it,
then so could he. He had thought to dry some sinew
for the purpose, but soon gave it up after a few unsuccessful attempts. Surely, he thought, there would be
some place to buy some good stout thread before he
left Arkansas. He would not only need a coat—his

trousers were beginning to become threadbare in the knees. That job might be a bit more of a challenge. He had little confidence in his ability to sew a pair of trousers. Adding to the list, both horses needed shoes. It was with all these concerns in mind that he came upon the settlement of Boiling Springs.

Pulling Blue to a halt on the brow of a low ridge that bordered the eastern side of the town, he sat for a few minutes surveying the scene. It appeared to be a lively little town, with a cluster of buildings gathered around a crossroads. There were a couple of wagons with mules standing before what appeared to be a general store on the south side of the crossroads. A few yards below it, he saw a blacksmith's forge. The road that lay in a north-south direction appeared to be a well-traveled route. Confident that he could find everything he needed here, Matt nudged Blue, and the big horse started down the slope.

As he had anticipated, Boiling Springs was able to meet most of his needs. A friendly storekeeper named Mathews supplied him with some stout thread, used to sew cottonseed bags, as well as a large needle used for the same purpose. Both horses were shod while he took his ease and made conversation with the smithy, an outspoken man named Bowers. If Matt had been of a nature to settle down, he would have given strong consideration to Boiling Springs. It was a peaceful place, and the two men he had met seemed friendly enough. According to Bowers, Boiling Springs was the exception to the state of things in Arkansas.

"I reckon you could say we were lucky. We had a couple of companies of Union infantry camped here, and their commanding officer was a kindly man. So they left things pretty much alone. Oh, they took everything that could be et or rode, but they didn't burn us down. Most of the men from around here were paroled in June over at Jacksonport, and I expect everyone whose comin' back is already home. God knows there's plenty of work waitin' for 'em. Without no men to work the land, most folks were damn-near starvin' to death in this county. Hell, there was more trouble from the damn guerilla bands than both the Union and Confederate armies combined. Stealin', burnin', destroyin' ever'thin' they couldn't use their-selves, they was the people caused Arkansas the most trouble."

For the first time in days, Matt was prompted to think about the folks he had left back in Virginia. Settling down in a place like this little settlement was no more than wistful thinking for an outlaw, he reminded himself. The main north-south road was the Little Rock Pike, and sooner or later a *Wanted* paper with his name on it would come riding down that road. So he bade them good-bye, Mathews and the smithy, and continued his journey west. Following the Arkansas River, he set out toward Fort Smith. According to Mathews, Fort Smith was the last place to buy supplies before crossing into Indian Territory.

Chapter 6

"Brance, somebody's comin'!"

Brance Burkett laid his cup aside and walked over to the ledge to see for himself. Thinking that it might possibly be the Tyler brothers coming back from their visit home, he stood gazing down at the river. Following the direction of Eli's bony finger, he stared at the trail that wound around the oak trees beside the river one hundred feet below. He was about to tell Eli that he was seeing things when a rider appeared, leading a pack horse. "I see him." He studied the approaching rider for a long moment before deciding he was not either of the Tyler brothers. "I ain't ever seen him before."

"Me neither," Eli said. "He's got a couple of good horses, though—bunch of hides and stuff on that pack horse, too."

"Snell!" Brance called back to a circle of men lolling around a campfire. One of them obediently got to his feet and started to climb up to the ledge. "Bring your rifle," Brance said, then stood impatiently waiting while Snell returned to the fire to get his weapon.

"Hurry up, dammit." When Snell joined Brance and Eli on the rocky ledge, Brance pointed to the rider making his way along the river trail below them. "Knock him outta that saddle."

Snell responded with a foolish grin. He was a simple man. Although nearly forty years of age, his brain had apparently stopped growing when he was twelve. His one attribute lay in his talent with a rifle. He had a better eye than any of the men who followed Brance Burkett and his band of bushwhackers. "Reckon if he's a Yank or a Reb, Brance?"

"It don't matter one way or the other, does it? Shoot him, dammit. I fancy that big ol' horse he's ridin'." Impatient to see the deed done, Brance added, "He ought'n to be ridin' through this part of the country by hisself, anyway."

Snell nodded his head in childlike glee. "I'll get him, Brance." He moved to the far corner of the ledge, and rested his rifle on a small boulder. As he did so, a handful of dirt and small pebbles was loosened and dropped to the bottom of the ledge. To a man with senses less keen, the small amount of gravel falling lightly among the rhododendron leaves might have gone unnoticed. But most of Matt's young life had been spent in the forest, hunting and trapping, and as a deer senses danger, he did not wait to react. He immediately dropped forward on his horse's neck and jerked the big blue roan's head toward the shelter of the cliff. The sharp crack of the Spencer split the quiet air of the hollow below the ledge, and he felt a slight tug as the bullet meant for his back lifted his hat from his head.

"Damn you, Snell!" Brance growled. "You missed him."

"He moved, Brance," Snell whined, fearing Brance's displeasure. "Somethin' spooked him."

"You missed him, you half-wit," Brance snarled in disgust. "Now we've got to go flush him out or we're gonna lose him." He turned at once and headed for his horse. "Eli!" he yelled. "You and Nate!" It was unnecessary to say more. The two men were already running for their mounts. "We'll cut him off below the ridge," Brance instructed on the fly, already charging toward the foot of the hill. Eli and Nate were soon on his heels. Behind them, the rest of the gang was scrambling around to join in the fun. Some—those who had unsaddled their horses—were left fumbling with their saddles in a frantic attempt to catch up.

Some one hundred feet below them, under the projecting ledge of the cliff, Matt had surveyed the situation as best he could. With no idea of what or who had suddenly attacked him, he sought the shelter of the cliff while he tried to decide what to do. Above him, he could hear the muffled shouts and the pounding of horses' hooves on the hard ground. From the sounds, it appeared that they were racing to cut him off. Without knowledge of who or how many assailants there were, he was uncertain as to whether he should make a run for it, or stand and fight. It could even be an army patrol, although his first inclination was that it was more likely a band of bushwhackers. His best course of action, he decided, was to go back the way he had come, and double back on them. Without hesitation then, he turned Blue, and staying close under the face of the cliff, rode back until he came to a ravine that led up the hill.

Churning through thick brush, the bay following behind, the big blue roan forged up the ravine to the brow of the ridge. Drawing his rifle from the sling, Matt dismounted and tied the horses in the trees. Not sure what he would find on the ledge, he moved the rest of the way on foot. After a distance of about fifty yards, he came upon a clearing and a campsite where two men were frantically cinching up their saddles in an effort to join their partners. "Hold it right there," Matt called out.

Although startled, both men acted as one. Pulling their pistols, they blazed away at Matt as he emerged from the trees. In their haste, their aim was wild, and bullets whined around him, but found no purchase as he dived for cover. Rolling over rapidly, he came up on one knee, the Henry leveled at his targets. Both men were cut down as Matt cranked out four shots in quick succession.

Looking quickly around him to make sure the two were indeed the only stragglers left behind by the others, Matt then ran to the far side of the cliff where the riders had descended the hill. Satisfied that he held the high ground against his attackers now, he positioned himself behind a boulder to await their return.

As Matt surmised, Brance Burkett reined his horse to a hard stop when he heard the gunfire behind him. "That son of a bitch," he cursed. "He doubled back on us. He's in our camp." Filled with rage, he turned his horse around and charged back up the hill past the stragglers of his gang still on their way down. "Turn around, dammit," he cursed as he passed them.

Up on the ledge, Matt heard them coming long before they came into view. There was no doubt in his mind that he had encountered one of the marauding gangs of outlaws that had preyed upon the people of Arkansas during the war. He was determined to make the meeting costly for them. Replacing the four spent cartridges, he got set to greet them.

Angry, but not a foolish man, Brance pulled up to let his men catch up to him. "We'll overrun him, boys! Rush him, and he'll turn tail and run." Not sure if the two men he had left behind were dead or alive, he started out again, firing his pistol blindly at the top of the hill. Brance's men followed his lead. Firing their weapons wildly, they charged up the hill while Brance held back a little to let others go out in front. His caution was justified, for the quarry they sought on that day was one the likes of which they had never encountered.

Methodically cranking out one deadly round after another, Matt laid down a blistering blanket of fire that emptied the saddles of the two foremost raiders and effectively halted the charge. Brance and the others were driven back by the barrage to seek cover in the trees. Matt took the opportunity to reload, and move to a rock on the other side of the small path.

"Brance!" Nate Simmons called out. "He got Tom and Luther."

"I know it," Brance called back impatiently. "Where is he? Can you see him?" Furious over having likely lost four of his men, he was almost in a rage to think that his intended victim now held the high ground.

"I think he's behind that big rock right at the top."

"See if you can work around to your right, maybe get a shot at him," Brance called out.

"I'll be damned," Nate shot back. "I ain't got nothin'

between me and that rock but this skinny little tree. I ain't movin'."

Brance's lip curled in a snarl of angry frustration. "Eli!" he yelled. "Can you see him?"

"I think Nate's right," Eli replied. "He's behind that big rock." For emphasis, he fired a couple of shots at the rock in question, the bullets glancing harmlessly off through the trees. "Sounds like he's got one of them Henry rifles. He's got us pinned down for sure."

"He's still just one man, dammit," Brance growled. The anger in him continued to build, knowing he was being held at bay by one man with a rifle. "Snell! Where are you?"

"I'm behind you, Brance." He parted the branches of a laurel bush to reveal himself.

"You ain't doin' no good back there," Brance said. "I believe you could get a shot at the son of a bitch if you drop down the hill a ways, and work around to come up beside him."

Snell's ever-present brainless smile widened a bit when he thought of the possibility of another chance at the man he had missed with his first shot. Without reply, he immediately slid back from the laurel bush and withdrew. Brance and the others waited impatiently while Snell made his way around the ridge to come up from the rifleman's flank. *The simpleminded fool might be lucky enough to catch him by surprise,* Brance thought. Even if unsuccessful, Snell might distract him long enough for the rest of them to advance on his position. He waited, his eyes locked on the big rock to the left of the path.

Moving carefully to avoid snapping a twig or displacing a pebble, Snell crept silently through thick stands of rhododendron bushes that rose higher than his head. When he estimated that he was even with, or a little past the boulder that guarded the path at the top of the ledge, he began a careful climb up the steep slope. With his Spencer fully loaded with seven cartridges, Snell dropped down and crawled the final ten yards to the top. All was quiet on the top of the ridge, save for the sound of a gentle breeze stirring the leaves of the hardwoods. He was confident that he had not been discovered.

Within a few feet of the boulder now, Snell made his move. Springing to his feet, he burst around the corner of the boulder, his rifle ready, only to find no one there. Baffled, he stood dumbly staring for a few seconds at the empty space where he had been certain his quarry waited. Then he glanced across the path to a smaller rock and into the steel blue eyes of the last man he was to see in this world. Snell was quick, but no match to win this contest with chain lightning. Matt pumped two slugs into the fumbling half-wit before Snell could bring his weapon to bear.

The rapid staccato of the Henry rifle as it rang out through the trees above them was sufficient to carry the grim results of Snell's assault to those waiting on the hillside below. "Dammit!" Brance roared. "I want that son of a bitch." There was no question of Snell's death. His Spencer had not even fired. There were no thoughts of regret that the simpleminded outlaw had been killed. There was only anger. In the course of little more than an hour's time, Brance's band of raiders had been reduced by five, leaving him with a gang of six—almost half his men killed by one man with a repeating rifle. It was not only inconceivable to Brance, it was infuriating. In the two years they had ridden together, raiding through Arkansas and Missouri, he had not lost one man—and now, five in one hour. Unable to contain his wrath, he yelled out, "You're a dead man, mister! You hear me? You're a dead man." His words echoing back through the trees and rocks were his only answer.

Brance was determined to kill Matt, no matter the cost. Even if he had to sacrifice one or two more men, he would not rest until the man was lying dead at his feet. "We're goin' up and get that bastard," he informed his men. "Nate, take Corbin and go 'round that side of the hill." He pointed toward the south. "Eli, you and Church go up the other side. Me and Spit'll go right in the front door. We'll give the son of a bitch more lead than he can handle. If we all come at him at the same time, he can't shoot in every direction at once. Wait till ever'body has time to get set, and when I fire, rush that damn rock with ever'thin' you've got."

The men began without protest, fearing Brance's wrath more than the deadly rifle at the top of the hill. They filed off up through the trees on foot, rifles ready. Brance, with blood in his eye and primed for a killing, started immediately up the narrow game trail that led to the clearing above. He was followed by a tall, doleful man called Spit. He was called Spit for the simple fact that he had a habit of almost constantly spitting. Not one of the gang knew his real name, nor cared to know.

Approaching the top of the hill, Brance moved as close to the boulder as he dared before taking cover behind a tree. Spit, following close on his heels, found a sizable pine a few yards to Brance's right. When he was in position, he spat and nodded to Brance. Brance waited a minute longer before raising his Spencer carbine and aiming at the suspected boulder. There was no more than a second's delay after his shot rang out when the forest around the hilltop erupted in a thunderous assault from three sides. Their bullets slashed the tree trunks and sang as they ricocheted from the rocks. "Let's get him, boys!" Brance yelled, and led the charge. There was no hesitation on the part of his men. With guns blazing they all converged on the boulder at the top of the trail.

"Hold your fire!" Brance ordered just as a yelp of pain was heard. When the smoke cleared, the six outlaws were left staring at a vacant patch of grass behind the rock. One of them, Church, was holding his shoulder as blood ran down his sleeve.

Spit stated the obvious—"Ain't nobody here"—then spat.

"One of you bastards shot me," Church whined, still clutching his shoulder.

"Let's see," Eli said, and pulled Church's hand away from the wound. "Hell, it ain't nothin'. You just got grazed."

Unconcerned with Church's wound, Brance scowled as he looked around the ledge that had served as their camp, and the five bodies that lay in awkward poses of death, the body of the foolish Snell close to where he stood. He started toward the far side of the ledge when he was stopped by the sound of pistol shots at the foot of the hill. "The horses!" Furious, he realized then that Matt had circled around them while they were climbing up the hill. "He's got to the horses," he yelled as he ran back down the path.

The object of Burkett's wrath was busy herding the horses he had found tied in the trees at the foot of the hill. Shooting his pistol in the air, he startled them into a stampede down along the river bank. Keeping after them, Matt ran the horses for a mile or more before watching them scatter into the hills. "That oughta do it," he remarked to Blue as he continued on his way to Fort Smith. *Assassin*, the word that had haunted his conscience when he was in the war, came to his mind again. Although he had taken the lives of five men, he felt no remorse. These were no doubt some of the bushwhackers that had preyed upon the innocent folk of Arkansas while their husbands, brothers, and fathers were off fighting for their country. And they had tried to murder him. He had no time for regrets over human trash.

Brance could feel one of his headaches coming on. They were occurring more frequently over the last two years, and they seemed to be triggered most often by extreme anger or frustration. They started with a dull ache, followed within a few hours by a steady pounding in his head that seemed to beat in time with his heartbeat. Sometimes that was as far as they progressed, subsiding gradually over a long period of time. But other times they continued to increase in intensity until he was almost blinded by the stabbing pain that threatened to crush his skull. It was during these episodes that his men had learned to stay out of his way, for in this state, he was likely to kill anyone who irritated him. He never told anyone of the excruciating pain he suffered. There was no doubt when he was in one of his spells, however. You could see it in his eyes. His men attributed it to a natural rage inside him that simply took control. "He's filled with the devil's bile," Eli explained to one of the men when out of Brance's hearing.

Eli had been with Brance since the beginning of the war. He had witnessed many of the violent rages that came over the cruel gang leader. The two had ridden with a group of Arkansas State Troopers that seized Fort Smith in April of 1861. When Union forces recaptured the fort in September 1863, the troop was split up. Most of the men joined up with Confederate troops. Brance and Eli decided it more to their advantage to range free in the Ozarks, taking what they wanted from the defenseless farms. Nate and Church had cast their lots with the two bushwhackers in the beginning. The other men came along over the years. In the summer of 1864, they were joined by the two Tyler brothers from Kentucky—two outlaws that could more than match Brance in evil intent. Since the end of the war, and the return of the menfolk to defend their homesteads, Burkett and his band of bushwhackers had found the pickings not so easy. Still, there were plenty of opportunities for ruthless men to take advantage of isolated farms. Like Brance, Eli was not at all pleased with the unfortunate encounter with the lone rifleman. A big part of the gang's success had been their number—a number that was now cut in half.

Chapter 7

Matt assumed he was approaching Fort Smith when he came upon a cleared field down near the river's edge. The occasional field he had seen up until that time had seemed long abandoned. This one had recently been plowed. He walked his horses around the hedgerow at the southern end close to the water. It had been a hard day's ride, and he stopped to water his tired animals. The bay was surviving very well on a diet primarily composed of grass, but Blue was showing signs of fatigue. "Spoiled," Matt stated as he rubbed the big stallion's neck. "You're just gonna have to get used to it, boy. Oats aren't always that easy to come by."

Back in the saddle, he continued along the river trail. In less than an hour's ride, he came upon a gathering of buildings that were the outskirts of the town of Fort Smith. Beyond this cluster of buildings, he could see the walls of the fort itself. The sight of the military post caused him to pause and reconsider. He had no desire to come into contact with Union soldiers, even though he figured there was little chance there would be any interest in him at this distant outpost. He would have bypassed Fort Smith altogether had it not been for his need to resupply himself with basic essentials before venturing into Indian Territory. And Fort Smith was the last opportunity for that. *Hell,* he thought, *I'll go on into town. There ain't much chance anybody will pay me any mind.*

Will Andrews looked up from the sack of flour he was sifting through when a shadow fell across him. The tall figure blocking his light from the doorway paused a moment to survey the room before stepping inside. "Afternoon," Matt offered in greeting.

"Afternoon," Will returned, squinting in an effort to recognize the visitor to his store. "What can I do for you?"

Matt looked around the room at the empty shelves. "I was hoping to buy some coffee and maybe some bacon or side meat. I've been eatin' a helluva lot of wild game lately, and a taste of salt pork would be welcome." When the storekeeper continued to gaze at him without answering, Matt continued. "I could use some forty-four cartridges."

Will appeared dumbfounded for a moment before replying. "Mister, where the hell have you been for the last four years?" He made a sweeping gesture toward his empty shelves. "I ain't had spit to sell since the damn Yankee army took over."

Matt shook his head thoughtfully, realizing then how naive his requests had been. "I'm not from around here. I was just hopin' you might have some supplies." He turned, preparing to take his leave.

"Hold on a minute, mister," Will said, his tone softening a little. "Times have been so hard around here that I reckon I forgot common courtesy." He got up from his stool and extended his hand. "Will Andrews is the name. I've got some green coffee beans I can let you have, and some of this flour if you want it. Don't have no pork at all. About the only meat I see lately comes in the flour sacks." He nodded toward a can on the floor beside the flour sack where he had been depositing the weevils he had been sifting from the flour.

"I reckon I could use the coffee," Matt replied, shaking Will's hand. "You know where I can get some oats for my horses?"

"You can try Sam Pickens down at the end of the street. He owns the stables and does some blacksmithin'. He might have some." While he talked, Will pulled the top off of a barrel, and scooped out some coffee beans. He paused to glance at Matt, waiting for his nod. Matt nodded when the sack was three quarters full, and Will tied it off and plopped it on his scale. "'Pears like you've been travelin' for a spell. Where'd you ride in from?"

"Back east," Matt replied. It was apparent that the storekeeper wanted to make conversation, but Matt figured the less talk, the better. He promptly changed the subject. "I've got a sizable stack of deer hides I'd like to trade somewhere."

Will shook his head slowly. "I don't know any folks around here that would have much use for deer hides."

"Well, much obliged," Matt said as he paid for his coffee, and turned to leave. Will walked out the door with him.

"You headed over to the fort?" Will asked.

"What?" Matt answered after abruptly pausing in the doorway. Realizing that Will was waiting for his answer, he blurted, "Ah, no, I reckon not." The cause for his momentary distraction was the display of notices tacked on the door. Down near the bottom was a *Wanted* poster for one Matt Slaughter, wanted for murder in Virginia. It featured a drawing of his likeness. He glanced at Will's face. The storekeeper paid no mind to the notices, continuing his conversation.

"Well, if you're lookin' for a place to settle down, there's plenty of good land around here, and cheap as you'll ever find it."

"I reckon I'll just be passin' through," Matt said, and packed his coffee sack away on his horse.

Will stepped back to allow room for Matt to turn his horse. "Well, stop in to see me again if you get back this way, Mister . . ." He paused. "I never did get your name."

"Shannon," Matt replied. "The name's Shannon."

"Well, good luck to you, young feller." He stood watching Matt as he rode down to the end of the dusty street toward the blacksmith. *Seemed like a nice enough young man*, Will thought. Then he went back into the store, still oblivious to the wanted poster on his door.

Sam Pickens took a moment to wipe the grease from his hands before propping the wheel against the bed of the wagon box that awaited it. A short, stocky man, he displayed a generous grin for the stranger standing in the open doorway. "Can I help ya?"

"I could use some oats for my horses if you've got any," Matt replied. "They been feedin' on nothin' but grass for a spell."

"Sure, I got oats," Sam said, obviously disappointed that the stranger was not seeking anything beyond horse feed. "I can give you a good price for shoeing them horses."

"Just had it done a few days back," Matt replied.

Sam nodded slowly. "You in town for a while? I can board them animals for four bits a day, includin' a ration of oats." When Matt hesitated to answer right away, Sam went on. "We got us a dandy hotel in town now—fixed it up proper since the Yankees like to burnt it to the ground—got a saloon downstairs."

It was tempting. It had been a while since he had slept in a bed, or had a drink of liquor. He didn't miss sleeping in a bed that much, but a drink of liquor might hit the spot. There was still enough money to splurge a little on self-indulgence. Still, there was the thought of that *Wanted* poster. He thought about the sketch of his face on the paper. It didn't look much like him, in his opinion. Will Andrews had not made the connection. After debating the issue for a few moments, he decided that he could risk a visit to a saloon. "Money's a little in short supply right now," he finally stated. "I'll leave my horses with you overnight, but I don't reckon I'll stay in the hotel."

"For a quarter a night, you can sleep in the stable with your horses," Sam was quick to suggest. "There's already another feller sleepin' here."

"You want fifty cents for a horse, but only a quarter for me?" Matt asked, somewhat amused.

"I don't have to feed you no oats," Sam replied, causing Matt to smile.

"What's your pleasure, mister?"

"Got anything that won't kill a man?" Matt replied to the bartender.

The bartender, a beefy Irishman with whiskey-flushed cheeks, responded with a wide grin. "Hell,

I've got some premium corn liquor, just come down from St. Louis. You're in luck, young feller, it's the first we've had that ain't homegrown for quite a spell."

"I'll risk it," Matt replied, and put his money on the bar while the bartender poured his drink. "Might as well make it a double if it's as good as you say."

"Smooth as silk," the bartender said, and slid the glass over toward Matt.

It was early in the evening, and there were no other patrons in the saloon except for a five-handed poker game at a table in the back corner of the room. Matt took a sip of his whiskey and blinked back the burn as the fiery liquid scorched his throat. *Damn*, he thought, *it's been a while.* He walked back to the poker table to watch while he sipped his drink. "Evenin'," he said. "Mind if I watch a few hands?"

They turned to look him over for a second, then quickly turned their attention back to the game—all but one. He had the look of a gambler, in his frock-tailed black coat and his string tie, with eyes deep set behind heavy brows. He took a bit longer to look the stranger over before responding to Matt's question. "Not if you don't stand too close—I like plenty of elbow room when I'm playin' cards." Matt nodded. The gambler continued to look him over for a few moments more. "Maybe you'd like to sit in for a few hands."

"Thanks just the same," Matt replied. "I'll just finish my drink and be on my way." String Tie gazed at him for a moment longer, then dismissed him from his mind, returning his concentration to the game at hand.

It *had* been a long time between drinks for Matt, and, with his empty stomach, he could feel the effects of the alcohol almost immediately. There was a definite tingling in his brain as the strong elixir rushed through his bloodstream. *I couldn't take much of this*, he thought. *I'd soon be on my ass.* He tried to concentrate on the card game, and determine who was winning and who was taking a beating.

After watching for only a few minutes, it was obvious that four of the players seemed to know each other. The fifth, a big man with a bald head and a full, bushy gray beard, dressed in animal skins, was apparently a stranger to the others—and also apparently the biggest loser. There was a sizable pile of money on the table, most of it before String Tie. The longer Matt watched, the more convinced he was that the stranger was in the process of being fleeced by the other four. String Tie was extremely deft when it came to handling the cards, and even with the alcohol buzz in Matt's brain, he was certain he saw a card come off the bottom of the deck when the man dealt. He also noticed that a couple of the other men busily engaged the stranger in animated conversation during every deal, keeping his glass full from a bottle on the table. *The poor bastard*, Matt thought, *like a lamb to the slaughter.*

The longer Matt looked at the bushy-faced loser, the more the man seemed familiar to him, as if he had seen him before somewhere. *It's probably the whiskey*, he thought. *Whiskey makes your mind think all kinds of things.* With that thought in mind, he decided it was time for him to get back to the stable. He didn't care to watch any more of the blatant fleecing of the burly stranger, anyway. He turned to leave when String Tie stopped him.

"What's your hurry, mister? You sure you don't wanna sit in a few hands?" He fashioned a wide smile for Matt's benefit. "I'm sure the boys here don't mind another player." His three conspirators grinned and nodded their approval, playing their parts. The bald, bushy-faced man simply stared blankly at the shot glass in his hand.

Matt couldn't suppress a wry smile at the thought of the invitation. The small amount of money left before the big man was sign enough that a new sucker would soon be needed. The four scavengers watched him like a pack of hungry wolves, staring at a calf. "I reckon not," he said. "I don't have money to spare."

"That's a mighty fancy-lookin' rifle you're holdin' onto there," String Tie said. "I'd be willin' to lend you a stake on that rifle."

Matt suddenly lost his patience with the blatant attempt to fleece yet another stranger. He knew he'd best just turn and walk away, but he was beginning to feel sorry for their victim, who appeared to be stunned at the moment by an overconsumption of alcohol. "I expect if I was to play poker, I'd prefer to take my chances with somebody who didn't deal from the top *and* bottom of the deck."

String Tie blinked hard, taken aback by the comment. He quickly recovered, however, and the thin smile returned to his face when he replied. "That's kinda hard talk, mister—kinda insultin' to me and my friends here."

At that point, the big bushy-faced man seemed to come out of his stupor. "You and your friends has been mighty damn lucky all right," he blurted. "Too damn lucky, if you ask me." He pushed his chair back from the table.

Anticipating the storm that was about to strike the saloon, String Tie took off his hat and began to rake all the money into it. "Just hold it right there," the game's victim warned, and got to his feet. "I knew you bastards was cheatin' me." His shoulders were as wide as an oxbow, but he was more than a little unsteady, a result of the quantity of whiskey he had consumed. His uncertain appearance caused one of String Tie's partners to make a faulty judgment. A sizable man himself, he kicked his chair back as he rose to his feet, and without warning, delivered a haymaker to the side of the victim's face. The blow resulted in little more than causing the bearded brute's head to turn slightly, and his eyes blinked several times as if just awakening. His assailant seemed momentarily stunned, staring at his fist as if checking a weapon to see if it was loaded. When he glanced up again, it was just in time to get a close look at the knuckles of the massive fist that flattened him.

Apparently having learned nothing after seeing his partner slide across the floor on his back, the man on the other side of Bushy Face took a swing at him. His results were similar to those of his partner, and he wobbled drunkenly before crumpling to the floor with a dislocated jaw. Seeing the folly in facing the enraged giant head-on, String Tie grabbed the whiskey bottle from the table and positioned himself behind his adversary while Bushy Face was occupied with the others. He was about to deliver a blow to the back of the brute's skull when the butt of Matt's rifle flattened his nose and sent him staggering against the bar. His hat dropped to the floor, spilling money in the process.

The rapid series of events, taking place within a few moments' time, left the last one of the card players with a decision, which he made without hesitation. Out the door he went, as fast as his legs could carry him. Taking advantage of the distraction caused by his partner's sudden sprint for the door, String Tie reached inside his coat and drew his revolver.

"I wouldn't," Matt warned the gambler, and leveled his rifle at him.

"You son of a bitch," String Tie hissed, but thought better of making a move.

"I expect it would be best if you and your friends dragged your cheatin' asses outta here," Matt suggested. Seeing the wisdom in the stranger's suggestion, the three struggled to their feet, realizing that they had been beaten. "Leave it," Matt warned when String Tie made a move to pick up the money. "You can have your hat. Leave the rest."

String Tie scowled like a cur dog. "That money belongs to me," he complained, his words garbled by the blood flowing from his broken nose.

"Not anymore," Matt replied without emotion. "Now, get goin'."

During this brief exchange, Bushy Face stared at the young stranger who had stepped in to help him. His face expressionless behind the full growth of whiskers, and with dull eyes, he watched the retreat of the remaining three of his adversaries. Matt glanced at him in time to see a spark of action in his eyes. A moment later, the big man made a sudden move toward him. Startled, Matt crouched, reacting as fast as he could to defend himself as Bushy Face threw a massive punch toward his head.

The fist missed by a wide margin, and Matt set himself to come up under the brute's chin with the Henry. An instant before he retaliated, he heard a dull grunt and the smack of a fist against flesh. Turning at once, he saw the bartender drop to the floor, a four-foot length of timber falling to clatter on the planks. Quickly shifting his gaze back to the huge man standing before him, he saw the whiskers part to reveal a wide grin. "He was fixin' to give you a real big headache," the huge man said.

"Damn, I reckon," Matt replied, looking down at the heavy piece of lumber. He picked it up and stood poised to use it on his assailant should the bartender wish to continue the fight. Choosing a wiser course, the bartender crawled behind the counter to try to shake off the effects of the big man's fist.

"I owe you my thanks, mister," he stated, and thrust out his hand. "Smith's the name. I believe those ol' boys was about to skin me good. Good thing you come along." When Matt shook his hand, he knelt down and began gathering up the money. "Yessir, they was fillin' me so full of that rotgut whiskey, I swear, I didn't know if I was comin' or goin', but I knew they had to be cheatin'."

Matt couldn't help but marvel at how suddenly sober the big man had become. "Shannon," he replied in response to Smith's introduction, and stood watching while Smith scooped up the money.

"Most of this is mine, anyway," Smith continued, giving Matt a wink. "But there's a little profit here that I reckon I'm obliged to share with you. You shore as hell earned it."

Less concerned with the money than the thought of retaliation, Matt moved to the end of the bar where he could see what the bartender was up to. He soon spotted what he was looking for, and reached over the bar to retrieve a sawed-off shotgun. Breaking the breech, he pulled the shells out and threw them across the room. Then he laid the shotgun on the counter. Glancing at the cowering bartender, he was convinced that the precaution had probably been unnecessary. "I expect we'd better get outta here," he said to Smith, "before your friends decide to come back for their money."

"Yeah, I reckon," Smith replied, a wide grin parting the beard. He was obviously pleased with the way the evening had turned out.

Outside the saloon, they both took a quick look up and down the street to make sure there was no surprise waiting for them. The street seemed clear, so they paused to shake hands again. "I owe you, Shannon, for steppin' in back there," Smith said, and pressed a stack of bills in Matt's hand. Matt tried to refuse the money, but Smith insisted. "You go on and take it. Hell, it belonged to them buzzards, anyway. I ain't got many friends in this world, and I reckon you're the only one I got in this town."

"All right," Matt relented. There was no doubt but what he could use the money. He stepped down from the boardwalk and turned toward the stable at the end of the street.

"You headed for the stable?" Smith asked. "That's where I'm goin'. I'll walk with you."

"I figured you were stayin' in the hotel," Matt said.

"Hell, no," Smith replied. "I ain't got no money to waste on a fancy bed. I need all my money to play cards." He laughed at his own comment.

They walked down the dusty street together, Smith in animated conversation about the card game, Matt scanning the street from side to side cautiously. He was not ready to believe that the likes of String Tie and his partners were prone to leave the fight without an attempt to recover their losses.

Matt's intuition was right on target. The gambler wearing the black frock coat and string tie, known to his partners as Shiner, was at that moment holding a handkerchief under his bloody nose. While the bleeding had slowed almost to a trickle, the nose was already swelling to double its normal size. "That son of a bitch with the rifle is gonna rue the day he set foot in this town," he muttered angrily as he led his two partners into the back door of the stable. The fourth member of his party, who had made the hasty exit from the saloon, was still nowhere to be found. The two that remained, Tasker and Bodie, had scores to settle for themselves. All three were determined to extract vengeance on the big bald man and his newfound friend.

Sam Pickens looked up when he heard the three come in the back of the stable. He recognized Shiner and his two friends immediately. Knowing they could hardly be up to any good, he called out. "What can I do for you, Shiner?" He noticed that all three were carrying rifles.

"We've got a little business to take care of," Shiner replied. "And if you don't wanna get hurt, I'd advise you to make yourself scarce."

Sam hesitated, looking from one to the other. He was a peaceful man and liked to avoid trouble. But this was his property, and he didn't like being ordered out of his own stable. "I don't know what kinda trouble you've been up to this time, Shiner, but I don't appreciate you bringin' it to my place."

Shiner possessed neither the time nor the patience to bother with Sam Pickens. "I ain't got time to fool with you, dammit. There's gonna be lead flyin' around in here in a few minutes, and if you're in the way, it'll just be your tough luck. So get the hell outta here before I decide to shoot you down just for the hell of it." He stood there, glaring at the stable owner for several long seconds, his rifle poised to back up his threat while Sam made up his mind.

Sam had attempted to demonstrate some backbone, but after thinking it over, he felt it wasn't worth the risk. Without another word, he turned to leave, deciding it far more sensible to find the deputy marshal, and let him handle it. When he had left, Shiner turned to give quick instructions to his men. "Bodie! Over there behind them hay bales—Tasker, you climb up there in the loft. I'm gonna be here in the last stall, so mind which way you're shootin'."

Matt and his newfound friend, the shiny-domed, bushy-whiskered man calling himself Smith, approached the stables just in time to see Sam Pickens coming out the front entrance. "Evenin', Mr. Pickens," Smith called out cheerfully.

Sam hesitated for only a step or two, staring at the two men as if he had never met them. He couldn't decide if he should warn them or just stay out of it, and let the lot of them kill each other off. He wavered for only a moment. "Evenin'," he muttered, barely above a whisper, and hurried away.

Matt and Smith turned to watch him depart. "Now, he's actin' kinda strange, ain't he?" Smith mused. He glanced briefly at Matt, then turned to stare at the front entrance to the stable. The soft glow of a lantern somewhere inside the building illuminated the entrance. "Looks like he left a light on for us," Smith joked soberly. Sam's behavior was warning enough, even if the stable owner had declined to speak a word of caution. Smith continued to stare at the doorway to the stable, unconsciously shifting the pistol in his holster to make sure it was free. "You any good with that rifle you're totin'?" he asked calmly.

"I reckon," Matt replied, equally calm. He had been almost certain that they were far from finished with String Tie and his friends. He would have preferred to avoid another confrontation, but his horses and all his gear were in the stable, and he had no intention of losing them.

"I expect if we go walkin' in the front door, we might find a little welcomin' party waitin' for us," Smith said. He took a few moments to consider. "There's a window in the tack room on the other side. You look a helluva lot younger and fitter that I am. Suppose you could climb in that window? I'm afraid I've got too much belly to tote."

"Yeah," Matt replied, "I can make it."

"All right, I'll sneak around and come in the back. Whaddaya think?"

"Sounds as good a plan as any," Matt said.

Matt propped his rifle against the weathered boards of the barn side while he pulled himself up to the windowsill. After a quick look inside to make sure there was no one in the room, he pulled his body up, and went headfirst through the window. Once inside, he got to his feet and reached back out the window where Smith was waiting to hand up his rifle. Smith nodded as Matt took the Henry, then turned and disappeared around the back corner of the building.

It was not yet a hard dark outside the stable when

Matt had climbed through the tack room window. Inside the small room, there was no more than a flicker of lantern light through the open doorway. It struck Matt as kind of careless for Sam Pickens to leave his stable with a lantern burning. The man had seemed to be in a bit of a hurry, all the more evidence pointing to an ambush waiting in the stable.

Matt moved silently across to the doorway where he paused to listen. There was no sound in the stable other than the nervous shifting of horses' hooves in the stalls and an occasional whinny. From his position inside the tack room door, he could see the front entrance to the stable, and the lantern sitting in the middle of the floor just inside. It was obviously set there on purpose to illuminate the entrance. He moved to the other side of the door, so he could look back toward the rear of the stable. Peering into the darkened rear of the building, his gaze shifted from the back stalls to a stack of hay bales in one corner. *A likely spot*, he thought, and unconsciously felt the hammer of his rifle with his thumb to make sure he had cocked it.

Dropping to one knee, he inched closer to the door frame, his rifle trained on the baled hay. In the next instant, the quiet interior of the stable exploded with gunfire, and flashes of muzzle blasts split the darkness like dueling lightning bolts as Smith suddenly charged through the back door. Matt pumped three quick rounds into the hay bales, aiming at the muzzle flash. One of his shots found its target, as evidenced by a sharp yelp of pain.

Matt ran across the open stable to take cover in an empty stall as another barrage of gunfire broke out near the back entrance. From the muzzle flashes, Matt could see that it was an exchange of pistol fire at close range. Afterward, there was a long period of silence. After a few moments more, he heard Smith call out. "Shannon, you all right?"

"Yeah," Matt replied.

"We got both of the bastards," Smith came back. "They was waitin' for us all right."

Matt was about to wonder aloud about the other two poker players when he was suddenly stopped by a fine rain of hay dust sifting through the boards over his head. "Look out!" he yelled, but it was not quick enough to warn Smith. From his position in the loft, Tasker opened fire with his pistol just as Smith walked out into the lantern light. The bullet caught Smith in the shoulder and spun him around. Matt's reactions were immediate, and Tasker fell from the loft, dead before his body crashed to the dirt floor with three .44 bullets in his chest.

Matt took a quick look at Tasker to make sure he was dead. Then he made sure of the other two before going to Smith's aid. "That was mighty damn careless, not checkin' the loft," Smith groaned as he held his shoulder.

"How bad is it?" Matt asked.

"Well, I've had worse, I reckon, but it hurts like hell."

"Maybe we can find a doctor in this town," Matt said.

"No—hell, no," Smith protested at once. "We'd best get our horses, and get the hell outta here before that feller Pickens shows up with the deputy marshal. Somebody's bound to come a'runnin' to see what all the shootin' was about." He looked around for something to stuff against the wound to slow the flow of blood. "I don't need no doctor, anyway. Just get me on my horse. I've got a place over in Injun Territory, and a woman who can take care of this bullet wound." He grabbed a rag from a nail on the side of a stall, and stuffed it inside his shirt.

A crowd of curious spectators was still gathering in front of the stables when the two riders galloped away into the night. Smith led the way, his body slumped slightly forward in the saddle, his left hand thrust inside his shirt in a makeshift sling for his wounded shoulder. Matt followed his new partner, leading both their pack horses, half expecting Smith to tumble from the saddle at any minute. The wound did not appear serious, but there had been quite a bit of blood loss, and Matt had seen men in the war faint from severe bleeding. Smith insisted that he was all right. Matt had to admit, the man seemed to be a tough old bird.

When Fort Smith was far enough behind them to let up on the horses, they slowed to a walk. As Smith led them along a trail that wound through the hills north of the town, Matt thought about the turn of events that resulted in this new direction his life had taken. He knew nothing about the man he was riding with, other than the apparent fact that he was an easy pigeon to pluck at a poker table, and a helluva man in a bar fight. Still, Matt had detected an honest-rogue quality in the man that somehow suggested a sense of fairness. Matt followed him into Indian Territory simply because the man was wounded, although Matt was beginning to believe Smith didn't need anyone to accompany him. Aside from that, Matt rode with him because he had no better plan. It didn't seem healthy to hang around Fort Smith after shooting three men, especially after having seen a *Wanted* poster with his picture on it.

Smith said he had a place in the Cherokee nation. Matt would go with him at least that far. Then he would decide where he would strike out from there.

They made camp with little more than three or four hours left before sunup, confident at that point that there was no posse on their trail. While Smith knelt by a small stream to clean some of the dried blood away from his shoulder, Matt gathered some wood for a fire. After he took care of the horses, he came back to the fire to join Smith. "You want me to take a look at that wound?" Matt asked.

"It's all right, just startin' to puff up a little. The damn slug's still in there, but Broken Reed can dig it out tomorrow. We oughta be at my place before dark."

"That thing's gotta be sore as hell," Matt said. "You sure you don't want me to try to cut it out?"

"Thanks just the same," Smith insisted. "But we're less than a day to home; I expect I'd druther have Broken Reed do it."

"All right," Matt shrugged. He gazed at the wounded man for a long moment. "Smith," he pronounced, as if sounding it for the first time. "What the hell is your real name?"

The big man chuckled before answering. "Ike," he said, "Ike Brister."

Ike Brister. The name triggered a thought in Matt's memory. No wonder the bushy-faced man had seemed familiar to him before. Ike Brister—that was the man on the *Wanted* poster he had found in Tyler's saddlebags back in West Virginia. So now he was not only an outlaw, he had partnered up with an outlaw—a murderer no less. "I saw your likeness on a

Wanted paper," Matt said. "It said you murdered somebody."

"I seen your'n," Ike returned frankly. "It said the same thing, only your name weren't Shannon."

"Matt Slaughter," Matt introduced himself. "They're sayin' I killed a Union officer, but it wasn't murder. It was an accident. The damn gun went off during a fight. He wouldn't be dead if he hadn't pulled the pistol."

"They're after me for killin' a soldier, too," Ike said. "Only it weren't no accident. I followed the son of a bitch all the way up into Missouri to kill him. He was a sergeant with a Union cavalry company. They burnt my daddy's house to the ground. And when Pap was finally smoked out, they shot him down, right there in his front yard. I reckon things like that happen in a war, but they wouldn't let my mama even go to Pap's side. This sergeant dragged her off, and hit her with his gun butt when she tried to pull away from him. If I'd been there, that sergeant wouldn't have drawed another breath. Mama never got over that blow to the head. Some friends of ours said she finally died two months later. It took me the better part of two years to find the bastard that killed her, but, by God, I sent him to hell where he belongs."

There followed a long period of silence as both men thought about the irony of their situations. Matt had not really committed the crime for which he was wanted, but in his mind he knew that he could not fault Ike for taking the action he did. In his place, he would have been likely to do the same thing. Finding it awkward to say much in response to Ike's confession, he shrugged and asked, "So you saw my picture on a poster, did you?" Ike nodded and smiled. "And you recognized me?"

"Hell, I knew you were wanted when you came in the saloon."

Matt thought that over for a few moments while he made a decision. He reached up and stroked his mustache. "I reckon I'll be shavin' in the mornin'."

They started out again at daybreak, Ike leading a clean-shaven Matt and the pack horses, continuing north until reaching a cross-trail that led them due west. They were well into Indian Territory now, and less than a day's ride from the Cherokee village Ike called home. Maintaining a steady pace, the two riders held to a northwest course that led through country with hills covered with oaks and hickories. Ike plodded along, never complaining about a wound that was obviously beginning to fester. Matt decided that his gruff new friend was more than a little skittish about someone he just met probing his shoulder with a knife.

True to his reckoning, a little after sundown on the second day, they struck a river that Ike identified as the Illinois. He led them down to the water's edge where he pulled up and waited for Matt to come alongside. They paused there to let the horses drink, and Matt took the time to admire the pristine beauty of the river. His gaze scanned the high bluffs on the opposite side, covered with oaks and giant sycamores. Downstream, a small rocky island, thick with brush and river birch, split the gently flowing crystal clear water. Matt decided that he had seen few rivers that were prettier.

"Come on," Ike said, breaking into his brief reverie. "We ain't got but two miles to go."

They picked up a trail that led along the river, and in a short time, Ike pulled up on a knoll overlooking a broad open meadow. Ike pointed to a cluster of log huts and skin lodges. "That there's Old Bear's village," he said. "He's my papa-in-law, although me and Broken Reed ain't never been officially hitched." He nudged his horse with his heels. "Come on. I'm gettin' hungry, and this damn shoulder is painin' me somethin' fierce."

Chapter 8

Jesse Tyler reluctantly stopped to water his horse, then only because of the real possibility he would soon be on foot if he didn't rest the tired animal. It had been a hard ride from West Virginia, through parts of Kentucky and Missouri, and now finally back in Arkansas territory. He had shown the weary horse no mercy in his urgency to track down the man called Shannon. Knowing his brother as well as he did, it wasn't hard to figure out what had happened. When Wesley had heard about the turkey shoot in the little hollow in West Virginia, he figured he was going to have that Henry rifle one way or another. When he failed to return, Jesse went there to find out why. It didn't take much persuasion to learn the man's name who had won the rifle. There could be little doubt that Shannon was the man who killed his brother. It made no difference to Jesse that his brother had trailed Shannon for the purpose of murdering him. Wesley was his brother, and nobody was going to get away with killing Jesse Tyler's brother.

It had been pure luck that he had picked up

Shannon's trail in the little town of Boiling Springs. He had been about to admit he had lost him when he decided to ride into Boiling Springs to buy a bottle of whiskey. A casual remark by the bartender caused Tyler to seek out the blacksmith and inquire about another stranger who recently passed through.

"Feller over at the saloon said you was talkin' about a stranger ridin' through here a few days ago."

The blacksmith, Bowers, turned to face Tyler. "Is that so?" he replied. This stranger in black asking questions made him cautious for some reason. The man had a look about him that some would call calculating. Others, less eloquent, would simply describe it as a cold, mean scowl. Bowers took an immediate dislike to the man. "I'd say it was more like a week or so," he said.

"What was his name?" Tyler demanded.

"I don't believe he give his name," Bowers said. "Leastways, I don't recollect that he did."

Tyler was suspicious. He had a feeling that the smithy had some reason to cover up for Shannon. He was beginning to lose his temper. He pulled out his pistol, and held it up before Bowers' face. "Would it help your memory if I was to stick this pistol up your nose?"

Bowers suddenly realized what manner of man he was dealing with, and an earlier sense of caution gave way to fright. The look on Jesse Tyler's snarling face bore testimony that he was not a man to cross. "There's no call to get riled, mister," he quickly replied. "Now that I think on it some, I believe his name was Shannon."

"Where was he headin' when he left here?"

"I don't know," Bowers stammered. Then, noticing the narrowing of Tyler's eyes, he hastily added, "He asked about the way to Fort Smith."

Tyler nodded thoughtfully, and holstered his weapon. "Headin' for Injun Territory," he said to himself, no longer interested in the blacksmith. Without another word to Bowers, he climbed up in the saddle and rode out of town. Bowers stood watching him, feeling a sudden need to empty his bladder, until he disappeared from sight, hoping it was the last he would see of the man.

Jesse Tyler was possessed of an evil determination. He was a born loner, even when his brother was alive and the two of them rode with Brance Burkett and his gang. Very few members of the gang approached him, due to his brooding nature. His brother had advised them that it was best to just leave him alone. Not long after the two brothers joined the gang, the rest of the men were witness to the depth of Jesse's determination.

Raiding along the Missouri border during the last months of the war, the gang happened upon a farmer named Miller, his wife, and two small children—a girl around nine, and a twelve- or thirteen-year-old boy. They were driving a wagon back from the little town of Neosho with a few meager supplies. When waylaid by Brance and his men, the father elected to reject the demand to hand over the supplies, resulting in his untimely death. Once the shooting started, there seemed no sense in leaving witnesses. The man's wife and the little girl were shot immediately. But the boy picked up a hammer that lay in the wagon, and hurled it at those approaching him. It grazed Jesse's arm. The boy dived over the side of the wagon, and was off through the brush like a rabbit.

"Hell, let him go," Brance called out. "We're headin' south, anyway."

"The little shit almost took my head off," Jesse growled, and turned his horse in pursuit. The brush, though easily penetrated by a small boy, was too thick for a man on a horse. Jesse cursed and kicked his horse hard, galloping down the road until he could swing around the dense thicket. Ignoring the calls from his brother to let the boy go, he searched the woods, trying to pick up the boy's trail. Once he found it, he trailed the youngster relentlessly until the boy emerged from the woods no more than a quarter of a mile from town. Jesse picked up the boy's footprints in the soft sand of the road, and followed them through the lower part of the town to the church.

An evening prayer service was interrupted by the sudden appearance of the frightened child as he burst into the church, seeking safety. Gasping for breath, he ran up the center aisle toward the startled minister and fell before the pulpit. Moments later, the congregation was jolted yet again by another abrupt intrusion upon their service, this time in the form of Satan himself, wearing a gun belt. Shocked speechless, not one of the good Christians in the tiny church was moved to take action against this flagrant invasion of evil. They watched, horrified, as Jesse drew his pistol and calmly walked up to the cowering boy. Without hesitation, he executed the defenseless lad, placing two bullets in the boy's brain.

The sudden explosion of the pistol shots ripped the

silence of the church like bolts of lightning, rendering every gentle soul in the congregation aghast in shocked paralysis. Those closest to the aisle would later recall the sulfurous odor of gun smoke that wafted slowly from the barrel of Jesse's revolver. With no show of haste, he turned, and with the weapon still drawn, walked back down the aisle toward the door. Stunned, each male member of the congregation averted his eyes as Jesse passed, fearful that he might intercept the evil one's gaze.

Outside the church, there were still no sounds of reaction from the stunned gathering inside. Feeling no sense of urgency, Jesse calmly stepped up in the saddle, wheeled his horse, and took his leave of Neosho, feeling that the boy's attack upon him had been met with sufficient retaliation. By the time the good folk of Neosho had recovered enough to inform the sheriff, and a posse was formed, Jesse and the Burkett gang were miles away to the south. This evil determination that relentlessly followed a twelve-year-old boy to his execution was now focused upon the man who had killed Jesse's brother—a man called Shannon.

"Yessir, we had ourselves some excitement around here about a week ago." Jake Barnhill, the bartender, polished a shot glass as he talked. The stranger at the bar seemed interested, so he continued. "Three fellers was gunned down over in the livery stable—the ones that did it was settin' right over at that table playin' cards, right where your friends is settin'." He went on to relate the events that led to the fight in the saloon. The stranger was keenly interested when he described the two men who had the altercation with Shiner and his cronies.

"And you say them two didn't come in together?" Brance Burkett asked.

"Nah, they didn't," Jake replied, folding the soiled cloth and laying it on the bar. "I don't think they even knew each other before they came in here."

"The younger one, you say you ain't never seen him around here before?"

"Nope," Jake said. "He was totin' one of those Henry rifles, and he looked like he might be pretty handy with it."

Jake's last remark caused Brance to raise an eyebrow. "And him and the other feller, the bald-headed one, they was the ones that gunned down three fellers in the stable?"

"Well, I reckon," Jake asserted. "Sam Pickens seen the two of 'em walk into his stable not five minutes before the shootin' started. And they sure as hell hightailed it outta town right after."

Brance couldn't help smiling to himself when he thought about the bartender's accounting of the shooting. It was him, all right—him and that fancy repeating rifle of his. "Did you get his name?" Brance asked, "The younger one."

"Shannon," Jake replied.

Brance smiled as he repeated the name to himself. *Shannon.* There was little question where Shannon and his partner had headed—Indian Territory, where most outlaws found refuge from the law. Brance and his boys knew something about Indian Territory. He just might meet up with Shannon again. Next time, it would be with a better consequence. Bringing his thoughts back to the conversation, he asked, "Didn't nobody go after them two? No posse or nothin'?"

"Oh, hell, yeah," Jake replied. "There was even a cavalry patrol sent out lookin' for 'em, but they never picked up their trail past Rottenwood Creek. Hell, them two is gone, most likely past the dead line."

"Maybe so," Brance said, thinking that it might take an outlaw to find an outlaw. He was more than casually familiar with the dead line, an imaginary boundary about ninety miles beyond Fort Smith. It was beyond this line that the odds a lawman could venture and still come back with his life were slim at best. "Well, much obliged," he said to Jake, and returned to the table to join his friends.

Brance sat down at the table next to Eli and poured himself a drink from the bottle in the center. "I'm thinkin' about a little ride over in Injun Territory," he said, "to do a little huntin'." He then proceeded to tell the story he had just learned from the bartender.

"Hell, we might as well," Spit remarked. "We sure ain't doin' nothin' around here." He leaned over and spat on the plank floor for emphasis.

"Well, I'll be go to hell," Eli suddenly exclaimed. "Would you look what the cat just drug in." Everyone turned to follow the direction of his gaze. A shadowy figure stood just outside the swinging doors of the saloon, looking the room over before entering. "Bartender! You'd best bring us another bottle," Eli ordered.

Seeing the familiar faces of his partners, Jesse Tyler stepped inside, into the light of the room. He stood there for a moment, his wide-brimmed, flat-crowned black hat pulled low on his forehead, showing almost no sign that he recognized the six men seated at the table. It was typical of Tyler's manner—devoid of expression, his face hard as granite. After a moment, he walked over to the table, his Spencer cradled in his arms. Each man nodded a respectful greeting as Jesse pulled up a chair from another table. Brance was the first to speak to him.

"Well, damn, Tyler, I see you missed us enough to come back." He craned his neck to look toward the door. "Where's Wesley?"

"Wesley's dead," Tyler replied without emotion. "Murdered by the bastard I'm on my way to kill."

"Goddam," Brance responded, shaking his head slowly. "Well, we're right sorry to hear that. Ain't we boys?" To a man, they all nodded slowly. "This feller, this walkin' dead man, has he got a name?"

"Shannon," Tyler answered.

"Shannon?" Eli exclaimed, unable to keep a smile from his face. "Small world, ain't it, Brance?"

"It is for a fact," Brance responded, then turned back to explain to the puzzled Tyler. "You ain't the only one lookin' for Mr. Shannon. We've got a little score to settle with that man ourselves. If you'll notice, there ain't but six of us settin' around here drinking liquor."

Tyler acknowledged the remark with little more than a shift of his eyes. He had noticed that half of the gang was absent, but he had not been interested enough to ask why. When Brance explained, the only emotion Jesse felt was a deepening of the determination he harbored to find Shannon and kill him.

"It's a wonder that ol' boy ain't feelin' shivers runnin' up and down his spine," Spit commented. "He's got plenty o' folks lookin' for his ass. You, us six, the deputy marshal, even the damn army is on his trail." He spat, and wiped the lingering spittle from his chin with the back of his hand.

"We was just talkin' about headin' out to Injun Territory," Brance said. "I expect that's where we might find this feller Shannon."

"I expect so," Tyler agreed. "I've been followin' the bastard all the way from West Virginia, and all along he 'peared to be headin' for the Territory." He fixed a cold eye on Brance. "I'm claimin' first rights on him. He murdered my brother. I figure that gives me a claim."

"Yeah, hell, we've got no problem with that, have we boys?" He looked around him, receiving nods of agreement from the others. "I don't rightly care who takes care of him, just so it's done."

"Injun Territory covers a helluva lot of ground," Corbin spoke up. Silent to that point, he was skeptical about their chances of tracking down two men in a parcel of land that stretched from Texas to Kansas Territory. "Them two might be hard to find."

Having eavesdropped on the conversation between the members of the gang up to that point, the bartender decided to offer a comment. He walked over to the table and placed a spittoon next to Spit's chair, hoping it might encourage him to use it. Spit got the point, and aimed his next expectoration at the brass vessel, barely missing it by an inch or so. He glanced apologetically at the bartender.

"You know, if it would help you fellers," Jake said, "Sam Pickens said he'd never seen the young feller before, but the big bald-headed one has put his horses up in his stable two or three times before." When he saw that he had captured their attention, he went on to elaborate. "Sam said he didn't know much about him, but he did say he was a squaw man—Cherokee woman. So I reckon he's most likely gone to one of the villages in the Cherokee Nation."

"That makes sense," Brance said.

"There's more'n one village in the Cherokee Nation," Corbin felt inclined to say. He was not as passionate for vengeance as Brance or Tyler. The five empty saddles Shannon had left meant a bigger share of their next score for the rest of them. "There ain't a helluva lot to go after in Injun Territory, anyway, unless you want some hides or beads or somethin'."

"There's squaws," Church replied with a grin.

Tyler shifted his lifeless gaze to fix upon Corbin. "Nobody's makin' you go, Corbin. If you ain't got the belly for it, stay here. The bastard killed my brother, and I aim to get him."

"Hell, Tyler," Corbin quickly replied. He had no wish to annoy the belligerent outlaw. "I ain't sayin' I don't wanna go. I was just pointin' out that there's a lot of ground to cover. 'Course I'm goin'."

"'Course he's goin'," Brance echoed. "We'll all start out first thing in the mornin'."

Chapter 9

"*Ma-du*," Broken Reed pronounced softly, and smiled as she passed Matt on her way to fill her water bucket.

Matt nodded and returned the smile. He watched the ample figure as she made her way down to the edge of the river for a moment before he turned to Ike. "She always says that, *Ma-do*, when she sees me. What does it mean? Is she callin' me a coyote or somethin'?"

The question caused Ike to chuckle. "Nah, she ain't callin' you nothin'. She's just callin' your name, *Ma-du*—that's Cherokee for *Matt*."

"Oh." Matt thought about that for a moment, then pronounced it again as it sounded to him, "*Ma-do*." He smiled at Ike. "I didn't figure there was a Cherokee word for Matt. You speak Cherokee?"

"*Tsalagi* is how they say it," Ike replied. "There ain't no *ch* sound in their language. Their real name, when they're talkin' about theirselves, is *Aniyunwiya*. It means *real people* or somethin' like that. I don't know but a few words—enough to let Broken Reed know what I want. She knows enough American so's I know what she's wantin'. We get along pretty good—sorta meet in the middle." He chuckled at the thought.

Matt sat down next to the cabin wall, letting the warm afternoon sun penetrate to his bones. The days were getting shorter. Ike said that chilly weather could probably be expected within three or four weeks. The thought caused him to look at the deer hides stretched out to dry. Broken Reed had taken over his hides, and was busy softening them. Not willing to wait for the stiff skins to cure, she had already begun sewing Matt's new clothes, using previously softened hides of her own. Like Ike, she felt there was little time left before the chilly breezes would come sweeping across the prairie, cutting through Matt's threadbare cavalry britches.

Following his new friend's gaze, Ike guessed what Matt was thinking. "It won't be long till you'll be all dressed up like a wild Injun. Broken Reed works fast. I seen her eyeballin' them boots of your'n, too— wouldn't be surprised if she didn't make you some warm moccasins for the winter."

"I'm obliged," Matt said. He had been warmly received by Broken Reed and her father, Old Bear. The old man lived in a lodge made of buffalo hides, attached to the cabin Ike had built for his wife. Ike said that Old Bear was the chief of this little band of Cherokees. He had walked the Trail of Tears from Carolina, when so many of his people had perished when the government forced them from their ancestral home. The only symbol of any authority he now wore was a small silver cross, given to him by a missionary. The cross was worn on a rawhide thong around the old man's neck. Thinking about it, Matt unconsciously reached up and stroked the tiny silver medal he wore around his own neck.

Old Bear's village was small, with no evidence of prosperity, but the people all seemed to hold Ike in high regard. Matt supposed their fondness for the grizzly bear of a man had a lot to do with the fact that Ike supplied the village with meat and hides. Most of the game around Old Bear's village had been hunted out, and the food rations promised by the government were slow in coming, and sometimes not coming at all. Ike complained that hunting trips were taking longer and longer, since the game was getting so scarce. When Matt asked why the young men of the village didn't do more to supply food, Ike responded. "Look around you. You see many young men?" He answered his own question. "Hell, there ain't no young men. Any that can, get the hell outta here as soon as they can. Wouldn't you?"

Matt had to admit that he would, given the circumstances. But then, he was a man prone to wander, anyway. He would most likely have left the Shenandoah sooner or later, even had he not been forced to run for his life.

For now, he was content to relax for a while, unburden his mind of serious thoughts, and let his horses fatten up a little on the rolling grassland. The bay and his big blue roan grazed with the Indian ponies, and Matt thought he could at last see some signs that Blue was learning to live without a constant portion of oats. The bay needed time to heal before Matt was ready to load a pack on him again. The horse had managed to wedge a granite shard inside the edge of its shoe, causing a bruise to develop. It was healing rapidly, but the horse still favored it. *Too bad the horse doesn't heal as fast as Ike*, Matt thought. The huge man barely favored his wounded shoulder—testimony, Matt supposed, to either an amazing healing capacity, or a magic touch by Broken Reed. Matt was beginning to enjoy this leisure life as he sat with his back to the cabin wall, soaking up the sun from a clear Oklahoma sky.

"*Hi-gi,*" Broken Reed interrupted his reverie, and he opened his eyes to see her smiling face. "*Hi-gi,*" she repeated. "Eat."

"Let's eat it before she throws it to the dogs," Ike said.

Yessir, Matt thought to himself, *a man could get plumb spoiled by this kind of treatment.* He could understand why Ike chose to live with his Cherokee wife. Broken Reed stepped back to allow the men to precede her, smiling at Matt as he passed by. When Ike followed, she reached out and patted his ample stomach. "*Ya-ni-sa,*" she teased, and giggled delightedly when the huge man grabbed for her. Too quick for his lunge, she danced away from him.

"I'll show you who's a buffalo," he threatened playfully, and chased her toward the cabin. Matt couldn't help but grin, watching the youthful antics of his big friend. Their play did, indeed, invoke the image of a buffalo bull chasing after a wolf pup. For a moment, Matt envied his friend. Though only half his age, Broken Reed seemed to glow in Ike's presence. It was a good marriage.

Before long, Matt's contentment with total relaxation waned, and he began to feel the itch to push on to country he had not yet seen. The rolling country around Old Bear's village had taken on a monotony that prompted him to think about the Rocky Mountains he had heard about. Ike fully understood his young friend's urge to see the high country. In his earlier years, Ike had succumbed to the same urges. He was just a boy when he followed his uncle out to Montana Territory, to Alder Gulch and many of the other little creeks, searching for gold. Like most of the other prospectors, they enjoyed spotty luck, finding dust here and there, most of which was squandered away by his uncle on strong spirits and card games. "I roamed the wild country for a few years," Ike said. "Saw a lot of the territory, the Bitterroots, the Wind River Mountains, the Bighorns." He paused to recollect, a misty look in his eye. "Hell, I reckon I'd still be roamin' around somewhere out there if I hadn't rode through Oklahoma Territory about seven years ago, and had Broken Reed throw a halter on me." He laughed at the thought. "I've thought about takin' her with me and headin' outta this place, but she's got relatives here she has to take care of. So I reckon this is where I'll stay till they put me in the ground."

"I expect it's time for me to move on," Matt stated. "It's gonna be gettin' into cold weather pretty soon, and I reckon if I'm gonna head to the high country, I'd best not waste any more time."

"You sure you don't wanna light here until spring? It gets mighty damn cold out on the high prairie. A man can freeze to death right quick."

"I'll be all right," Matt assured his friend. "Broken Reed has fixed me up with some dandy winter clothes." He paused to laugh. "Besides, if I lay around here much longer, I might get as lazy as you."

Once the seed of adventure had taken root in his mind, it was not long before Matt developed an itch to be on his way. He had no particular destination in mind; he just had an urge to see what lay beyond the

horizon. He had always been like that. When his folks
were killed, he insisted that Owen should inherit the
farm. He had been satisfied with the small parcel
down by the river, knowing at the time that he was
bound to leave it sooner or later. Had it not been for
the war, he probably would have already been west of
the high prairie. Now, he reminded himself, there was
an additional reason to keep moving: an arrest warrant back east. It was his hope that he had left those
who might be searching for him behind.

Ike interrupted his thoughts. "One of the young
boys, Crooked Foot, and some of his friends told Old
Bear they saw deer sign aplenty while they was
huntin' over near the Flint Hills. Whaddaya say you
hang around a little longer, and we'll do a little
huntin'?" It was obvious to him that Matt was turning
the prospect over in his mind, so he was quick to encourage the idea. "Most of the whitetails around here
have been scared off. Crooked Foot said it looked like
a sizable herd on the move. It's a little early for the rut-
tin' season to start. I expect the bucks ain't hardly
started to claim their does yet. They'll all be fat and
sassy, carryin' their summer weight. Whaddaya say,
Matt? We could use that rifle of your'n—be a good
chance to pack in a lot of meat and hides for the
village."

The prospect was tempting. Matt always enjoyed
hunting, but the last comment Ike had made convinced him. It would be a good opportunity to help
supply the village with meat, and he felt obliged to the
people in Old Bear's camp. They had made him feel
welcome, and thanks to Broken Reed's deft hand, he
was now outfitted for the coming winter in warm

buckskins. "I reckon," he finally answered. "Hell, I ain't on any time schedule."

Ike's face immediately lit up with a wide smile. Gazing at the happy reaction from his friend, it struck Matt that he had come to be quite fond of Ike in the short time they had known each other. He was going to miss the man.

The hunt was quickly organized, with every able male member of the tribe eager to join. Due to the lack of young men in the village, it was a party of old men and boys. They all turned to Ike to lead the party, and with Crooked Foot acting as guide, they started out early the next morning. After taking a final look at Ike's shoulder wound, Broken Reed nodded her satisfaction with the progress of the healing. She then cast an appraising eye at Matt's buckskin shirt and trousers, again nodding her satisfaction with the results of her efforts. Though no more than half her husband's age, Broken Reed tended to fuss over Ike in a fashion more motherly than wifely.

Riding a paint pony, Crooked Foot led them north after crossing over the river, then veered off to a more northwesterly course. According to Ike, if they were to hold that course for a couple of days, it would eventually lead to the Flint Hills and the tall-grass country. The deer Crooked Foot had discovered were far short of that, moving slowly through the hills, feeding on plants and grasses along the many streams, bedding down during the middle of the day in the ravines and dry washes. Once they reached the area where Crooked Foot had first encountered the deer, however, they discovered that the herd had moved farther north. "They ain't far ahead of us, though," Ike commented, examining the sign. Crooked Foot nodded in agreement.

Matt had to admire Crooked Foot's ability to read sign. Only fourteen years of age, the Cherokee boy seemed to know what the deer were thinking just by examining the sharp hoofprints and the droppings. According to Ike, Crooked Foot was born with a deformed ankle bone, causing his right foot to toe in, resulting in a slight limp. His disability failed to hamper him in any activity. In fact, he had come to be admired by both his peers and the elders of the village as a responsible young man.

Confident in his own skills as a tracker, Matt studied a set of tracks that led away from a stream where the deer had stopped to drink. "Looks like they're splittin' off into small groups," he decided. "This looks like a bunch of does, judging by the tracks." He stood up to scan the terrain ahead. "I'd bet they headed for that patch of woods at the foot of those hills." He pointed out a stand of cottonwoods about a quarter of a mile ahead. Crooked Foot nodded. The deer were seeking shady havens to rest in before looking for food in the cool of the evening.

There were a multitude of tracks near the tiny stream. Crooked Foot had been right in estimating a good-sized herd passing through the area. "Bucks there," he said, pointing to a set of tracks heading off in a different direction. The hunting party decided to stalk the does, both for the quality of the meat and the softness of the hides. They divided into two groups. The first was led by Crooked Foot, and started out following the tracks heading toward the cottonwoods. Ike and Matt led the remainder of the party in a wide

circle toward a low pass about five hundred yards beyond the grove of trees. Crooked Foot and his boys
would flush the deer and drive them toward the pass
where Matt and Ike would be waiting with their rifles.

In a short time, the ambushing party was in position. There was little doubt that the two white men
would account for the major harvest of meat, but the
old men and boys that lay in wait with them would
take a respectable share with nothing more than bows.
They had all barely gotten set when they heard the
whoops and yells of Crooked Foot's party. "East or
west?" Matt asked casually as he cranked a cartridge
into the chamber.

"East," Ike replied, equally casual, and shifted his
rifle around to sight along the left side of the pass.

Ike had already developed a fondness for this quiet
young man from the Shenandoah Valley. He was soon
to discover Matt's proficiency with a Henry repeating
rifle. With both men concentrating on the narrow pass,
the deer suddenly appeared. There were seven, all
does, and they burst through the opening, darting this
way and that, but generally bolting up the western
slope out of the pass. Matt rose to one knee and took
aim. Methodically, with no waste of time between
shots, he knocked down four of the deer—all kill
shots—before the rest of the frightened animals disappeared into the trees on the slope. The waiting hunters
immediately gave chase. Matt and Ike remained.

"Damn," Ike remarked, still marveling at the show
of marksmanship, easing back on the hammer of his
rifle, the barrel still cool. "You don't need no help a'tall,
do ya?"

"They broke on the western side," Matt replied contritely, thinking Ike was complaining that he didn't get a shot.

Ike laughed and got to his feet. "That was some shootin', partner," he said, shaking his head in awe.

Crooked Foot and the others ran two of the remaining three does to ground, killing them with their bows. Later in the afternoon, the hunters flushed another bunch from a pocket of oaks farther along the line of hills, taking three young bucks. With a harvest of nine deer, the small hunting party decided it was time to call an end to the hunt, and get about the business of skinning and butchering. The final score was five killed with arrows and four by Matt's rifle. Ike had not fired a shot. Although he made a show of unconcern, he could not totally hide his aggravation. Crooked Foot seemed especially amused by Ike's lack of success, and could not help but tease his white friend.

"Next time, maybe we try to catch an old buck, and tie him to a tree. Then you can shoot him."

Ike laughed, taking the teasing good-naturedly. He knew Crooked Foot actually held him in high esteem. In fact, the boy looked upon the older white man much like an uncle. Still, it bothered him more than he would ever admit that he had not killed a deer. His chance for redemption came unexpectedly, however, and almost as a gift. Riding back to the four does, Ike caught a flicker of movement in the trees on the western slope. Realizing that no one else had noticed it, he kept an eye on the clearing below the trees, and quietly cocked his rifle. Sure enough, the surviving doe of the original seven emerged from the foliage. Frightened and confused, the doe had evidently been chased in circles by the Cherokee hunters. The sharp crack of Ike's rifle dropped the unfortunate doe at the edge of the clearing, bringing the total kill to an even ten.

"Most times you'll get more meat if you keep your eyes open instead of your mouth," Ike told Crooked Foot, with a wink for Matt.

Now the real work began as the hunters began the skinning and quartering. Soon all ten carcasses were hanging from tree limbs, gutted. When most of the blood had been drained, they were cut down and quartered, and readied for the trip back to the village. This time of year it was especially important to dry the meat as soon as possible to preserve it, so the hunters wasted little time in starting back. They had ridden a meandering trail while tracking the deer. On the trip back, it would be a shorter, more direct route.

Some nine miles away, Broken Reed paused for a few moments to listen. She had suddenly felt a sense of foreboding—something she could not explain, as if aware of an approaching storm. She put a half-finished basket aside and got to her feet. Outside, the sky was crystal blue, with no sign of a cloud. Looking back toward the other lodges and huts, she saw nothing amiss in the tiny village. The women were getting ready for a busy time when the hunters returned. Still, the sense of apprehension would not leave her mind, so she walked down by the river and stood for several minutes, looking toward the hills to the west. She wished that Ike would return soon. The hunters had been gone for two days now. She hoped that they had not had to trail the deer for too long, and might be back before another day had passed.

Broken Reed felt safe from all danger when Ike was at home. Standing now on the bank of the river, she pictured the great hulk of a man with his almost ever-present smile all but hidden in his bushy beard. She knew that Ike was born with an incurable wanderlust, and when he took her for his wife, she expected that one day she would turn and find him gone. But she discovered after seven years of marriage that the huge man possessed a faithful soul. And while the urge to wander sometimes overcame him, he always returned, usually with presents for her and her father. After a moment, she shrugged, shaking the feeling of dread from her mind. Ike and his new friend would soon be back, she told herself. Then she turned and retraced her steps to the cabin, unaware of the gathering evil that was about to strike her peaceful little village.

"It ain't much of a village." Nate Simmons remarked as Brance rode up beside him to take a look.

The two were soon joined by the rest of the gang, and the seven outlaws formed a line on the low ridge overlooking the valley. Brance studied the modest cluster of tipis and log cabins. Then he looked at the few ponies grazing on the far side of the river. "It's a sorry lookin' village all right," he finally commented. This was the third village they had discovered after having followed the Illinois for over twenty miles. At first glance, they all looked about the same, devoid of any sign of prosperity. Brance was beginning to lose interest in his search for revenge. Each little Indian village they came to offered nothing to compensate for their long ride through the Cherokee Nation. The rest of the men were already grumbling among themselves, complaining about the tedious journey with no opportunity for reward—all but one.

Tyler gave his horse a sharp kick, and the animal started down the ridge. "We ain't gonna find the bastard settin' up here lookin'," he snarled.

The others made no move to follow his lead, hanging back to complain. After waiting until the violent man was out of earshot, Church voiced the complaint that was on everyone's mind. "Dammit, Brance, this ain't gettin' us nowhere. There shore as hell ain't nothin' in the whole damn Injun Territory worth stealin'. How long are we gonna follow that mad dog? Them two we're lookin' for might not've headed back here, a'tall. For all we know, they mighta headed on north to St. Louie, and right now they're settin' in a saloon somewhere while we're out here eatin' dust."

His comments were met with mumbled echoes of agreement. Eli nodded thoughtfully and turned to his longtime partner. "Church is right, Brance. We sure as hell could be doin' somethin' a whole lot less wearisome."

Brance gave it some thought. Although his passion to settle with the young fellow called Shannon was admittedly cooling somewhat, Brance still felt some reluctance to let him get away. What Church said was true—Shannon and the man he took up with might not have ridden this way at all. "I don't know," he finally admitted. We've rode a helluva long way to give up now." He nodded toward Tyler, already halfway down the ridge. "Tyler sure as hell ain't thinkin' about turnin' back."

"Hell," Spit chimed in, "let Tyler do whatever the hell he wants." He spat to punctuate his remarks. "That crazy son of a bitch might keep ridin' till he hits the Pacific Ocean."

Sensing that he might be seeing signs of dissension among his men, Brance glanced at his lieutenant. Seeing Eli's nod, he made a decision. "All right," he said, "we'll ride on down and look this little village over. If Shannon ain't hidin' out here, we'll say to hell with it, and head toward Missouri." That seemed to meet with everyone's approval, so they started down the ridge after Tyler.

Surprised to see riders approaching their village, the people walked forward to see what manner of white men would have reason to be in this part of the Cherokee Nation. Past experience had taught them to be wary of whites traveling the territory, so it was with a somewhat guarded posture that Old Bear greeted Brance's gang. Reading the eyes of the foremost rider, Old Bear sensed a need for caution. The man had the look of a hunter of men.

"Hey, old man," Tyler demanded, "you speak white man's talk?"

"Some," Old Bear replied.

"We're lookin' for two white men that maybe come ridin' through here. You see any white men in the last week or so?"

Anxious to hurry the strangers along, Old Bear answered. "No, no white men," he replied.

At that moment, Brance and the others pulled up beside him, the men gawking at the old people standing stoically in the center of the camp. "He says he ain't seen no white men," Tyler called back to Brance.

"He ain't, huh? Well, I wonder if he'd tell us if he had." Looking from one side to the other, he answered his own thought. "I don't see nothin' that would be worth hangin' around here for. I expect he's probably tellin' the truth." He pulled back on his reins, preparing to leave.

"Hold on a minute, Brance," Corbin remarked, catching a glimpse of Broken Reed peering at them from the cabin door. "Maybe we oughta take a look in these huts. There might be somebody hidin' out."

Following Corbin's gaze, Church saw at once what had caught his eye. "Yeah, Brance, we might as well see what's here."

"Maybe we could get somethin' to eat," Spit added, not yet aware of the real interest behind his two companions' remarks.

"There ain't nobody hidin' out in this damn hole," Tyler blurted, before Brance had a chance to reply. "We're wastin' time."

"Maybe the boys are right," Brance retorted. "Wouldn't hurt to take a little rest before we ride again."

"I ain't got no time to rest," Tyler shot back. "Let's get movin'."

Brance decided it was time to demonstrate who was the leader of the gang, and consequently, who called the shots. "Well, Tyler, I reckon you'll be movin' on by yourself. The rest of us are gonna see what we can find in them huts."

The two headstrong outlaws locked eyes for a long moment in a test of wills, each man intent upon intimidating the other. It might have developed into a power play, but Tyler knew the men would back Brance and not himself. Knowing this, he finally shrugged it off. "Suit yourself," he said, and rode off toward the river.

Brance watched him for a few moments before turning back to Old Bear. "Now, then, old man, let's take a look in them shacks."

A sense of alarm surged through the small gathering of Cherokees as they watched the heavily armed white men dismount. Old Bear attempted to stand in the way when Corbin and Church started for Ike's cabin. "Get outta the way, Grandpa," Corbin said, shoving the old man aside, a malevolent grin of anticipation fixed upon his face. There was immediate reaction from the Indians, and several of the men stepped forward, but any thoughts they had of resisting the invasion of their village were stifled by the drawn guns of the outlaws.

"Now, don't go gettin' riled up," Brance warned, his pistol leveled at the closest Cherokee. "We're just gonna have a look-see in them huts. If you behave yourselves, we'll just take what we want, and be on our way." He was about to say more when he was interrupted by the sound of hooves behind him. Turning around, he discovered Tyler driving straight for him at a gallop. Brance's first reaction was to bring his weapon to bear on the charging man, thinking that Tyler had decided upon a power play after all. Tyler ignored him, however, and pulled his horse to a sliding stop in the midst of the Cherokee villagers, causing them to scatter to avoid being trampled under the hooves.

Leaping from the saddle, his face twisted with rage, Tyler grabbed Old Bear, and pulled the startled old man up close to his face. "That's my brother's bay stallion down there with them Injun ponies! Where is that damn Shannon? Where is he?" When Old Bear did not respond immediately, Tyler cracked him across the head with the barrel of his pistol. "Where is he?" Tyler demanded again. Old Bear, dazed by the blow, could not reply at once. "Damn you!" Tyler shouted, his face a mask of unbridled fury. He stuck the barrel of the pistol against the side of Old Bear's head, and pulled the trigger. The gathering of Indians gasped as one as they witnessed their old chief slump to the ground in death.

A cry of anguish rang out from Ike's cabin, and Broken Reed burst through the doorway, running to her father's side. "Well, lookee here," Corbin chortled delightedly, catching Broken Reed's arm as she passed. "Where you goin', sweetie?" He looked around to gloat at his friends. "Look what I got." His comment was specifically aimed at Church, in light of the competition between them to get to the face they had seen through the open door. His gloating was short-lived, however, for in the next instant his smile suddenly froze on his face, then turned to a look of horrified shock as Broken Reed's long skinning knife sank deep under his rib cage.

Releasing Broken Reed's arm, Corbin staggered back a couple of steps, and stared down stupidly at the bone handle protruding from his shirt. Broken Reed wrenched herself away from Church's outstretched hand, and ran past him to her father. Everything had happened so suddenly, and without warning, that the spectators, both outlaw and Cherokee, were momentarily stunned. Brance was the first to recover, and with no further hesitation, walked over and methodically put two bullets into the grieving woman's back. Broken Reed slumped across Old Bear's body, dead.

Confusion reigned for the next few minutes. With nothing more to fight with than their bare hands, several men of the village attempted to attack the intruders. The outlaws quickly responded, shooting two of the men at point-blank range. This effectively stopped the Cherokees' attack, but not the revenge-crazed Tyler. He promptly started shooting every Indian in sight—women, old men, even children. The result was a bloodbath, as some of the others in the gang joined in the massacre. Those who could fled toward the river, but few escaped the blistering curtain of lead.

After no more than five or ten minutes, the storm of gunfire subsided, and in the eerie quiet that followed, only one sound pierced the silence: Corbin screamed in terrified pain when he tried to remove the steel blade from his innards. Staggering around, half crazed with shock, he babbled incoherently while he sought in vain to relieve his agony. The blade, however, refused to come out, having evidently wedged against a rib.

"Damn, Corbin," Spit remarked with no show of compassion for the suffering man. "I reckon you didn't figure on that, did you?" He seemed mildly fascinated by Corbin's dilemma, although he was not moved to offer help. He turned his head momentarily to spit on the corpse of an old woman near his feet. "A man has to be careful messin' around with Injun women," he offered as he turned to join the others who were already pillaging the huts. Walking past the bodies of Broken Reed and her father, he glanced down to notice the silver cross hanging from the rawhide thong around Old Bear's neck. Grinning to himself for being the first one to notice it, he knelt down and removed it from the corpse. "Hell, I could use a little of the Lord's protection, myself," he said aloud. Then he chuckled and spit when he added, "Seeing as how it did so much good for you."

The only member of the gang to offer assistance to Corbin was Nate Simmons. He lingered behind the others to help the suffering man as Corbin's strength began to desert him. With Nate holding onto one arm, Corbin sank heavily to the ground, staring at the patch of blood that was rapidly spreading across his shirt. "It pains somethin' awful, Nate," Corbin whined. "I'm afeared I'm dyin'."

"Maybe not," Nate said, effecting as gentle a tone as a man of his rough nature could create. "You just set quiet for a spell, and then we'll see about gettin' that knife outta your belly." He knelt beside the wounded outlaw for a long moment, watching him closely. "You know, just in case things don't turn out for the best, I've always admired that brace of pistols you're wearin'. I'd appreciate it if you'd let the boys know you'd like for me to have 'em." Corbin, in no condition to answer coherently at that point, merely stared up at Nate with eyes wide with terror. "You just rest here a spell," Nate said after a few moments, then left to join the others in the search for plunder.

The search failed to yield much of value for the gang of outlaws—a little food, some trinkets of little worth, and some cooking utensils. Tyler stormed from lodge to lodge, looking for further indication that the man he hunted was somewhere near, or might be planning to return. There was nothing but the bay stallion grazing with the Indian ponies on the other side of the river. But at least that gave him hope that Shannon would return to the village. It was unlikely that he would have traded the bay for one of the Indian ponies.

"Well, that weren't hardly worth the ammunition we spent, were it?" Eli looked around him at the dead bodies lying like bundles of rags upon the bare ground. "The rest of them Injuns took off."

"I reckon," Brance replied as he casually reloaded his pistol.

"Reckon what we oughta do about Corbin?" Eli asked.

Brance paused to think. He had forgotten Corbin for the moment. "I guess we'd better take a look at him," he finally decided, "if he's still alive."

"He's still alive," Eli said, nodding toward the stricken man lying on the ground.

Together, they walked over to Corbin. In a few minutes, they were joined by the others. All gathered around the suffering Corbin to gawk and voice their speculations on his chance of survival. No one was inclined to offer any suggestions as to what should be done to ease his pain. Finally, Brance, feeling it his place to take action, pushed the others aside, and bent low over Corbin to take a closer look. "Well," he decided, "the first thing we gotta do is get this damn knife outta him." That said, he promptly placed his boot in the middle of Corbin's chest, and taking the knife handle in both hands, exerted all his strength upon the reluctant blade.

Corbin's agonized scream pierced the still air as the deadly blade was suddenly released. Brance jumped back quickly to avoid the spurt of blood that followed the withdrawal. Holding the bloody blade up for the others to see, Brance said, "Ain't that a nasty-lookin' pigsticker?" He then wiped it clean on Corbin's shirttail. "We'd best stop that bleedin', or he's gonna die sure enough."

No one moved right away, content to let one of the others do something to help poor Corbin. "I expect he'd lay more comfortable if we took them pistols off'en him," Nate Simmons suggested, and knelt down to unbuckle Corbin's gun belt.

"Here," Eli said, tossing an Indian blanket at Nate. "Stuff a corner of this on that wound before he bleeds to death." Nate did as he was told, but it was too late for the tormented man. Corbin's eyelids began fluttering, and his babbling became more and more faint.

"What's he sayin'?" Church asked.

"He's talkin' to the devil," Spit quipped. "He's sayin' save a place at the supper table for ol' Church."

Spit's remark brought a chuckle from the rest of the group—all except Tyler, who was unable to acknowledge humor in any form, no matter how awkward the situation. "He's a dead man," he offered, scowling. "We'd best be thinkin' about Shannon."

Corbin offered no resistance when Nate pulled the gun belt from under him, even though it dragged his body a couple of feet. "Whaddaya reckon we oughta do about him?" Nate asked as he got to his feet again.

"Nothin'," Brance stated matter-of-factly. "Like Tyler said, he's a dead man. And don't go gettin' no ideas about them pistols. I expect we'll draw straws for 'em."

Nate immediately complained. "Corbin wanted me to have these here pistols. He as much as said so a few minutes ago when the rest of you went lookin' in them shacks, and I was the only one lookin' out for him." He dropped back on one knee beside Corbin, and shook the dying man by the shoulders. "Ain't that right, Corbin?" Corbin, already on the devil's doorstep at that point, made a gurgling sound as his final breath struggled through the blood in his throat. Nate looked up hopefully at Brance. "See, he's tryin' to tell you."

"We'll draw straws for the pistols," Brance declared emphatically. "Right now, though, let's drag all these bodies into one of the huts if we're gonna camp here a while. We can set the hut on fire, and burn 'em up. If we don't, they're gonna start to stink before too long."

"Corbin, too?" Nate asked.

"If he's dead," Brance replied, no longer concerned with his former comrade. "But I suspect it'd be a good idea to get our horses outta sight. Spit, why don't you and Church take 'em over behind the huts, on the other side of that rise yonder."

The outlaws followed Brance's orders—with the exception of Tyler, who stood watching the activities with the ever-present scowl etched into the lines of his face. He had not as yet made up his mind as to whether he was content to sit in the Indian village and wait for Shannon to return. What if he didn't return? Then Tyler would have wasted precious time while Shannon rode even farther away, consequently increasing the chances he would never be found again. Brance might be content to wait here in ambush. That was more like Brance's style. But Tyler was a hunter; he preferred to stalk his quarry. Still, there was the matter of Wesley's bay stallion on the far bank. Tyler wheeled his horse to face the riverbank, and sat there for several minutes, studying the horses on the other side, especially the bay. Standing several hands higher than the smaller Indian ponies around him, the bay was far and away too good a horse to leave behind. Maybe Brance was right. Shannon would probably be back for the horse. *But not if the stallion had gone lame,* he thought. He decided to cross over and take a closer look.

The bay shied away from the ominous figure approaching from the river, limping noticeably as it loped along the bank. Tyler pulled up immediately. He had his answer. The horse *was* lame. Shannon had probably just passed through this little village. Tyler immediately started scouting along the river, first one side, and then the other until he found what he searched for. There were many tracks, some old, some new, heading in many different directions. But there was one trail of a dozen or more horses, one of which was shod. This was the trail he sought. There was no way to tell, but he guessed that the shod horse was not part of a party of ponies, merely riding along the same trail. He took one look in the general direction in which the trail pointed, and started out immediately. Behind him, he could hear whooping and hollering as Brance's men fired the hut. He didn't bother to look back.

Chapter 10

With the pack horses loaded with meat and hides, the Cherokee hunting party prepared to start back to the village. They decided to return on the eastern side of the river. It would be a more direct route back, and should save them almost half a day's travel. Matt rode at the front of the party between Ike and Crooked Foot, listening to tales of buffalo hunts that Ike used to participate in when he was a younger man. "There's still buffalo aplenty," Ike declared, "but not around here no more. You've got to go north of here, and west, to the High Plains, to get buffalo now." Matt listened with great interest as his friend told of seeing wide valleys filled with a virtual sea of the grunting beasts as they flowed through the high country, hooves thundering, tails flying. It was a sight he told himself he would like to see.

Starting out late in the afternoon, the hunters were in the saddle for only a few hours before the sun sank behind the hills and a campsite had to be selected. They settled for a spot by a narrow stream, bordered by a line of willows, and went about the business of tending the horses and building a fire. In short order, there was deer meat roasting and coffee boiling.

After eating his fill, Matt poured a second cup of the strong black coffee, and sat down beside Ike. Ike offered up some conversation for a few minutes, but before long the weight in his stomach began to pull at his eyelids, and soon his head started nodding. In a matter of minutes, his chin came to rest on his chest, and Matt figured that was the end of his friend's chatter for one day. He turned to comment on it to Crooked Foot, but the Cherokee boy was peering out into the twilight to the south, obviously distracted.

"What is it?" Matt asked.

"Someone is coming," the boy answered in Cherokee. Then, in English, he said, "People come."

Matt instinctively reached for his rifle, but Crooked Foot did not appear to be alarmed, merely curious. The Indian boy said something in Cherokee, and several of the others within earshot answered. Soon the entire hunting party was on its feet and looking toward the prairie to the south. One of the older men nudged Ike, and he sat up. Then, from the willows on the other side of the stream, a voice called out. It was immediately answered by the hunters. Soon the air was filled with excited voices.

"What is it?" Matt asked for the second time, looking to Ike for explanation.

"Bad news," Ike responded, as the visitors emerged from the willows. "These folks is from our village. They're sayin' some white men with guns attacked the village. A lot of folks are dead." His words were short and cryptic, as he thought about his wife and the danger she might be facing. Her safety his one concern, he scrambled to his feet and ran to meet the stragglers from his village. "Broken Reed?" Ike called out to them. "Broken Reed?"

"Gone under," someone answered his anguished cry, "Old Bear, too."

The words stopped Ike in his tracks, and for a moment, his brain refused to function. "Come on," Matt said, laying a hand on his friend's shoulder. "Let's get the horses saddled." After a long moment, Ike nodded his head, and without a word, followed Matt to the horses. Leaving a few of the boys behind to tend the pack horses and the meat, they started out under a moonless sky. Grim and silent, the band of hunters rode behind the two white men as they followed the river in the darkness, each man and boy gripped by thoughts of what they might find.

"Is he awake?" Eli asked when he walked back up from the river.

"Hell, I reckon," Nate answered with a shrug of his shoulders. "I looked in the window a while ago, and he was still settin' there in the corner, holdin' that damn pistol. It looked like his eyes was open, and he was starin' with that damn look he gets when he's seen the devil."

Church winked at Spit, and said, "Why don't you go on in there and get him up, Nate?"

"Why don't you?" Nate shot back. "I ain't that anxious to get myself shot."

Eli listened to the senseless banter for a few moments before going to the window of Ike's cabin to take a look for himself. Of all the gang, Eli had ridden with Brance the longest and had witnessed many of

Brance's spells. Unlike the others, he did not believe Brance was in direct contact with the devil—a concept that he knew Brance encouraged. Something was wrong inside his partner's head. Of that, there was no doubt. But whatever overcame the man, Eli was convinced that it was debilitating to the extent that Brance could not control it. That was the reason he always backed into a corner and drew his pistol, Eli figured. He had an idea that Brance was blinded by whatever went on inside his head, and that was the reason anyone who approached him was likely to get shot.

Not anxious to get shot himself, Eli took an extra minute to observe the gang leader huddled in the corner of the cabin. When Brance's gaze slowly shifted toward the window, Eli knew that he was out of his spell. Satisfied that it was now safe to approach him, Eli stepped away from the window and opened the door. "There's coffee on the fire, and the boys found some dried meat of some kind. You about ready to get goin'?"

Making an effort to appear rested after a night's sleep, Brance slid his pistol back in the holster and got to his feet. Eli noticed that he held onto the log wall to steady himself. After a few moments, Brance seemed to regain his balance, and the drawn expression on his face relaxed to present his normal appearance. "I get a little stiff when I fall asleep crouched up like that," he offered in excuse.

"I reckon," Eli replied. He watched his longtime partner for a few moments more before commenting again. "Why don't we get the hell outta here, Brance? To hell with that damn Shannon. He ain't worth chasin' all over hell and back when we could be somewhere where's there's somethin' worth stealin'. Besides, there's no tellin' how many Injuns has already seen the smoke from that cabin. We might have half the Cherokee Nation on our asses if we hang around here much longer."

Brance didn't answer at once, his head still fragile after hours of a pounding headache. He stepped outside to squint painfully at a rising sun. Then he looked at the others sitting around a campfire, all staring at him. "What the hell is everybody gawkin' at me for?" he finally said. "I need some of that coffee." He walked over to take the cup Church held out to him. "I need a shot of whiskey in it," he grumbled. "Nobody find any whiskey in this whole damn village?"

"Nary a drop," Spit answered and spat in the fire.

"Not no whiskey, nor anythin' else worth a damn," Nate commented.

Brance sipped cautiously from the hot metal cup, hoping that no one noticed his trembling hand. He knew from countless times before that it would become steady in a short time, and he would be recovered from the torment that occasionally overcame him. He thought for a few moments about Eli's comments inside the cabin. It appeared that the rest of the men shared Eli's opinion that it was time to move on to better pickings. He looked at the charred timbers of the funeral cabin, still smoking from a few little pockets of flame. Eli was probably right. The thin column of smoke could most likely be seen by anyone for miles around. Setting the cabin on fire was not the brightest thing to have done. Brance thought about the man he knew only by the name of Shannon. There was no denying the satisfaction he would enjoy by tracking the man down and killing him. But his desire for revenge had been dulled by days of riding from one desolate Indian village to the next. The men were becoming restless for something more satisfying to their lustful instincts, and less interested in punishing Shannon.

Eli watched Brance as the somber man continued to sip his coffee in silent contemplation. He had willingly followed Brance for several years now, mainly because the brutal bushwhacker's ideas had always been in line with his own. The two may have reached the fork in the road where it was time to make a change. Eli could understand Brance's passion for catching up to Shannon, but he remembered the last encounter the gang had with the mysterious stranger—five empty saddles. Sometimes it was best to leave a rattlesnake alone, and get on about your business. Eli had made his decision. He was leaving with or without Brance.

Brance suddenly broke his silence. "Seen anythin' of Tyler?"

"That crazy son of a bitch is probably halfway across Kansas Territory by now," Church answered.

Brance nodded, the beginnings of a faint smile nudging the corners of his mouth. "I expect so," he said. "Maybe he'll run Shannon down." He looked at Eli and winked. "I expect it's time for us to pack up and head for someplace where there's some whiskey. Whaddaya say, boys?"

By their reaction, there was little doubt that the men were ready to do just that. Eli nodded his approval, and without a word, turned to get his saddle. In his mind, however, he knew that he had come close to splitting with his longtime partner, and he had been prepared to handle whatever trouble that parting might have sparked—even if it had come to a confrontation with guns.

A short time later, the gang filed out of the Cherokee village, passing by the smoldering logs of the cabin and the charred bodies of the dead.

After a seemingly endless night, the first rays of the sun found the hunting party within a mile of the village. Already tired from the prior day's hunt and the sleepless night, Ike signaled a halt to decide how best to approach the village. If the raiders were still there, it would require some plan to surprise them and negate their edge in weapons. In a matter of minutes, the sky began to accept the sun's light, and the eastern hills appeared and took shape.

"Look!" Crooked Foot exclaimed, pointing toward a thin gray column rising up into the morning light.

"Smoke," Ike confirmed, and a new sense of urgency took hold in the party of hunters. Everyone prepared to ride again at once.

"Wait," Matt said. "They said there were only seven white men. I think we would have a better chance if just the two of us slipped up on them. If we can surprise them, we can probably cut the odds down before they knew what hit 'em. I think we'll have less chance of gettin' more of your friends killed. If we go chargin' in there with this bunch, we're bound to lose a few more."

Ike thought about it for a brief moment before agreeing. It made sense to him. He'd already seen a demonstration of how quick and accurate his young friend was with a repeating rifle. His heart still leaden with grief over the death of Broken Reed, Ike was in a revengeful mood, for a precious part of his life had been ripped from him. He wanted to kill every man of the raiding party himself, but he knew that was not a likely prospect. With just the two of them, he was bound to get his share, however. He preferred not to have to be concerned with the rest of the survivors. They would only be in his way. He and Matt were all that were needed to erase this gang of scum from the face of the earth.

It was settled then, although most of the hunters argued that they, too, had a score to settle. Ike convinced them that he and Matt had a better chance with their repeating rifles if they went alone—all but one. Young Crooked Foot was adamant that he should go with them. His mother and father were among those reported killed, and he argued so persistently that it was difficult to deny him. When finally he threatened to go on his own, Ike relented. "All right," he said. "You can go along, but you better do like I tell you, and don't go off like a wild Injun." Leaving the main party behind, the three rode off toward the column of smoke.

Crossing the river above the village, they worked their way down along the bluffs until they had the huts in sight. Dismounting and leaving the horses there, they moved in closer until they were no more than two hundred yards away. There they paused to plan their assault while they watched the camp.

Matt scanned the cluster of dwellings, settling his gaze first upon the smoking ruins of the burnt-out cabin, then shifting back to the others, one by one. There was no sign of a living soul among the cabins. Glancing over toward the other side of the river, he could see no horses grazing. The village was deserted. "We're too late," he said, stating the obvious.

Ike could not contain a painful cry of frustration at the thought of the gang of murderers riding free. "We'll get 'em," Matt promised, trying to reassure his grieving friend. "First, we'll see if anything can be done for those poor folks down there." Crooked Foot ran back for the horses, and Matt fired three shots in the air to summon the rest of the hunters.

It was a dreadful sight that greeted the three when they rode into the deserted village. The burnt-out cabin had served as a poor funeral pyre, leaving a sickening pile of blackened bodies in the center of the charred logs. Those on top, though burnt almost beyond recognition, had served to insulate those beneath them. The smell of burnt flesh was one that Matt would remember for a long time. When he attempted to pull one of the bodies from the top of the pile, the flesh of the arm came free from the bone, causing him to step away to get a breath of fresh air. After a minute to collect his wits, he took a length of timber, and using it as a pry bar, he and Ike began uncovering bodies.

Slowly, as the outer covering of human bodies was removed, the corpses beneath became more recognizable, although bloated and swollen. Crooked Foot's parents were near the top of the pile, recognizable but badly burned. The shock of seeing his mother and father so horribly disfigured was too much for the boy. He cried out in despair, turned, and walked away, unable to look at their corpses. Matt wished at that moment that they had made the boy remain with the rest of the hunting party. The image of his parents in death would be permanently burned into Crooked Foot's memory.

Finally, near the bottom of the pile, they uncovered Old Bear's body, and just beneath, Broken Reed. Ike staggered back, reeling under the shock of seeing her. Her dress had been cut away, leaving her exposed, obviously done for no other purpose than to gaze upon her nakedness. "They cooked her," he gasped before a sob choked his throat, leaving him unable to continue.

"Go on outside," Matt said. "I'll cover her and carry her out of here."

Ike just stood there. "They cooked her," he sobbed again, his brain paralyzed by the image that still burned in his mind. Matt took him by the arm and turned him away. Ike dutifully stepped over the charred timbers and walked out of the cabin.

"Go find somethin' to dig graves with," Matt said, thinking it best to give the devastated man something to occupy his mind. "We've got to get these people in the ground." Ike nodded silently and started toward his cabin for a shovel, leaving Matt to finish the grim chore of uncovering the remaining bodies.

The last body was that of a white man. Matt paused to speculate on the circumstances that caused the body to be among those of the Indians. Corbin's corpse showed no evidence of seared flesh like the others. Having been insulated by the bodies on top of him, his corpse showed only signs of puffiness from the heat. Matt found it interesting that the man's boots were missing. *There were seven*, he thought, *now there are six.* He knew that he and Ike would be tracking the six raiders as soon as the burying was finished. It was such a senseless massacre. What would any ruthless gang of outlaws have to gain by attacking a peaceful, defenseless village of mostly women and old men? There was nothing in Old Bear's camp of great value. Matt found it impossible to understand such wanton violence. One thing he knew with certainty, however: the act must not go unpunished. Had he known that the reason for the attack on the poor people of Old Bear's village was to kill a man named Shannon, the burden of guilt might have been devastating.

Broken Reed and Old Bear were in the ground by the time the rest of the hunters arrived. Amid the chorus of grieving survivors, Ike and Matt helped Crooked Foot bury his parents. Once that was done, the two wasted little time preparing to go after the outlaws. Once again, Crooked Foot insisted he was going to accompany them. Feeling they had no right to deny him, they made no protest. Packing what essentials they could find, they started out, following an obvious trail that led to the northeast. As they left the river behind them, Crooked Foot took one long look back at the village of his family and friends. Ike never looked back. That part of his life was ended. He would forever be thankful for the time he had been allowed with Broken Reed, and her memory would be with him always.

Chapter II

"If we don't find a damn town pretty soon, I'm gonna go plum loco," Church complained. "My ass is gettin' calluses from this damn saddle, and my shoulder hurts where one of you bastards shot me. I need a drink of likker bad."

"Hell, Church, you're already loco," Nate teased, riding along beside him. "Look at ol' Spit up there. He don't care if the sun don't shine." A few yards ahead of them, Spit rode along the wagon track, patiently following Brance and Eli. Thinking no farther than the present moment, Spit contented himself with the feel of his new boots, posthumously donated by the late Dick Corbin. As far as Spit was concerned, it was a good trade: Corbin's life for the hand-tooled boots. As if punctuating Nate's remarks, he turned his head to the side and spat.

"I swear," Church felt compelled to comment. "Where the hell does he get all that spit? My mouth's so dry you could start a fire in it." Dropping the thought immediately, he returned to his original complaint. "I hope to hell this road leads to a town somewhere."

"Well, if it don't," Nate replied, "then it wouldn't make a helluva lot of sense, now would it?"

The band of outlaws had struck the wagon track earlier in the day, and Brance had decided to follow it, feeling certain it would lead to a town. The two-rut trail tracked northward along the western edge of the Ozarks, and appeared to be well traveled. They had passed a farmhouse a few miles back. It was little more than a shanty. Sitting far back from the road, it was barely visible through the trees. Nate and Church were in favor of riding over to see if there was anything worth taking, but Brance was against it. His reasons were simple. If there was a town at the end of this road, they might decide to stay there a while to really look over the prospects. And it wouldn't do for some neighbor of the farmer to come riding in to report a robbery—or worse, a murder. "Don't look like there could be much worth takin', anyway," Eli commented, backing Brance's decision.

Toward the shank of the afternoon, the road made a long curve around an outcropping of granite to reveal a gathering of rough structures about a quarter of a mile ahead. "Well, there she is," Spit announced, "just like you said." Following the road down to the town, they passed a small church with a cemetery just beyond. Past that, they crossed a series of small springs, and Spit summoned a saliva missile for each one. "Don't look like they're liable to run outta water in this town," he observed.

Beside a log bridge that had been built over the largest of the springs there was a weathered sign that extended a welcome to the town of Neosho, county seat of Newton County. It didn't appear to be an especially lively town. The half-dozen buildings were almost barren in their plainness, with weathered gray siding and shingle roofs. Beyond these buildings, there appeared to be ruins of burnt-out structures where perhaps the major part of the town had once been. They were now grown up in grass and tall brush. Brance took all of this in as the five outlaws crossed over the bridge. He glanced at Eli. "Ain't big enough to have a bank," he said, disappointed. "I was hopin' there'd be a bank."

Looking down the street at the largest building in the town, Eli answered, "I reckon the general store will have to do."

They continued along the street, gaping at the few people they saw as they passed the post office and the land office. The blacksmith paused in his work to stare at the five riders as they ambled past his forge. Eli nodded, and the smithy nodded in response, although his face reflected the sense of wariness he no doubt felt inside. "He looks like he seen a snake," Church said aside to Nate, and chuckled.

At the large building near the end of town, they pulled up at the hitching rail. Dismounting, Brance stepped up on the boardwalk, and looked up and down the almost-deserted street. He nodded to Eli, who had walked out into the middle of the rutted dirt thoroughfare to have a look back the way they had come. Eli nodded in return. The two outlaws seemed in agreement that the town was theirs for the taking. The other three had little more on their minds than finding a drink of whiskey. They entered the store as soon as they dismounted.

BANNERMAN'S, the sign over the door proclaimed. Eli

and Brance followed the others inside. "Afternoon, gentlemen," Roy Bannerman greeted his visitors. It was apparent by the disappointment on their faces that neither dry goods nor horse feed were what they were looking for. "If you're looking for a drink," Bannerman said, "the saloon's in the other side of the building." He motioned toward a door on his right. "You can go right through there. Barney's over there, he'll be glad to help you."

"Much obliged," Brance replied, looking Bannerman over. Seeing no real threat from the store owner, his face broke into a wide grin. "I reckon we could use a little somethin' to cut the dust. We'll be needin' some supplies later." The other four followed him into the saloon.

"I reckon you'd be Barney," Brance said to the white-haired man reading a newspaper spread out on the counter.

"Yessir, I'm Barney. You fellers lookin' for a drink?"

Brance fixed the old man with a grin. "Why, this here's a saloon, ain't it, Barney?" Looking around him, he saw one round table in the back corner of the room. "Just bring us a bottle of the best you got, and set it right down on the table there, Barney." The five outlaws filed around the table and sat down.

Barney brought a bottle and five glasses, and placed them on the table. Then he stood there a moment studying their faces before speaking. "This here's the best in the house. This is the brand of whiskey that Sheriff Wheeler always drinks. He'll most likely show up pretty soon now for his evenin' drink." Barney wasn't real comfortable with the five strangers. They had a rough look about them, and he figured it might be a good idea to mention the sheriff's name.

"Is that a fact?" Brance replied. He shoved his glass over toward Spit, who was doing the pouring honors. "I wouldn't have even thought a town no bigger'n this would be able to pay a sheriff."

Barney hesitated, not sure if he should explain. "He don't sheriff full-time," he finally admitted. "Makes his livin' as a blacksmith, but he does a dandy job keeping the peace."

"Blacksmith?" Brance questioned. "We passed his place on the way in—young feller."

"Bert's a young feller," Barney replied. "Strong as an ox, too."

Eli interrupted the conversation. "You need a lot of law around here? The town don't look like there's enough folks around to stir up mischief."

"Well, that's a fact, I reckon. We are a peaceful town. Bert don't have to work at sheriffin' too often, but when trouble starts, he can handle it."

Back in the dry goods section of the store, Roy Bannerman's thoughts were running along the same lines as Barney's. The five strangers looked like trouble searching for a place to light. Saddle tramps in appearance, they looked like some of the free-ranging raiders and bushwhackers that had roamed Missouri and Arkansas during the latter years of the war. The more thought he gave it, the more convinced he became that it would be wise on his part to take precautions. He called his son from the back room, and told him to fetch the sheriff. "Tell Bert there's some suspicious-lookin' strangers in the saloon, and it might be a good idea to stop by just to let 'em know there's law in this town. Tell him it wouldn't hurt to wear his gun." As soon as the boy was gone, Bannerman walked over behind the counter and pulled his shotgun from the shelf beneath. Breaking the breech, he dropped two shells in and propped it against the back of the counter where it would be handy.

Beyond the door that separated the two sections of the store, Brance and his gang were feeling the effects of the raw whiskey. The conversation at the table began to grow in intensity until it approached a raucous chorus of laughter and swearing. Brance called a nervous Barney over to the table and ordered another bottle.

"Look, fellers," Barney pleaded respectfully, "I'd really appreciate it if you'd hold it down a little. There's womenfolk and children that come in the store, and we wouldn't wanna offend them."

"Is there any womenfolk in there right now?" Church immediately asked, grinning lecherously.

Before Barney tried to answer, Brance interrupted, amused by the bartender's tentative approach. "Why, sure, Barney, we'll try to keep it down. We don't wanna be insultin' none of the good women of Neosho."

Equally amused by the cat-and-mouse game Brance was embarking upon, Eli grunted his indifference, pushed his chair back and stood up. "I'm 'bout to bust. I've gotta take a leak."

"There's an outhouse out back," Barney quickly offered, almost afraid the sinister-looking stranger might decide to relieve himself right there on the floor. Eli grunted again and disappeared out the back door.

Eli had been gone no more than a minute or two when Bert Wheeler walked in the side door from the store. Wearing his badge pinned on his shirt, and his revolver strapped around his waist, he presented a formidable figure as he strode casually into the room. "Evenin', Barney," he greeted the white-haired bartender, to which Barney returned a loud and enthusiastic, "Evenin', Sheriff."

Bert stood there for a moment, then walked over to the table. "Evenin', fellers," he offered. His greeting was met by a line of wide grins and no verbal response. "You fellers just passin' through town?"

There was still no response beyond the drunken grins for a long moment. Finally, as Bert began to find the silence uncomfortable, Brance answered him. "Why we ain't decided yet. Have we, fellers?" He looked around him to acknowledge the grunts of confirmation. "We might decide to stick around for a spell to get to know the folks."

There was no hiding the fact that the strangers were toying with him, and Bert was smart enough to know that he had better show some sign of authority. "I don't expect there's much here that would interest men like you. The folks around here are law-abidin' farmers. You might wanna ride on over to Springfield or some bigger town."

"Are you tellin' us to get outta town?" Brance responded at once, the smile disappearing from his face.

Bert sensed a showdown—the last thing he wanted with the odds stacked so heavily against him. He thought carefully before answering. "Why, no, I'm just sayin' that there ain't much in Neosho unless you're thinkin' about buyin' some land to farm." As soon as he said it, he was afraid it would obviously be seen as backing down.

Brance laughed out loud. "Well, we might be

thinkin' about doin' some farmin' at that." His three partners continued to sit there with foolish grins in place, entertained by the game. When the part-time sheriff seemed totally undecided as to what he should do, Brance said, "Hell, set down, Sheriff, and have a drink."

Mistaking the invitation as a sign of capitulation, Bert decided his show of authority had won the battle of wits. "Thanks just the same, but I reckon not," he said forcefully. Glancing briefly at Barney, who was watching wide-eyed, he turned back to Brance. "I expect you boys had best finish your drinks and ride on outta town. The folks around here like to keep a kinda quiet town, and you boys don't strike me as bein' that type."

"Why, bless my soul," Brance mocked. Pretending to ignore the sheriff, he turned to Church. "I believe the sheriff here has misjudged us. Whaddaya think, Church? Ain't we the most peace-lovin' folks around these parts? I believe he owes us an apology."

"You're damn right he does," Church responded gleefully, his eyes riveted on the sheriff. "He oughta beg our pardons right now."

"Damn right," Brance huffed, looking around the table at the leering faces of his gang. Then he turned his attention back to land on Bert Wheeler. "We all think you owe us an apology," he said.

Bert was in too deep now to back out without losing face. He didn't like the direction this was heading, but he tried to show some backbone, even if his heart wasn't in it. "I'd appreciate it if you boys would finish your drinks and head on outta town."

Still wearing a smile on his face, Brance answered.

"Me and the boys are pretty much used to leavin' a place when we're damn good and ready." He locked his gaze firmly on the sheriff's eyes, baiting him outright. "I expect we'll hang around a while, since I don't see nobody who can do anything about it."

There it was, laid out and thrown at his feet. Young Bert Wheeler knew at that moment that his test of courage was now, in this place. His nerves turned to ice, and he could feel his pulse pounding away at his brain. He knew he was standing before the life-altering decision that confronted many men. There were four of them. He could walk away from it, or he could call what he hoped was a bluff. Either choice would forever reflect how he was remembered by his family and friends. He made his decision. "I'm not givin' you any choice. Settle up with Barney, and get on your horses. Your kind ain't welcome in Neosho."

With his eyes fixed on the sneering face of Brance Burkett, he didn't see it coming. The heavy silence that had descended upon the room was suddenly ripped apart by the shock of a pistol shot. Bert never even had a chance to go for his revolver. He took a step backward, clutching at his chest with both hands, staring with disbelieving eyes at the gun in Nate's hand. He stood there for a brief moment before collapsing to the floor, with a bullet through the heart.

All eyes at the table calmly turned toward the bar to gauge Barney's reaction. There was little to fear from that quarter. The frail old bartender was stunned into paralysis, staring stupidly at the body of Bert Wheeler sprawled awkwardly in the middle of the barroom floor. Spit stood up, and walked casually over to the bar to help himself to another bottle. He grinned at the

befuddled old bartender as he passed. On his way
back to the table, he paused to look at the corpse on the
floor. Seeing no signs of life, he spat on the body and
sat down at the table.

Roy Bannerman was startled by the shot inside the
saloon. He froze for a long moment, waiting to hear if
more were to follow. Thinking it unwise to charge
through the door, he decided to stay behind the
counter with his double-barreled shotgun trained on
the doorway. He could only imagine what had taken
place on the other side of the door, but he told himself
that if anyone other than Bert or Barney came through
it, he was going to cut them down, and ask questions
later.

There was another who had heard the pistol shot inside the saloon. Eli stopped to listen when he heard the
shot. Standing outside the outhouse, he decided against
returning through the saloon's back door. Looking toward the corner of the building, he saw another door
that obviously led to the back of the dry goods section.
As a precaution, he decided to go that way. When no
additional shots followed the first, he was not overly
alarmed. One of the men might have fired at a cockroach
or a rat, or just for the pure hell of it—or Brance might
have taken a notion to shoot the old bartender. Still, it always paid to exercise a little caution. So he turned the
knob slowly, and carefully pushed the door open. He
found himself in a small storeroom lined with shelves.
Passing through the storeroom, he paused in the doorway to the main store. He paused again when he spied
Roy Bannerman, his back toward him, crouching behind
the counter. The storekeeper held a double-barreled
shotgun trained on the door to the saloon. Eli gave the

situation no more than a moment's thought before he drew his pistol and pulled the trigger.

Bannerman jerked upright when the bullet slammed into his back. He grabbed for the edge of the counter to keep from falling. The shotgun clattered harmlessly to the floor. Eli kept his pistol trained on the wounded man as he watched him slide down the corner of the counter, half turning toward his assailant as he crumpled to the floor, his eyes wide and staring in shock. Eli spent another bullet, this one in Bannerman's forehead.

Moments after Eli's second shot, the door to the saloon was suddenly flung open, but no one came through. "It's all right," Eli called out. "It's just me." As he said it, he caught a flicker of movement near the front door of the store. Without consciously thinking about it, he immediately spun around and dropped to one knee, his pistol ready to fire. Bannerman's young son stood frozen by the front door, terrified, having just seen his father shot down before his eyes. Eli rose to his feet again, the pistol still aimed at the stunned boy. After a long moment, Eli said, "Bang!" and laughed delightedly when the youngster bolted out the door.

"What was all the shootin' about?" Nate asked as he preceded the others through the saloon door.

Eli nodded toward Bannerman's body near the end of the counter. "He was fixin' to give you a double load of buckshot when you walked out that door." He glanced at Brance when he followed Nate out the door. "What was the shot I heard outside?"

"The sheriff came to call while you was in the outhouse," Brance replied.

"I expect we'd best pack up everythin' we can take,

and clear outta here while we've still got a little daylight left," Eli advised. "Somebody most likely heard the shootin', and if they didn't, that young'un that just run out of here will go for help."

"Why didn't you shoot him?" Brance wondered aloud.

"I don't know," Eli answered, replacing the two spent bullets. He looked up at Brance and smiled. "I reckon I'm just gettin' softhearted."

"That'll be the day," Church commented.

"Won't it, though," Spit said, and spat on Bannerman's body.

Church shook his head and grinned. "Why do you always spit on ever' corpse you see?"

Spit shrugged his shoulders, puzzled that Church would ask the question. For want of a better answer, he said, "It ain't polite to spit on the floor."

Chapter 12

It was not a difficult task, following the white raiders; they made no effort to hide their trail. But if they had, Matt was convinced that Crooked Foot would have been able to follow them anyway. He was impressed with the quiet confidence of the young Cherokee. Crooked Foot exhibited a maturity far beyond his fourteen years. Ike, by nature a competitive soul, and one who was accustomed to relying upon his skill as a tracker, sometimes found Crooked Foot's quiet demeanor exasperating. Matt could not help but be amused by the difference of opinion between Ike and the boy over the number of white men they were tracking.

Ike was convinced that they were trailing six men and two pack horses. Matt figured that Ike was certain of that because there had originally been seven outlaws, according to what the people of the village had reported. With one dead, that left six. That much was true, Ike insisted, but he maintained that he had confirmed it by sorting out the tracks of eight horses, six carrying riders. Crooked Foot merely gazed at Ike through lifeless eyes, and when Ike was through arguing, he would simply insist without emotion, "Five riders, two pack horses."

"Well, where's the other rider, then?" Ike demanded. "There wasn't but one dead white man back yonder."

"Five riders, two pack horses," Crooked Foot repeated stoically.

"Hardheaded young pup," Ike complained, frustrated with the boy's unflappable manner. "I was readin' sign before you was on your mama's tit."

"Five riders, two pack horses," Crooked Foot said softly and climbed back on his pony.

Matt slowly shook his head. It was of little concern to him whether there were five or six, even though the matter seemed to be of great significance to Ike and Crooked Foot. At least the argument served to free Ike's mind from thoughts of Broken Reed for a time.

Whether left by seven horses or eight, the trail led to a point where it intercepted a well-used wagon track west of the Ozarks, and then followed it northward. There was no disagreement on that. It was late in the afternoon when they saw the buildings of Neosho. Riding past a modest church with recently whitewashed siding, Ike called their attention to the little cemetery beside it. "Looks like they been here," he said, pointing to two obviously fresh graves. Unnoticed by the three riders, a man carrying a shotgun stepped out the door of the church after they had passed, and walked after them toward the town.

"Neosho." Matt read the sign by the bridge as the big blue roan started across. There were only a few buildings in the town—a smithy, a carpenter's shop, a small post office, a few others—and they all seemed to be closed. With evening shadows stretching across the dusty street, there should have normally been a lantern or a candle here and there. But that was not the case. The windows remained dark, and Matt had the feeling that there were people in every building, watching them as they rode through the silent town. The only sign of life came from a large building at the end of the street, where lantern light could be seen flickering through the open door. The three riders made for it.

Pulling up at the rail before Bannerman's, they dismounted. As Matt threw a leg over and turned to step down, he spotted the lone man following them on foot, a shotgun draped over his arm. Matt caught Ike's eye, and nodded toward the man. "I see him," Ike said. "He came outta the church back there." Matt pulled the Henry from the saddle sling. Ike smiled at him. "Town ain't got a real friendly feel to it, has it?"

"Reckon not," Matt replied. He stepped up on the walk. Looking back again, he caught a glimpse of a face peering from the doorway of the carpenter's shop. It immediately disappeared again. Across the street at the post office, a man stepped out and locked the door behind him. He carried a rifle. Looking in the other direction, past the general store, he spotted another man coming from the stables, also armed. "Looks like they don't care much for strangers around here," Matt remarked. "I expect they've got their reasons, and those fresh graves back there might have a helluva lot to do with it."

"Wonder how they feel 'bout Injuns," Crooked Foot mumbled, causing Ike and Matt to laugh.

"Let's go see," Ike said, and headed for the open door.

As Matt had surmised, the people of Neosho had plenty of reasons to distrust strangers in the wake of

Brance Burkett's visit. When she turned to see the three figures dressed in buckskins appear in the doorway, Roy Bannerman's widow involuntarily drew a sharp breath and backed up to the counter. A boy of perhaps eleven or twelve ran behind the counter and picked up a double-barreled shotgun.

"Whoa, son," Ike said, holding both hands up before him. "You won't need that shotgun. We mean you no harm."

The boy, unsure of himself, looked to his mother, then back at the strangers, still holding the shotgun as if ready to fire. "Ma'am," Matt said softly, "we've not come to cause you any more grief." Judging by the black dress she wore, he guessed that one of the fresh graves might be the final resting place for someone of the woman's family, possibly her husband.

"Papa," Myra Bannerman called out. Her eyes were still wide with fright, never leaving the face of the broad-shouldered young man who spoke to her in a reassuring tone. A few moments later, a white-haired old man appeared in the doorway leading to the saloon.

"The store ain't open today," the old man said, with as much authority as he could muster.

"We ain't lookin' to buy nothin'," Ike started to explain.

"What *are* you looking for, then?" The voice came from the open doorway behind them. A tall, thin man stepped into the room, cradling a shotgun in his arms. Matt recognized him as the man who had followed them from the church. With deep-set dark eyes peering menacingly from under heavy black eyebrows, the man looked to be no one to be taken lightly. For a few moments, the room was leaden with tension. Then another voice came from just outside the door. "I'm right behind you, Reverend."

Matt realized that the situation could get completely out of hand, touched off by no more than the smallest of sparks. It was obvious that the little town had suffered tragically from the outlaws' visit, and they were determined not to be taken advantage of by a second visit. There were nervous fingers on the triggers, and any false move might set them off. Without turning to look at the men behind him, Matt answered the reverend's question, "We were wonderin' if we could buy some hard candy."

"What?" The preacher exclaimed, not sure what he had just heard. "Candy? All you're wanting is candy?" The razor-thin face almost broke into a smile, and the shotgun was lowered a fraction.

Ike looked at Matt, wondering if his young friend had suddenly lost his mind. When he glanced behind him to see the preacher and the carpenter step into the store, he realized that the explosive air of tension that had threatened moments before was suddenly defused.

"We don't generally greet strangers in this manner," the tall dark man said. "We've just suffered a great loss to our town, and I reckon we're kinda on edge right now. Myra's husband and Bert Wheeler, our sheriff, were gunned down by a band of outlaws, and we weren't sure you three weren't part of their gang. I hope you fellows ain't offended."

"Can't say as I blame you," Ike replied. "Just so happens we're trailin' the bunch that hit your town. A few days ago, they hit my village—killed my wife and her daddy. We've been trackin' 'em for the best part of four days."

"Then we'll share your sorrow along with our own." He stepped forward and extended his hand. "My name's John Sewell. My farm's the first one you passed coming in. I'm also the pastor for our little town." He turned to nod to the man who had stepped up beside him. "This is Waymon Roberts. He's the man to see if you need any carpenter work done. And this is Mrs. Bannerman. Her husband was one of the men we buried yesterday. That's Barney Morgan in the door there. He's Mrs. Bannerman's father." They were joined a few moments later by the other two men Matt had seen on the street.

Ike shook hands with the preacher, then introduced Matt and himself. "Smith's my name. This young feller's Shannon." He shot a glance in Matt's direction to warn him. Matt understood Ike's caution. This was Missouri. They were no longer in Indian Territory. He nodded, and Ike continued. "And this young pup is Crooked Foot. He lost some folks, too."

"Well, Mr. Smith, I'm right sorry you and your friends didn't show up a couple of days sooner. We got hit hard. Ain't nothin' like that happened around here since the last years of the war when the Miller family was murdered by bushwhackers. Roy Bannerman is gonna be missed by the folks hereabouts. Barney and Myra are gonna try to run the store, but Roy was the man who got things done for the town. Bert was our sheriff, although it was only a part-time job. He was a blacksmith by trade. We're really gonna miss him." He paused to stroke the stubby beard on his chin, then continued. "Barney, where's our manners? Why don't we go in the saloon and get a little something to cut our thirst. These fellows have been traveling, and are probably a mite dry. I know I could use a drink. I don't mind telling you, I had a touch of dry mouth when I saw these fellows ride by the church." Remembering then that there was a lady present, he quickly said, "Excuse us, Myra."

"I never turn down a drink," Ike responded, and led the way through the saloon door.

Walking up to the bar, Reverend Sewell said, "Barney, how about some of the good stuff." Feeling the need to explain himself, he said, "I never touch the stuff when I'm doing the Lord's work, but I ain't on duty now." Then he shot a glance in Crooked Foot's direction. "Is he a full-blood?" Ike said that he was. "Then I reckon Barney can't serve him no whiskey."

"Don't matter," Ike replied. "He don't drink, anyway."

The drinks were poured and downed. When the glasses were refilled, the conversation was quickly returned to the matter most pressing: catching up with the raiders. Ike explained that the three of them had nothing to go on beyond the tracks in the dirt that they had followed from Oklahoma Territory. In fact, Barney was the only one of them who had spent time in the presence of the outlaws. He tried to give them as much information as he could recall.

"Brance was the name of the boss of the gang," Barney remembered. "I heard the others call him that. I don't remember if I heard any of the other names." He paused while he tried to think of anything that might help. "One of 'em spit a lot. He wasn't chewin' tobacco. It was just spit." Barney's eyes brightened as he recalled one other that was unusual. "One of 'em was sorta peculiar-lookin'; tall and thin as the reverend here, but he was as peeled as an onion, didn't have no hair on his face or the top of his head." Barney glanced at Matt. "And he was kinda like Shannon there. He didn't do much talkin'."

Ike laughed. "Yeah, Shannon don't say much, but he listens like hell." Serious again, he asked, "Can you tell us where they headed when they left here?"

"They didn't waste much time after they murdered Roy and Bert," Waymon Roberts volunteered. "I was workin' on a bedstead for Wilford Collins when I heard the shots. I wasn't sure that's what I heard for a few minutes. When I thought about it, I decided I'd best go see. By the time I walked out in the street, I saw the bunch of 'em ridin' off past the stables."

Barney spoke up then. "Waymon's right. They didn't waste much time. They ransacked the store, takin' everything they could load on their horses—coffee, flour, the little bit of money in the cash drawer, every forty-four cartridge on the shelf. We ain't figured out everything that's missin' yet."

"My guess is they probably headed for Springfield," Reverend Sewell said. "That's about the most godless town around these parts, just right for the likes of them. Drinking and gambling, whoring and killing, Springfield's got all the devil's pleasures. Just last July, some fellow named Hickok shot it out with another gambler over an argument about cards over there. They gave him a trial, and the jury decided in his favor. Self-defense, they said it was, and let him go. And people are now talking about him like he was some kind of hero or something. Yessir, that's the kind of place that would most likely attract this bunch of murderers."

"How many in the gang?"

The question came as a surprise. They had almost forgotten Crooked Foot was there. Sewell had assumed that the Cherokee boy spoke no English. He looked at Barney for confirmation as he answered, "Five." Barney nodded in agreement.

The stoic expression did not change, but the Indian boy turned his gaze to settle on Ike. "Five," Ike sputtered. "Five or six . . . can't no man say for sure when you're trackin' that many horses . . . it's mostly a guess."

Matt smiled, but the thought also occurred to him that it meant that one of the gang that hit Old Bear's village was not accounted for. He would give it more thought later. At the moment, he was more interested in the whereabouts of the other five. It was possible the missing member of the gang may have been one of the many bodies stacked in the smoldering ruins of the cabin.

Several more men of the town wandered in the saloon before the three strangers left, each one with an apologetic alibi for being too late to help when Brance Burkett's gang gunned down two of their fellow citizens. Matt couldn't help thinking that they would have been too late this time as well if Ike, Crooked Foot, and he had been part of the gang of cutthroats.

Since it was too late in the evening to start out for Springfield, Ike and Matt decided to wait until morning. After a final round of drinks, they said good night to the preacher and his friends, promising to bring back any news of success in tracking down the murderers. They made camp by one of the many springs in the area about a half mile out of town, on the road to Springfield.

With the first rays of the morning sun, the three were up and preparing to get underway. Crooked Foot searched the road for any recognizable sign that might confirm the trail left by Brance's gang. It proved to be a futile exercise. It had been too long. The tracks were old, and there were too many to distinguish one from another. Ike and Matt talked the matter over. The men they were after may have started out on this road—it was the only road out of town in this direction. The speculation that they were heading for Springfield was just that: a speculation. They could have decided to leave the road at any point, and head in any direction. With no trail to follow, the three were left with no option but to go to Springfield in hopes of finding the raiders there. According to Reverend Sewell, Springfield was a good sixty miles to the northeast of Neosho, and the road was little more than a narrow wagon track for a good portion of the way. "Whenever you come to a crossroads or a fork," he had advised, "always hold to the northeast, and you'll get there." So they broke camp, and started out on a journey that should take two days at best, all three keeping a sharp eye on the trail in search of sign that might indicate the outlaws' departure from the wagon track.

Matt poured himself a cup of coffee from the metal pot sitting in the coals of the fire. It had been a long day in the saddle, and as best he and Ike could figure, they may have covered half the distance to Springfield. Though late summer, the trees were already showing signs of an early fall. Cold weather was not far away, and he thought about how his plans had changed since his path had crossed that of a man

whom he knew now by the name Brance. True, he had
no particular destination when he left Virginia, only a
notion to see the plains and the Rocky Mountains.
Now it seemed likely he would spend the winter in the
hills of Missouri or Arkansas. That possibility did not
seem to be especially wise in view of the fact that he
was wanted by the law in those states. Ike had warned
him that winter on the high plains could be fatal, and
no time for a man to be traveling west. Maybe, when
this mission he had set for himself was completed, he
would go back to the Cherokee Nation with Ike and
Crooked Foot. The prospect was not particularly ap-
pealing. *I'll decide after this thing is done,* he told himself,
and turned his attention to the Indian boy seated
across the fire from him.

Sensing Matt's eyes upon him, Crooked Foot
looked up, meeting Matt's gaze for a few seconds before returning his attention to the strands of sinew he
was patiently weaving into a new bowstring. Ever
stoic in expression, Matt wondered if the boy ever
smiled. It occurred to him then that he was glad
Crooked Foot had insisted upon riding with them. He
was far and away a better tracker than Ike—although
Ike would never admit it—and his deadly skill with a
bow provided them with most of the small game they
ate, saving precious .44 cartridges in the process. It
was sometimes easy to forget that the boy was only
fourteen.

Hard luck, he thought, *losing your parents at that age.*
It occurred to him then that he had not been much
older than Crooked Foot when his mother and father
were killed. He and Owen had ridden up into the
mountains, hoping to kill a deer. Gone for two days,

they returned to find the smoldering ruins of what had been the family home, the bodies of their parents trapped inside. The memory of it still brought a feeling of grief. He could imagine that the grief felt by Crooked Foot and Ike was even more devastating due to the circumstances surrounding their loss. The men who perpetrated these wanton murders had to be stopped. It was difficult for Matt to understand how men, no matter how depraved, could kill innocent people without cause or conscience. He would have been even more dismayed had he known that Crooked Foot's parents and Ike's wife had perished because of him. The men that committed these foul deeds were not simply raiding at random. They were looking for him when they rode into Indian Territory and happened upon Old Bear's village.

"We oughta be in Springfield tomorrow night," Ike said, interrupting Matt's thoughts.

"I reckon," Matt replied.

"Look at ol' Nate," Spit exclaimed, "dancin' with that big ol' woman." He shook his head and chuckled. "Hell, she looks old enough to be his mama . . . and dancin' him into the floor."

Brance looked up from his cards long enough to give Nate a glance. Then he returned his attention to the hand he had just been dealt, not really interested in the high-stepping shuffle Nate tried to pass off as dancing. "I'd like to see one decent deal tonight," he complained, too disgusted to even think about bluffing. He glared intensely at his hand, trying to see something to bet on. One queen, one ten, and three low clubs—it was the kind of hand he had drawn all evening, and he was getting fed up with his cold streak. Spit, on the other hand, seemed to be drawing all the cards, and was accumulating a sizable pile of cash on the table before him. It galled Brance more than a little because he considered himself a much smarter poker player than the simpleminded Spit.

Laughing cheerfully, Spit opened the bidding with five dollars. The man to his left, who claimed to be a dairy farmer, studied his cards for a moment before calling Spit's bet. Opposite Brance, Eli nodded silently and pushed five dollars into the pot. He was not a winner like Spit, but he was breaking about even. This, too, irritated Brance a bit. He seemed to be the only one losing big. He shifted his eyes to the man on Eli's left, the owner of the saloon. Brance wanted to say he was cheating, but if he was, he was cheating himself as well, for he was doing no better than breakeven.

The bet around to him now, Brance bit his lip and tossed five into the pot from his rapidly dwindling pile. He thought about raising the bet, but Spit was too dumb to go for the bluff. "I'm in," he mumbled, and tossed the three low clubs into the center of the table. *We need to get some more money*, he thought as he watched the discards tossed in, cursing silently when Spit only discarded one. Eli had visited the bank that morning to take a look at the layout. According to what he saw, it would be an easy job: two tellers, one gray-haired manager, and one old man in the inner office. Brance had planned to enjoy the stay in Springfield for a few more days, but his luck at the poker table was going to dictate an earlier departure.

The son of a bitch drew out on us! He fumed silently when Spit picked up his new card and placed it carefully in his hand, making an effort to keep a grin off his face. Brance didn't have to see the grin to know Spit had drawn the card he needed. The simple fact that the man had not spit in the last few minutes told him that in his excitement his mouth was dry. He barely glanced at his queen-high nothing before throwing it in, even before Spit bid again. Disgusted, Brance turned his attention to the dance floor, where Nate and Church were competing to see who could make the bigger fool of himself.

Like two wooly-faced, awkward otters, the two outlaws stomped and whooped as they lurched to the razor-sharp notes of the fiddle. Their dance partners appeared to be stepping to a different rhythm as the ladies, both over-ripe and past forty, skipped daintily around the two sweating and puffing men. The fiddler, a bone-thin, silver-haired man, displayed no emotion at all as he sawed away at his instrument, oblivious to the antics of the dancers cavorting drunkenly before him. The scene struck Brance as amusing—watching the two bouncing around like children at play, their foolish grins belying the fact that either of them would slit his own mother's throat for a paltry profit.

His thoughts were distracted then, and his attention shifted to someone across the crowded room. Two men and what appeared to be an Indian boy stepped inside the front door of the saloon. White men, they wore buckskins and carried rifles. Brance was immediately alerted by the manner in which the two men surveyed the room. Forgetting the card game and the dancers for the moment, he studied the men's faces, trying to remember if he had seen them before. They were obviously searching for someone, but he could not recognize them. He looked back at Eli, and Eli nodded to indicate that he, too, was curious about the three. One of them, the younger white man, carried a Henry rifle, and Brance's thoughts went briefly to a rocky cliff in Arkansas when a single man with a Henry rifle damn near depleted his gang. That man, however, was not wearing buckskins, and he never got close enough to see his face plainly. They were not lawmen. That much was obvious, so Brance decided they were probably of no concern to him. But he would keep an eye on them just the same. While he watched, the bartender walked over to speak to the three. He couldn't hear what was being said, but he could guess.

"Evenin', fellers," the bartender greeted them. "You fellers is strangers around here, so I'm gonna have to tell you we don't serve no likker to Injuns."

Ike responded. "Me and him ain't Injuns, so I reckon you can pour me one." Nodding toward Crooked Foot, he said, "He don't touch the stuff, anyway. How 'bout it, Matt? You want a little shooter?"

Matt shook his head no. Like Crooked Foot, he did not come looking for a drink. "You go ahead. I'll just look around." This was the second saloon they had entered, and it was by far the busier.

The bartender hesitated for a moment, stopped by the grim expression on the face of the broad-shouldered young man, before he said, "If it's all the same to you fellers, we'd druther the Injun wait outside."

"He'll stay with us," Matt shot back. "We'll only be a minute, and then we'll all leave."

The bartender aimed a nervous glance in the direction of the poker table where his boss sat playing cards. "Listen, fellers," he pleaded, "I don't make the rules. If it was up to me, he could stay—and have a drink, but my boss is settin' over yonder at that table. I'll be in trouble if the Injun don't go outside."

Matt turned his head to take a look at Crooked Foot as if considering the request. In a moment, he turned back to the bartender. "He stays," he stated flatly.

Deep inside, a cautious voice told the bartender that it might be foolish to even consider insisting. "I reckon it wouldn't hurt for him to stand by the door here," he conceded, "but if anybody says anything, he'll have to go."

"Obliged," Matt said, and stepped around the bartender. His gaze sweeping the crowded saloon, he squinted hard, trying to see through the blue-gray haze of tobacco smoke that hung over the noisy room. He and Ike made their way around the room, searching the faces seated around the small tables. In reality, they weren't sure what they were looking for. They had no real means of identifying the men they sought. They only knew that they numbered five, and they would probably hang together.

It appeared to be a futile exercise. There was no obvious group of five men that stood apart from the rest of the noisy crowd. They had just about decided that the men they were after were not there, when Ike walked by the poker table in the back. He almost went on past, but something caught his eye, and he stopped in his tracks. Raising his rifle to a ready position, he took a step back. "That's a mighty unusual cross you're wearin' there, friend. Mind if I ask you where you got it?"

Action at the poker table immediately stopped. All turned to look at the small silver cross hanging from a rawhide thong around Spit's neck. For a man who had made many a mistake in his life, Spit now made his biggest. Riding what he thought was a lucky streak, he sneered at Ike, and spat. "I took it offen a dead Injun," he snarled, and reached for the pistol in his belt.

Ike did not hesitate. His rifle ball slammed into Spit's chest before the unfortunate man could clear the revolver from his belt. Spit went over backward on the floor. What happened after that took place in less than a minute's time. The sudden report of the rifle sent the saloon patrons scattering in every direction. Matt immediately whirled around, ready to cover Ike. Church shoved his stunned dance partner aside and drew his pistol, only to drop to the floor when Matt's Henry cut him down.

Trying to look in every direction at once, Matt did not notice Nate in the far corner, still holding onto the ample figure of his dance partner. He was in no hurry to get the same hand that Matt had dealt Church. He hesitated, and when Matt turned his attention to the table where Ike was still searching the faces, Nate carefully eased his Colt Army revolver from the holster. Keeping the terrified woman between him and the table, he slowly raised the weapon to take aim at Matt's back. Just as his finger began to squeeze the trigger, he was suddenly dealt a solid blow between his shoulder blades, causing his pistol to discharge and send a bullet into the ceiling. Stunned and confused, he staggered forward a couple of steps, holding onto the woman's shoulder for support. A second blow to his side pounded his ribcage like a strike from a hammer, and everything went black before his eyes. The woman screamed and jumped back in fright as Nate crumpled to the saloon floor, two arrows protruding cruelly from his body.

In the general pandemonium of the sudden violence, those nearest the door bolted, most of the others dived under tables or flattened themselves against the walls. The saloon floor was now cleared of everyone except Matt, who stood in the center, poised to strike at anything that moved. The stunned patrons, some of whom were armed, lacked the time to make a decision to act or not. The acrid aroma of gun smoke mixed in with the tobacco smoke and lay like a thin gray cloud over the center of the floor.

Ike, his eyes still focused on the card players at the table, warned everyone in the room. "No need for all you folks to get nervous and get yourself killed. We're just lookin' for five murderers that killed a lot of innocent people. The rest of you ain't got nothin' to fear from us." He directed his next remarks back to the table. "There's two more that come in with them three." He shifted his gaze from one face to the next, set to react to the slightest movement.

Brance was not foolish enough to make a play for his pistol after having witnessed the lightninglike reaction from the buckskin-clad rifleman. Keeping a blank expression on his face, and daring not to glance at Eli, he met Ike's gaze when it settled upon him. The owner of the saloon was the first to speak up, identifying himself at once. He was followed immediately by the dairy farmer who proclaimed that most everyone in the saloon knew him.

Eli, deadly calm in every situation, had sized his situation up exactly as Brance had. "Friend, I don't know any of these folks here. I'm just on my way back from Kansas City—thought I'd play a few hands of poker." Ike hesitated a moment as he studied the man. Eli's gaze met his, steady and unblinking. After a moment, Ike turned his eyes on Brance.

"I've got a wife and young'uns camped outside of town," Brance proclaimed in mock innocence. "I don't know nothin' about the men you're lookin' for." Inside, he was struggling to hold his anger, knowing it would be suicide to lose control of it now.

Ike turned to the saloon owner again. "Point out the two that come in with them three."

The man hesitated for a brief second, looking to his right and left, obviously nervous. He started to speak, but checked it abruptly when he felt the hard steel barrel of Eli's derringer pressed against his gut, the hand that held it hidden from Ike's view by the edge of the table. The message clear, the owner of the saloon swallowed hard before he forced the words out. "I don't see them right now," he managed.

"I think they left about an hour ago," Eli spoke up, his gaze calm and deliberate.

The dairy farmer started to speak, but Brance was quick to interrupt. "That's a fact," he said. "They went out the door a while back." He shot a hidden glance toward the farmer that needed no interpretation.

Ike looked at the farmer. "Was you gonna say somethin'?"

"No," the man blurted. "Like he said, they're not here."

Watching the interrogation from the center of the room, Matt was not sure he accepted the story the players told. He had a feeling that the other two outlaws were still in the saloon. And for that reason, he kept a constant watch over the spectators, alert for any sudden motion. He felt a certain reassurance knowing that

Crooked Foot's sharp eyes were behind him as well. It appeared that he and Ike faced a stalemate with no way to properly identify the two they sought. They were there—he knew it in his gut. Matt turned, about to question one of the frightened spectators, only to find himself staring at the sheriff and two deputies, their rifles leveled at him. Crooked Foot was nowhere to be seen.

Matt's reaction was almost automatic, but he checked himself hard, reluctant to fire on a man wearing a badge. "This little party is over," the sheriff announced and directed his deputies to take Matt's and Ike's weapons. Neither man resisted, unwilling to endanger innocent lives. The sheriff looked around the room until his eyes settled on one of the spectators. "Pete," he instructed, "you and a couple of the boys lend a hand to haul these bodies outta here."

Brance stole a quick glance in Eli's direction with just a hint of a smile on his face. Like his partner, he now had his revolver pressed against the farmer's ribs. A din of excited voices returned to fill the saloon once again as several men dragged or carried the three bodies toward the door. The four poker players remained seated at the table until the sheriff and his deputies escorted their two prisoners outside.

"You done real good, friend," Eli hissed into the saloon owner's ear. "You just saved your life. I expect you and your friend here best stay right where you are until we leave." He and Brance stood up then, and calmly made their way to the door, leaving the owner and the farmer properly frightened for their safety. Once outside, the two lost no time in getting to the stable and their horses.

"Who in the hell was them two?" Eli asked as they

hurried down the street. "And how come they're rag-gin' our asses?"

Brance was pretty confident that he knew. "That one with the Henry rifle was the same bastard we tried to jump down in Arkansas—cost us five men."

"Damn!" Eli exclaimed. "You're right." He shook his head, thinking of the irony of the situation. "Hell, I thought we was chasin' him—not the other way around."

"I reckon it's on account of that little party we had back at that Cherokee village—musta been some folks he knew. They had that Injun with 'em." Brance thought about the man with the repeating rifle. "He's cost me a helluva lot," he mumbled under his breath. Then he looked at Eli and grinned. "But I expect he ain't goin' nowhere for a spell now, and we'll be long gone even if they let him outta jail."

"That may be," Eli replied. "But we'd better not lose any time gettin' outta this town. Them two we was playin' cards with ain't gonna wait long before tellin' the sheriff we was with Nate and the others."

"Hell, we didn't shoot anybody."

"All the same, they might start askin' questions. Ain't no sense in hangin' around."

"I expect you're right," Brance conceded.

As the two outlaws walked toward the stables, they were generally ignored by the curious people they met, who were hurrying toward the saloon and the source of the gunshots—except for one shadowy fig-ure in the alley between the post office and the general store. Crooked Foot knelt on one knee in the darkness of the alley, watching the saloon door. By the light of the saloon windows, he recognized Brance and Eli as two of the men who had been playing cards with the man Ike killed. Thinking it significant that the two were the only ones hurrying away from the scene of the shooting, he reasoned that they were the two he and his companions had come looking for.

When the lawmen had suddenly appeared, he slipped out of the saloon. The first thing he did was take the horses and lead them out of sight behind the stores. Once he was confident they were safe from confiscation, he returned to see what was to happen to Ike and Matt. When they were escorted from the saloon by the three lawmen, he started to follow. But within a matter of seconds, Brance and Eli appeared in the doorway, and he had changed his mind about following his friends.

Feeling confident that they were the final two in the gang that murdered his people, he notched an arrow and positioned himself at the corner of the post office building, and waited for his opportunity. When the two men were opposite the mouth of the alley, he took steady aim at the one closest to him and drew his bowstring. A fraction of a second before releasing his arrow, his view was suddenly blocked by several young boys who were running up the street to see what the shooting was about. With his bowstring still drawn fully back, he waited until the boys had passed. It was too late. He no longer had a clear shot. Releasing the tension on the bow, he moved out of the alley, and followed the two outlaws toward the stables.

In the shadowy light of the main street, he passed unnoticed by the few people still converging upon the saloon. When he got to the end of the street, he was just in time to see the two figures disappear into the stables. Looking around him then, he tried to select a suitable place to wait in ambush. There were no buildings close to the stables, and very few choices for concealment. Concealment was important, since his only weapon was his bow, and the two outlaws were armed with rifles. With that in mind, he chose the only tree of any size across from the front opening of the stable. Settling himself behind the oak, he notched his arrow again, and waited.

Several long minutes passed, and Crooked Foot began to wonder if perhaps he had been wrong in his presumption that the two were in the process of fleeing town. His thoughts shifted to Ike and Matt, and he wondered about their fate. In the next instant, he was startled by the sudden appearance of two riders charging from the stable at a full gallop. For some reason, he had not expected them to emerge in such haste, and he hurried to draw his bow. They did not offer an easy target, and he scolded himself for not being ready. There was only one slim chance for a shot, and he took it in desperation. Brance and Eli rode off into the darkness, oblivious of the arrow that passed behind them and embedded itself in the side of the stable.

The opportunity lost, Crooked Foot ran out into the dark street, his eyes following the rapidly departing figures. His horse was too far away to be of any use at that moment. With no other choice, he started running after the outlaws. They soon left him far behind, but he was able to determine the direction they took when they reached a fork in the road north of town. He remained standing there where the road split, staring into the darkness, waiting for his breath to return to normal. They had come so close to exacting complete vengeance upon the ruthless murderers, only to permit the last two to slip through their fingers.

Chapter 13

"Mornin', Jim," Sheriff Grayson Taylor greeted his deputy. "Any trouble with the prisoners?" The sheriff hung his hat on a peg behind the desk, and slipped out of his coat. "It's gettin' a mite chilly these last few mornings. Winter's gonna be here before you know it." He stepped over by the stove to warm his hands.

"I expect you're right," the deputy replied. "We're gonna need to bust up some more firewood, too." He poured a cup of coffee from the gray metal pot sitting on top of the stove, and handed it to the sheriff. "No trouble from them two," he answered Taylor's question. "They've been pretty much quiet all night."

Taylor nodded and took a tentative sip of the steaming hot coffee. "Damn, that pot's been settin' for a while. It's stronger'n mule piss."

Jim laughed. "I made it about five o'clock. I reckon it has got a little stronger since then. I guess I'd better make another pot, so we can feed our prisoners some breakfast. It wouldn't do for word to get out that our prisoners don't get fresh coffee with their breakfast."

"I'll check to see if I've got any paper on them two

before I go see Judge Harris. You can stop by Farmer's and tell 'em to send over two plates of food." He thought twice about it, then said, "Make it three plates. I ain't had that much to eat myself." He took his coffee back to his desk and sat down. Taking another sip of the hot liquid, he made a face and cursed, "Damn, that's rank." Setting the cup aside, he pulled a drawer open and took out a stack of *Wanted* bulletins, and started shuffling through them. Selecting a few that he wanted to look at more closely, he got up and climbed the stairs to the upper floor where the cells were located.

"Well, I hope you boys are enjoying our hospitality," Sheriff Taylor mocked, stepping up close to the bars. "You be sure and let us know if everything ain't comfy." His sarcasm was met with silence, which seemed to amuse him. "Now, lemme see," he went on. "Which one of you is Smith, and which one is Shannon?" There was still no response from the prisoners. "Just one name for both of you—you boys musta come from poor families—couldn't afford first and last names. Well, don't matter much. Them three fellers you killed didn't have no names neither."

He shuffled through his handful of papers, stopping to study one in particular. Then he nodded his head toward Ike. "I'm gonna call you Ike Brister. This drawing sure looks like you, with that face full of whiskers and that bald dome." He paused to read the bulletin. "This one's over a year old. Fits you to a tee, though. Puts you at about the right age, too." He shook his head in mock celebration. "Damn, this is the first time I've ever caught somebody that was on one of these papers. All right, so we got us a Mr. Ike Brister."

He turned his attention to Matt then. "Now, you . . . I ain't quite sure. I don't see nothin' that fits you." He looked up from the paper and smiled. "Suppose I just oughta turn you loose?" He frowned and turned his chin toward the ceiling as if concentrating hard. "Nah, I reckon not." Then, having amused himself sufficiently, he turned deadly serious. "You see, young feller, I don't stand for nobody coming into my town and shootin' three men down. I don't care what they did, murderers or whatnot. I'm the law in this town, and to me, you ain't no better'n them you killed. I expect we'll have a hangin' after Judge Harris rules on you."

"I'm goin' now, Sheriff," the deputy called from the downstairs.

"All right, Jim," Taylor called back. "Tell Farmer to put extra potatoes on one of them plates." Aiming his question at Matt then, he continued. "All right, Mr. Shannon, there's one thing we ain't settled yet. One of them dead men had a couple of arrows in his back. I know an Injun came into the saloon with you. The bartender told me he made him stand by the door. But when me and my deputies came in, I didn't see no Injun. It might go easier on you with the judge if you was to tell me where I can find that Injun."

Matt shrugged his shoulders indifferently. He and Ike had exhausted themselves the night before trying to convince the sheriff that he was letting two murderers escape. They had explained why they had followed Brance Burkett and his men to Springfield, but Taylor was not sympathetic to the degree that he would let them go. Vigilantes were not tolerated in Springfield, Taylor had explained, and they would be tried before a judge like any other bushwhackers.

"If he's got any notion of springin' you boys, he's a dead Injun," the sheriff said. "Might as well tell me where he's hidin'."

"I expect he's probably halfway back to Indian Territory by now," Matt replied.

Taylor gazed steadily into Matt's eyes for a long moment, trying to decide if it was worth questioning him further. "We didn't find no horses. You boys didn't walk over here from Oklahoma Territory, did you? I reckon your Injun friend took off with your horses while you set here in jail."

Matt shrugged again. "Well, he's an Injun, ain't he?"

"Suit yourself," Taylor sighed, and turned to leave. "You boys shoulda stayed in Oklahoma Territory." He called back over his shoulder as he started down the steps, "I'll have you some breakfast in a minute or two."

Matt waited until the sheriff had left the cell block, then he asked softly, "What do you expect happened to Crooked Foot?"

"Most likely gone to the hills," Ike said with some confidence. "I'm glad he had sense enough to get the horses outta town. Right now, I expect he's tryin' to figure out what the hell he's gonna do." He walked over to the window and tested the bars. "I know one thing, we've gotta get the hell outta here. Them two bastards is layin' out prairie behind 'em, and we can't afford to let 'em get too much lead on us." He tugged at the steel bars. "And these bars are too stout to pull out, even with a horse." The chances of escape looked pretty slim.

Evening shadows lengthened as nightfall approached. It had been a long, exasperating day for the two prisoners upstairs over the sheriff's office. Taylor or one of his deputies had looked in on them from time to time during the day. And the sheriff stopped by one last time before going home for the night, bringing the news that their trial was already scheduled for the following week. "The town council don't wanna go the expense of feedin' you boys for long," he said. "We'll get her done, so you boys won't have to wait for your hangin'."

"Much obliged," Matt replied facetiously, causing Taylor to chuckle as he descended the stairs.

The cells were soon drowned in darkness, the only light a faint glimmer of moonlight through the window. The prisoners sat on their wooden bunks, deep in their personal thoughts, feeling no need for meaningless conversation. Matt considered the possibility of an early death by hanging. He didn't fear death, never had, but he did regret never having made it to the Rocky Mountains and the high meadows. He wasted no thoughts on the unfairness of his pending death. He had killed, more than once—some he had felt guilty about, but that was during the war. Maybe he really was an outlaw, for he had taken it upon himself to punish those who had committed murder. He was about to dismiss the subject from his mind when he heard a faint sound. "What?" he said, thinking Ike had whispered something.

Ike didn't answer, but got up from his bunk and went to the window. "It's Crooked Foot," he whispered.

Matt joined Ike at the window. Down behind the building, in the deep shadows, he could just barely make out the form of the Cherokee boy. Crooked Foot took a long look at the back of the solidly built building.

Then he went to the corner, and took hold of the overlapping siding, testing it to see if he could climb it. He managed to pull himself up about six feet before losing his grip and sliding back to the ground. Determined to climb up to the window, he tried several more times, each try meeting with the same result as before.

"Ain't no use," Ike whispered. "You ain't gonna climb that wall—wouldn't do you much good if you could. They built these damn bars to stay put."

Stymied for the moment, but still determined, Crooked Foot studied the back wall of the jail for a few moments more before deciding to retreat. "I'll be back later," he promised.

"You'd best watch yourself—they're lookin' for you," Ike cautioned. "We ain't aimin' to set around here and let 'em hang us. One of 'em will make a mistake sometime, and we'll get our chance." He glanced over at Matt. Both men realized that the chances were pretty slim. He whispered down to Crooked Foot again. "It ain't healthy for you to hang around here. Somebody's liable to spot you, and then we'll all be settin' in this jail. Me and Matt'll think of somethin'. Take the horses up that little crick we crossed over south of town. Find you a spot back up that ridge somewhere. If we don't show up in two days, you hightail it on back home."

Crooked Foot stood silent in the shadows below for several long seconds, considering Ike's instructions. Making up his mind then, he said, "I'll be back." Then he turned and disappeared into the night.

"I'm afraid that boy is gonna wind up gettin' hisself shot," Ike said as he sat down on his bunk again.

*   *   *

Jim Tarpley got up from the desk, and replaced the whiskey bottle behind the file cabinet in the corner where Sheriff Taylor kept it hidden. As a matter of habit, he checked the front door to make sure it was locked. Then he picked up a lantern and walked up the stairs to make a final check on the prisoners before he turned in for the night.

In their bunks, neither man bothered to sit up when the light of the lantern played across the steel bars of the cell. "Looks like you boys is all set for the night," Jim remarked. "Keep it real quiet, and I'll see you get a good breakfast in the mornin'." His remarks were met with silence. Satisfied that all was well on the second floor, Jim went back down to settle in for the night.

Something seemed to be hammering away at the deputy's head, and he awoke with a start. Confused at first, he was not certain if he was still dreaming or not. The room was totally dark, and the hammering began again. He now realized that the noise he heard was someone pounding on the door. His mind cloudy and sleepy, aided in great measure by the generous toddy he had sneaked from the sheriff's whiskey bottle, he reached for the lantern on the desk. The pounding continued as he fumbled for a match. Once he had some light, he looked at the clock on the wall, thinking he must have overslept.

"What the hell?" he mumbled when he realized that it was only two o'clock in the morning. "Who the hell . . ." he started, then yelled, "All right! Dammit, wait a minute." He pulled his pants on over his long johns, grumbling to himself, "Some damn drunk lookin' to sleep it off."

"Who is it?" The deputy called out at the door, but there was no reply on the other side, only the incessant knocking that was by this time echoing in his skull. He threw the bolt, and opened the door just enough to peer through. He was immediately startled to discover the young Cherokee boy standing there. He did not see the Springfield rifle propped against the wall beside the door.

"You been looking for me?" Crooked Foot asked.

"What?" Jim stammered, his mind still foggy with sleep. It took a few seconds to register that he was gaping at the Indian boy who was responsible for the arrows in one of the dead men. When it finally hit him, he opened the door, and blurted, "I sure am. You done the right thing, givin' yourself up."

Crooked Foot stepped inside, grasping the rifle as he did. Jim stepped back to permit the boy entry, only to find himself staring into the barrel of the Springfield. "Damn!" he exclaimed, and took another step backward, "Easy, boy, take it easy with that damn thing!"

"Get the keys," Crooked Foot ordered.

"Boy, you're in enough trouble already. The best thing for you is to give me that rifle, and maybe the judge will be easy on you, seein' as how you're so young and all." He held out his hand for the rifle.

Crooked Foot raised the rifle, aiming it at the deputy's head. "Get the keys," he repeated.

"All right, all right," Jim replied at once. "Just take it easy with that rifle." He wasted no more words on an obviously useless endeavor. The boy had not hesitated to put two arrows in one man's back. There was no reason to believe he would hesitate to pull the trigger. "I'll get the keys," he said, and went to the desk. He was about to pull the desk drawer open when Crooked Foot stopped him.

"No!" The Indian boy commanded, and with the rifle, gestured toward a ring with two large keys, hanging on a nail near the stairs.

"All right!" Jim exclaimed. "I'm goin'. I forgot they was hangin' on that nail."

He moved away from the desk at once. Crooked Foot followed him around the desk, stopping to open the drawer. As he had suspected, inside lay one of Mr. Colt's fine Navy revolvers. Crooked Foot withdrew the pistol and stuck it in his belt. "Light," he commanded, pointing toward the lantern.

Upstairs in the cell, both men were awake, having heard the noises from below. Half expecting a midnight lynch mob, they stood watching the stairs as the light from the lantern ascended toward them, casting shadows through the bars. In a moment, the head and shoulders of the deputy appeared at the turn of the stairs. He was carrying the lantern, and as he came on up the steps, another figure followed behind him. "Crooked Foot," Ike and Matt uttered the name almost simultaneously.

No one had to tell the deputy what to do. He dutifully unlocked the cell door and stepped aside while the prisoners filed past him. Fear for his life compelled him to stare wide-eyed at the Springfield rifle still pointing at his head. These were desperate men, who had wantonly gunned down three victims in the saloon before dozens of witnesses. What would one more corpse mean to men like these?

Seeing the fear in the deputy's eyes, Matt spoke.

"We're not cold-blooded murderers. The only reason we came to Springfield was to rid the world of five men who *were* murderers. Sometimes things don't turn out to suit everybody, so step inside the cell. We'll leave the key downstairs, so the sheriff can let you out in the mornin'. You might as well go on back to sleep. It'll be a while yet before sunrise."

Emboldened by the prisoners' apparent lack of evil intent, Jim was encouraged to remark. "You boys might wanna think about what you're doin'. Breakin' outta here only makes it look worse for you, and you know there'll be a posse comin' after you at first light. This time, they most likely won't bother bringin' you back here. They'll probably just hang you on the spot." He paused a moment to complain. "Does that crazy Injun have to keep that rifle pointed at my head? I didn't give you no trouble." At this point, he feared the boy might accidentally pull the trigger, and he could imagine what the .58-caliber bullet would do to his head.

Ike couldn't help but smile, looking at the stoic countenance of the Cherokee boy. "We got no reason to shoot you."

"Maybe I shoot him anyway," Crooked Foot growled, threatening, the rifle still aimed at Jim's forehead. And before anyone could stop him, he pulled the trigger. The deputy's face froze in horror as the firing pin clicked sharply on the empty chamber. A smile crept slowly across the Cherokee boy's lips.

Matt shook his head, amazed by Crooked Foot's brazen bluff with the late Wesley Tyler's Springfield rifle. "There's cartridges for it in my saddlebags," he said.

"Damn!" Jim swore, already certain that he would make no mention of the absence of a cartridge when the sheriff arrived to release him in the morning.

"Let's go, boys," Ike said, winking at Matt. "It's a long piece back home to Oklahoma Territory."

With no desire to waste more time, the three went down to the office, where they recovered their weapons from a cabinet behind the sheriff's desk. While Matt looked his Henry rifle over to make sure it was still all right, Crooked Foot asked Ike, "We go back?"

"Nah," Ike said. "We got two more weasels to run aground, and I'm hopin' maybe that posse will take off in the opposite direction."

With weapons secured, the two escapees left the jail, and followed Crooked Foot to a grove of trees where the horses waited. In the darkness of early morning, they galloped out of Springfield, taking the west fork toward Kansas City.

Chapter 14

The lone rider stopped to read the sign by the narrow bridge that spanned a clear-running spring. Ignoring the bridge, he guided his horse down to the water to let it drink. When he thought the animal had had enough, he jerked the sorrel's reins back, gave it his heels, and Jesse Tyler rode into the peaceful town of Neosho.

Riding down the dusty street at a slow walk, Tyler took notice of every building he passed: the church, the blacksmith's forge, the post office, a carpenter's shop. The place had a familiar feel about it, but he felt sure he had never been there before. He didn't give it a great deal of thought. So many of these little towns looked alike, and Tyler had seen a lot of them when he and Wesley were raiding along the Missouri border with Brance Burkett's gang during the war.

Like his late brother, Tyler worked both sides of the law, depending upon which promised the greatest reward at that particular time. He and Wesley had collected a fair amount of reward money over the past few years, but nothing close to the sum they had robbed from innocent citizens. This manhunt was different. There would be no bounty collected when he finally caught up with Shannon. But the satisfaction he anticipated upon killing the man would be reward enough. Jesse thought about him every day and night, especially when seated before his campfire, unable to sleep because of the bitter bile of hatred that seemed to have filled his veins. His life had evolved into one single quest, to kill the man that killed his brother. Nothing else mattered.

When he had left Brance and the others back in the Cherokee village, he had been confident that Shannon had ridden west toward the Flint Hills. He had felt so strongly about it that he continued on after finding no real trail to follow. Finally realizing that his hunch was in error, he had turned around and returned to Old Bear's village. Deserted, the Cherokee camp had still possessed a sense of death. The funeral pyre was no longer there, the bodies long since recovered by their families—all save one. Tyler had snorted contemptuously when he gazed at the remains of Corbin, already bloated and rotting.

Brance and the gang had left an obvious trail when they departed the village. With nothing else to go on, Tyler had followed after them, hoping that Brance had found some sign of Shannon's trail. Now as he walked his horse slowly through the sleepy settlement of Neosho, he could imagine that there was nothing here that would invite a lengthy visit. Bannerman's store, near the end of the short street, looked to be the only place showing any signs of activity.

Myra Bannerman sat on a cane-bottom chair behind the counter, altering a pair of her late husband's trousers. Her father, Barney, could wear Roy's pants, but he needed the legs shortened a good inch or two. She looked up from her sewing when she heard the little bell on the front door jingle, announcing a customer. One glance at the dark frowning eyes, surveying the room from under the wide-brimmed hat, caused her to suddenly catch her breath. During the past few weeks, Neosho had attracted more than its share of strangers. Unfortunately, especially for her, they had brought nothing but sorrow to the peaceful little town. The sinister-looking stranger standing in her doorway now appeared to be more of the same grief.

"May I help you, sir?" Myra dutifully greeted Tyler, putting her sewing aside and getting to her feet.

Tyler didn't answer right away as he glanced at each corner of the room before stepping inside. In his business, he had learned to always be sure there were no surprises, no matter how innocent the scene appeared. Satisfied, he shifted his gaze back to the woman standing at the counter. He took note of the fact that she was dressed in black—a sure sign that Brance and the gang had passed this way. The thought brought a grim smile to his face. "I'm lookin' for somebody," he finally announced. "Five men. They shoulda come through here three or four days ago, maybe more."

So, she thought, this was one more in the dangerous string of strangers come to threaten honest people. She was about to reply when a voice came from the doorway behind the stranger. "Were they friends of yours?"

Tyler started, his hand dropping to the handle of his

pistol, but recovering almost immediately, when he saw the badge on the man behind him. "I ain't got no friends," he answered, and stepped to one side, so he could face the lawman head-on.

Waymon Roberts was not cut out to be a lawman. He was a carpenter by trade, and accepted the position of sheriff temporarily after Bert Wheeler was gunned down. At this moment, locked onto the deadly gaze of a born assassin, he couldn't help but wish he had not seen Tyler ride in. It was not unlike staring into the eyes of a rattlesnake. Tyler, long on experience facing dangerous men, read the fear and uncertainty in Waymon's eyes, and relaxed the hand on his pistol. "Well," he said, "have you seen five men passin' this way, or not?"

Waymon bolstered up his courage, and strived to inject a degree of authority in his response. "Oh, they passed through all right. They left two dead men behind them—one of 'em this lady's husband."

Tyler shot a quick glance at Myra Bannerman, unconcerned for her loss. Looking back at Waymon, he asked, "Which way'd they go when they left here?"

"Took the road to Springfield," Waymon said. "At least that's the direction they left in." Tyler nodded thoughtfully. Waymon continued. "'Course I'll tell you, same as I told them other fellers, they coulda turned off in any direction after they left town." This caught Tyler's attention in a hurry.

"What other fellers?" Tyler demanded, his eyes flashing with excitement.

"Two men and an Injun boy," the sheriff replied. "They said they were trailin' them five for shootin' up their camp."

Tyler tensed, certain he was on the right trail now. "Their names," he demanded impatiently. "The two men, what were their names?"

Waymon's freshly summoned bravado began to fade in the face of Tyler's sudden mood swing. "I don't remember," he stumbled, turning to Myra for help. "Smith, I think the big one called himself. The other . . ."

"Shannon," Myra said.

"Shannon," Tyler repeated, allowing a smile to gain access to his sinister features. He was confident now. The last few days had been spent with concern that Shannon might be riding out across the prairie somewhere, getting farther and farther away. "So now the fox is chasin' the hounds," he said, amused by the thought. His sense of urgency was immediately intensified by the fear that someone else might kill Shannon before he could get to him. He turned away from the acting sheriff, and gave Myra some gruff orders. "Give me five pounds of salt pork and about a peck of oats for my horse, and some coffee—sugar if you got some. And make it snappy. I'm in a hurry."

Feeling small after being so abruptly dismissed, Waymon felt compelled to assert his authority as sheriff, if only to save embarrassment before Myra and her son, Nathaniel. The boy had slipped quietly in from the saloon when he heard the conversation in the store. "I'm gonna have to ask you a few questions, friend. We've had more trouble in our town lately than the folks here wanna tolerate. What did you say your name was?"

"I didn't," Tyler replied bluntly, his cold gaze locking on the sheriff's.

The cruelty lying behind that gaze was enough to discourage Waymon's feeble efforts toward assuming authority. He hesitated for a long moment, trying to find a way to retreat without losing face. "Well," he stumbled, "I expect you've got the money to pay for them things."

Amused by the lawman's obvious lack of backbone, Tyler again allowed a wicked grin to spread across his dark features. "I expect that's between me and the lady here, and no business of yours. Ain't that right, lady?"

"Let it go, Waymon," Myra said. "It ain't worth causing a fuss over." She could see that the situation might escalate into something ugly, maybe even deadly.

"Yeah, Waymon," Tyler chided, exaggerating the pronunciation of the name. "Let it go." He sneered contemptuously at the hapless lawman. "How many of your friends were killed? Two? Well, the count is gonna go up one more if you don't get outta here right quick. I'm tired of lookin' at you."

Waymon flushed red, mortified by the blatant bully. Knowing that he could only save face by standing up to Tyler, he could not summon the courage to do so. He stood there helpless until Myra Bannerman told him to leave, that he was not needed. "Go on, Waymon. I'll call you if I need you."

With nothing left of his pride, Waymon muttered, "Well, I reckon there ain't been no crime committed." He turned abruptly, ignoring the wide grin on Tyler's face. "Send Nathaniel for me if you need me," he mumbled, and never looked back again.

When the sheriff had left, Tyler turned to Myra and asked, "How much do I owe you?"

Genuinely surprised that he offered payment, she quickly totaled his purchases and took the money, half expecting him to snatch it back and laugh at her. He waited patiently now while she wrapped his bacon in paper and tied it with string.

Leaving Bannerman's, Waymon marched straight to his shop, feeling the hot burn of humiliation between his shoulder blades. He hated his cowardice, hated it to the point where he felt nauseous. Upon reaching his door, he stalked inside, and ripping the badge from his shirt, flung it across the room. Hounded by a failure to act on that fatal day when Roy and Bert were murdered, his mind was now overburdened with guilt and disgust for his weakness. He had heard the shots fired inside the saloon, and rushed to his door in time to see Brance Burkett and his four companions as they emerged from the building and unhurriedly prepared to mount up. There was time for him to act, and he had tried to. He grabbed his shotgun, and returned to the door, but he hesitated when he saw the outlaws talking and laughing as they stepped up into their saddles. He closed his eyes and grimaced painfully as he remembered how he had slinked back inside and waited until the outlaws were riding out of town.

No one had blamed him for his lack of response, never questioning his explanation that he had been too late to take action. But it had been something that he had found difficult to expel from his memory. Feeling an obligation to the town, and especially to Myra Bannerman and Frances Wheeler, he had accepted the position of sheriff, even though he insisted it would be temporary. Now, the first time he had been called upon to confront a man who was obviously of the same ilk as the gang that murdered and robbed, he had backed down. The shame was eating away at his brain. He should have run Tyler out of town without explanation beyond the fact that vermin like him were not welcome in Neosho. His eyes came to rest upon the shotgun propped in the corner, and he knew what he must do.

Tyler took his change from Myra Bannerman, stoically watching as she counted it out. A jar containing peppermint sticks caught his eye, and he helped himself to one, and thrust it in his mouth. He glanced at Myra then to see if she was going to ask for payment. She did not, preferring to hurry him out of her store. He grunted his amusement, and gathering up his packages, left the store.

Looking over the rump of his horse, he was surprised to see the sheriff coming from his carpentry shop down the street. Curious, because the lawman was now carrying a double-barreled shotgun, Tyler watched him closely as he dropped his supplies into his saddle bags. Not sure what Waymon had in mind, Tyler reached down and slipped his pistol from the holster. "Hold still," he warned softly when the sorrel stamped its hooves nervously. Tyler shifted the piece of peppermint candy from one side of his mouth to the other, his eyes never leaving the lawman now obviously heading straight for him, the shotgun clutched before his chest with both hands.

When he had approached within ten yards of Tyler, Waymon stopped and hesitated for a few seconds before speaking. Looking into the insolent gaze of the outlaw, his resolve, so recently summoned, began to evaporate, and he had to force his words to come. "I just wanted to make sure you were leavin' town," he managed without stumbling over the words.

Shifting the stick of candy over to the opposite side of his mouth once more, Tyler grinned. "What did you say?" He had clearly heard what Waymon had said. He just wanted to make him say it again.

"As sheriff," Waymon stammered, "I'm tellin' you to leave Neosho and don't come back."

"You're runnin' me outta town?" Tyler asked, as if clarifying the sheriff's directive.

"That's right," Waymon replied, suddenly aware that his hands felt sweaty on the stock of the shotgun.

"What if I ain't ready to leave?"

There it was, the response that Waymon had hoped and prayed he would not hear. He wished at that moment that he had remained hidden in his shop like the time before. Fighting the impulse to turn and run, he forced himself to say, "Then I reckon it's my job to make you." He moved the shotgun ever so slightly. It was enough to signal his fate.

Without hesitating, Tyler brought his pistol up from behind his horse's rump, and fired three times in succession, all three bullets slamming into the stunned lawman's chest. Waymon staggered backward several steps, his face a mask of utter astonishment. He stood there for a brief moment, staring into the leering face of his assailant. Then the shotgun dropped from his hands, and he crumpled slowly to the ground.

The shots brought Myra Bannerman and Nathaniel running to the door. Tyler looked at the frightened woman and her son. Seeing that they offered no threat, he holstered his pistol, and stepped up in the saddle. "You can see it was self-defense," he commented smugly. "He was gonna use that shotgun on me." Turning the sorrel away from the hitching rail, he touched a finger to the brim of his hat in a contemptuous salute to the lady. Then he looked back at the frightened boy, and it triggered an incident in his memory of another frightened boy—one who had the audacity to throw a hammer at him and then seek refuge in a church. He had been in Neosho before this. The memory of it caused him to laugh. He kicked the sorrel hard, and crunched the last of the peppermint stick between his teeth. "Hell, I've been to church in this town."

Chapter 15

Eli bent low over his horse's neck, driving the buckskin gelding hard. The big horse's hooves beat out a hollow tattoo on the hard-packed sand along the edge of the creek that echoed back from the bluffs. He took time to glance over his shoulder at Brance, who was gradually falling behind. Brance's Morgan could not stay with Eli's buckskin over a great distance. The Morgan was a stout horse, but it lacked the stamina and determination of the buckskin. Knowing it was only a matter of minutes before Brance yelled for a halt, Eli let up on his horse, pulling him down to an easy lope until Brance caught up.

It was time to rest the horses, anyway. They had been ridden hard all day, and even Eli's buckskin was showing the strain. When they had galloped out of Springfield, they intended to put as much distance as possible between them and their pursuers. Even though the two buckskin-clad men were on their way to jail when Brance and Eli last saw them, there was something about the pair that made Eli want to leave them far behind. Brance, although scoffing at the potential danger, nonetheless made no objection when Eli said it was best to leave the territory.

"Gawdam," Brance swore when he pulled up beside Eli. "I thought I was gonna have to shoot that damn horse of yours to get you to stop. We're gonna have to make camp before it gets too dark to see."

"This is as good a place as any," Eli replied, looking around him. Satisfied, he dismounted.

"I don't know why we've been runnin' so hard, anyway. Hell, there ain't nobody after us," Brance said as he led the big Morgan stallion down to the water's edge.

"Maybe," Eli allowed. "But I don't trust them two—especially that one with the Henry rifle."

Brance looked at his partner and shook his head in wonder. "I ain't never seen you get spooked by anybody before. You ain't losing your edge, are you?"

"I ain't spooked," Eli replied, and turned to look Brance in the eye. "But my gut feelin' tells me it's a lot healthier to be where he ain't."

Brance couldn't believe he was hearing this kind of talk from Eli, especially in light of the fact they had been searching for this man, Shannon, for weeks. Maybe Eli was getting soft. But one look into the cold, hard eyes of his longtime partner in crime told Brance that this was not the case. "Hell, Eli, there ain't but two men comin' after us, and that's sayin' if they ain't locked up in jail."

"There's the Injun, too," Eli said.

"All right," Brance allowed impatiently, "the Injun kid, so there's two and a half men after us." He snorted his contempt. "I, by God, don't plan on turnin' tail and runnin' halfway across Kansas when there ain't but

two men and an Injun boy on my tail." The more he
thought about it, the more inflamed he became. It had
been a real streak of bad luck that began when he decided to bushwhack the lone rider on the blue roan
near the Arkansas River. He had been the leader of a
sizable band of outlaws. Now his gang was reduced to
the two of them—and they were on the run. All because of one man—Shannon. The sudden wave of
frustration that swept over Brance served to trigger a
slight aching in his brain, and he decided that it was
time to put an end to this running.

"I ain't runnin' another damn step from that son of
a bitch," he informed Eli. "He's cost me too damn
much. I say we hole up right here, and see if they're
still comin' after us. If they don't show up in a day or
two, then, by God, I'm goin' back and killin' that son
of a bitch, if I have to walk right in the jail to do it."

Eli fixed his gaze on Brance for a moment while he
considered his words. He had a serious feeling about
the man called Shannon. The other one, the big one,
merited serious consideration as well. But there was a
deeper ominous feeling about Shannon, and Eli be-
lieved that it was just a matter of time before a showdown. Somehow he knew that Shannon would keep
coming until that final moment. Brance was letting his
temper talk for him, but after more thought, Eli decided that what his partner proposed was the best solution to their problem. It would be better to be the
hunter instead of the hunted. "You're right," he finally
said, "we'd best finish up what we started out to do."

After some discussion, they decided that the spot
where they had stopped was fine for a campsite, but
not necessarily suited for ambush. Seeking better

concealment, they mounted up again and walked their
tired horses about a mile farther up the creek, where
they found what they were looking for. The creek took
a sharp turn where the bluffs were steeper and closer
to the water's edge. The top of the bluffs were cut by
numerous slashes and gullies of various depths and
aptly suited to hiding the two bushwhackers as well as
their horses. They found the spot ideal for watching
their back trail while affording a protected position
from which to fire.

"Hell, we could hold off an army from here,"
Brance boasted as he sighted his rifle on the sandy
creek bank below them.

Eli busied himself with collecting dead branches to
build a fire. When he felt he had collected enough, he
selected a spot for the fire in the deep end of the gully,
where there would be less chance of smoke giving
away their presence. "We'd best take the horses on
around the bend of the creek—see if we can find some
grass." He looked at Brance, and paused for a moment. Brance was in the process of making himself
comfortable at the rim of the gully, showing no signs
of moving. Eli shrugged and got to his feet. "I reckon
I'll take 'em. You keep your eyes peeled." *He's gone
back to being the boss again,* Eli thought as he led the
horses up out of the gully.

Brance heard Eli's remarks, but he chose to ignore
the obvious hint that he should help with the horses.
At that particular time, his mind was occupied with
more pressing problems. The mild headache that had
been triggered by his anger and frustration was pro-
gressing into something more worrisome, as the dull
pounding in his head increased to match the rhythm of

his heartbeat. Not all of his headaches progressed in intensity until taking control of his entire brain and rendering him helpless before the debilitating pain. In fact, he reminded himself, very few of them developed into that paralyzing stage. The sobering realization struck him that he could not afford to have one of his spells at this crucial time. It was a helpless feeling, for there was nothing he could do but wait it out, and he cursed God for damning him with this weakness.

He tried to make himself as comfortable as possible, forcing himself to concentrate on the wide sandy bank of the creek below him and the gentle flow of the water. Now that his gang had been reduced to only Eli and himself, he had to wonder if Eli would stand by him if he became helpless with the pain. He promptly pushed that question from his thoughts. He and Eli had ridden together too long, covered each other's backs too many times for Brance to concern himself with questions of Eli's support. He gently turned his head to follow his partner as Eli led the horses across the gullies to a patch of grass a few yards away. Much to his relief, the turning of his head failed to bring on the spinning sensation in his brain that usually signaled the onset of a spell. He returned his gaze to the creek behind him, still with no dizziness, just the pounding in his brain. In a few minutes, the pounding eased off to a dull throb, and he knew from experience that the point of danger had passed.

It was not difficult to follow the trail left by the two outlaws. There had been some effort to disguise the general direction after they had taken the left fork in the road just north of town. But Crooked Foot found their tracks after a careful search turned up two sets of fresh prints leaving the wagon track about two miles north of Springfield. From that point on, there appeared to have been no efforts to cover their trail—and judging by the length of the strides, speed was the major consideration.

Haste had to be a prime consideration for Matt and his two companions as well, for they could well anticipate a posse coming after them as soon as the deputy was found in the jail cell. It figured that a posse could follow the same trail they followed. So they stayed with the trail until darkness forced them to camp. Back in the saddle as soon as it was light enough to see, they continued following the two outlaws north, figuring that Brance and Eli were probably headed to Kansas City. But around noon that day, the trail veered more to the west, where the tracks ended at the bank of a narrow river. Crooked Foot swam his pony across, and motioned for Ike and Matt to follow when he picked up the trail on the opposite side.

"Now where the hell are they headin'?" Ike wondered aloud. Of the three, he was the only one who had ridden this part of the country before. "Now that I recollect, there is a little town up this way called Topeka. Maybe they're headin' there. It's on the Kansas River—Topeka Landing, they used to call it. Riverboats run back and forth on that river."

Matt and Crooked Foot were not particularly interested in the history of Topeka. They were more impressed with the fact that the tracks they followed appeared to be somewhat fresher in spite of the obvious lengthening of the stride. The men they chased were at a gallop again. "We gettin' close," Crooked

Foot announced when the tracks descended to a creek bank, and followed the course of the water north. After following the creek for the better part of a mile, they came to a point where the tracks stopped.

"Well," Ike said, "they stopped runnin'." He peered ahead toward a crook in the creek where it turned around some steep bluffs. "Looks like they musta stopped here and parlayed for a spell." He looked at Crooked Foot to see if the boy disagreed. Crooked Foot nodded, and Ike continued. "Watered their horses and started again, but this time at a walk." Ike nodded his head, agreeing with his own assessment of the situation. "I'd say we'd best watch our behinds from here on."

"How close?" Matt asked. Like his companions, he had a strong feeling that the two outlaws had paused here to have a discussion about something. And it was a good possibility that the subject might be to lay in wait for anyone following them.

"Pretty damn close," Ike replied. "These tracks is pretty fresh."

Matt glanced at Crooked Foot. The Cherokee boy was in agreement. Matt turned to study the steep bluffs at the bend of the creek. "If a man was planning to ambush somebody, those bluffs up ahead would be a damn good place to do it."

"That's what I was thinkin'," Ike said.

"Might be wise to circle that bend, and scout it from the other side," Matt suggested.

Ike and Crooked Foot concurred, so they turned and rode back the way they had come until reaching the cut where they had descended the bluffs that bordered the creek. Riding up into the bluffs again, they stopped momentarily before proceeding. A long ridge ran parallel to the bluffs, but there was very little cover in the way of trees, so Ike suggested they should cross over the ridge and take a wide swing around it, maybe finding better cover on the other side.

As Ike had hoped, the ridge they crossed was one of a series, running more or less parallel and offering protection from any eyes watching from the bluffs. They guided their horses along the base of the second ridge until reaching a point they guessed was approximate to the steep bluff at the creek's bend. "Best leave the horses here in these trees," Ike suggested.

On foot now, they spread out and started making their way carefully up to the bluffs again. Keeping low to the ground, Matt moved cautiously, but rapidly, to the crest of the ridge where he flattened himself on the ground, and scanned the broken line of bluffs some fifty yards before him. From where he lay, there was nothing but open ground between the trees on the ridge and the gullies and cuts that ran down to the creek. Crooked Foot crawled up beside him, and tapped him lightly on the arm. When Matt turned his head toward him, the Cherokee boy pointed to a small, dark object that appeared to be lying on the ground at the edge of one of the deeper gullies. Matt looked at it, then turned back to Crooked Foot, puzzled.

"Hat," Crooked Foot stated softly, and patted his head with his hand.

Matt looked again at the object, focusing his gaze upon it as Ike crawled up to join them. Crooked Foot pointed the object out again for Ike's benefit, and the big man settled himself between them, squinting his eyes in an effort to focus. Matt was about to question the Indian boy's imagination when the object suddenly moved, revealing the flat crown of a black hat before disappearing completely from their view. "Damn," Matt uttered in awe of the boy's keen eyesight. "It is a hat."

"I seen it right off," Ike said, causing both Matt and Crooked Foot to give him a sideways glance.

It was certain now. Their quarry had, indeed, stopped running, and was now waiting in ambush. One thing was without question: they had picked a good spot to lay in wait. From the deep gullies, the outlaws could watch the creek below them, as well as the open area behind them toward the ridges. It would be foolhardy to attempt to cross that open ground in daylight. "I reckon we'll be waiting for dark," Matt said.

Seated with his back against the hard, sandy side of the gully, his eyes focused upon the bank of the creek some thirty feet below them, Brance Burkett complained. "We've been settin' here all day. I believe if them bastards are on our trail, they'da been here by now. Hell, we were just lettin' ourselves get spooked by that son of a bitch with the Henry rifle. They're coolin' their heels in the Springfield jail."

"Maybe," Eli replied. He squinted up at the sun now rapidly settling toward the western hills. "There ain't much daylight left. We might as well stay put right here, and move on in the mornin'."

Brance was in agreement. His headache had eased off considerably since sitting quietly at the head of the gully. The only thing that kept a spark of the throbbing alive in his head was his disappointment at not being able to settle with Shannon once and for all.

Eli dug down in his saddlebags to find some bacon to fry, unaware that Brance was patiently waiting out a headache, hoping to avoid one of his spells. Brance had not moved from his position at the head of the gully during the entire time Eli had taken the horses to water, come back, and put some coffee on to boil. In fact, his partner had uttered no more than a few grunts in response to Eli's comments. Finally Eli was moved to inquire. "What the hell's wrong with you?" Then the thought struck him. "You ain't fixin' to have one of your spells, are you?"

Brance didn't answer at once. The pain that had eased off an hour before was now back with a vengeance, and it gave indication that it was going to continue to increase in intensity. He finally answered, his words soft and drawn out, each one seeming to echo in his brain. "No," he mumbled, "just leave me be." He knew by then that it was a lie. He *was* going to have one of the debilitating headaches, and he knew it would render him helpless. Already, his head was beginning to spin, and the pain was slashing between his eyes like jagged bolts of lightning. Pretty soon the nausea would come. He wanted to retire to some place where he could be alone to wait out the ordeal, but he was too sick now to get to his feet. He closed his eyes tight, trying to shut out the pain. When he did, he could feel his eyelids grating across his dry eyeballs as if thousands of nerve endings were suddenly exposed.

Although the tormented man remained motionless, Eli could tell there was something wrong. He stood over him, staring down, unable to avoid a feeling of disgust for his partner's apparent weakness. "Can you eat something?" Eli asked. "Maybe drink some of this coffee?" The suggestion was enough to bring a wave of dry heaves over Brance, who fell against the side of the gully, fumbling for his pistol. Eli stepped back then. Brance was taking his usual defensive position. If he was not already, he would soon be virtually blind and prone to shoot at any sound approaching him.

From experience, Eli knew it was not safe to remain where a bullet might be accidentally sent flying his way. He said not another word, picked up the coffeepot and the frying pan with the bacon, and left that particular gully to his inflicted partner. Better to sleep in a cold blanket than to chance getting shot by a half-crazed maniac, he thought. He settled himself down near the horses, close to the creek. Maybe Brance would sleep it off, he told himself. *If he don't, I'll leave the crazy son of a bitch in the morning.* He had finally had enough of Brance's insane spells.

Crooked Foot sat near the base of a tree, watching the clearing that separated him and his two friends from the bluffs. As he waited, he cradled the Springfield rifle across his lap, his hand unconsciously tracing the outline of the wooden stock. The rifle, once the possession of an outlaw named Tyler, had been a gift from Matt after Crooked Foot had used it to bluff his way into the jail. He had never owned a rifle before, and as he sat awaiting the darkness, he thought about how proud his father would have been to see his son in possession of such a weapon. Then the picture of his mother and father tossed carelessly upon a funeral pyre returned to his mind, and his hand tightened upon the trigger guard of the Springfield. *You will be avenged before this night is over,* he silently promised.

Shifting his eyes momentarily from the clearing, he glanced at Ike, stretched out under a scrubby oak, in all appearance seeming perfectly at ease. Crooked Foot knew that Ike's appearance was deceptive, for the grizzled old warrior was as thirsty for revenge as himself. He shifted his gaze back toward the gullies. The thin ribbon of smoke that had pinpointed the outlaws' campfire was lost now against the dark shadows of the night. It was time to move. He had no sooner had the thought when Matt returned from checking the horses. He knelt down beside the prone figure of Ike.

"Let's get at it," Matt said softly. Ike responded immediately.

Under a deep, moonless sky, the three spread out several yards apart, and moved silently across the expanse of open ground. Upon Ike's insistence, he was in the middle, moving straight for the head of the deep gully from which the smoke had come. Matt and Crooked Foot flanked the huge man. If luck was with them, they hoped to find the two outlaws asleep by the fire, making their execution quick and neat, although the thought of a long torturous death had entered Ike's mind.

Halfway across the clearing, they paused to listen for sounds from the camp. All was quiet—not even the sound of horses came to them in the stillness. The thought occurred to Matt that the three of them might be walking into an ambush. If that were the case, he could expect the sudden flash of gunfire to erupt at any second. But there was nothing. A few yards farther and they were approaching the first of the series of gullies. Crouching low in the darkness, Ike motioned for Matt and Crooked Foot to move into position to converge upon the camp. No more than a few feet from the brow of the gully, Ike waited until they were ready. Then he flattened himself upon the ground and eased his body forward until he could see over the rim.

There was no one there. A couple of saddlebags lay near the dying embers of the fire, but there was no sign of the men who owned them. Ike was immediately alert to the possibility that he might be in the midst of an ambush. He hugged the ground, looking quickly to either side, expecting the worst.

Crouching back in a deep slash at the head of the gully, his knees pulled up before him, Brance Burkett strived desperately to endure the debilitating hell that had seized him. The stabbing pain that relentlessly assaulted him left him blind and helpless, and he pressed his spine as far back against the cold clay of his cocoon as he could. Always afraid that someone might take advantage of his helplessness, he gripped his pistol tightly while his head rolled from side to side with the pain. A slight sound penetrated his torment. Fearing he was being attacked, he fired the pistol, emptying the weapon into the darkness against an unseen assailant.

The sudden barrage of gunshots startled Ike, and he dived for cover below the rim of the gully. Matt and Crooked Foot hit the ground, searching frantically for the source of the firing. From his side of the gully, Crooked Foot was the first to realize that the shots had come from a hollowed-out crevice in the head of the deep cut. He raised up on one knee, and fired into the dark hole. Following his lead, Matt pumped three more rounds into the cut. They waited then. All was silent. After a few long moments had passed with no return fire, Matt dropped down into the gully by the campfire. Picking up a half-burnt limb, he tossed it into the crevice. There was still no response. The limb offered very little illumination, but it was fairly evident that whoever had been hiding in the hole was done for.

Down by the creek, Eli sat up in his blanket when he heard the barrage of pistol shots. His brain still half asleep, his immediate reaction was to roll out of his blanket and reach for his rifle. He paused then as his brain cleared. *Something spooked the crazy bastard*, he thought. *It's a damn good thing I didn't stay up there.* He was about to return to his blanket when he heard the distinct sound of a Springfield rifle, followed by the rapid fire of Matt's Henry. "Shannon!" he blurted.

Ike stirred up the fire until he generated a stout flame on one of the limbs. Then, using it as a torch, he went to the crevice and thrust it inside. "There ain't but one of 'em in here," he warned, "but he's deader'n hell." Matt and Crooked Foot immediately reacted. Expecting an attack from below, they set themselves ready to fire. There was no sound for a moment, then one shot rang out from the bottom of the gully. Crooked Foot grunted dully when the bullet struck his breastbone. He staggered backward a couple of steps, then sank to the ground. Ike sprang to his side.

Leaving Ike to tend the wounded boy, Matt moved quickly down the dark ravine to the water's edge. He got to the creek in time to hear the beat of hooves as Eli's horse thundered away into the darkness. Searching frantically, it took several precious moments before Matt sighted the dark form of the horse and rider against the black tree line on the other side of the creek. By then it was too late to get off a good shot. But he took it anyway, purely out of frustration. As he expected, his shot was wasted. "Damn!" he swore, for his horse was on the opposite side of the second ridge.

With no thought of giving up the chase, he did not hesitate. Scrambling back up the gully as quickly as he could manage, he paused for only a moment when he got to the top where Ike was doing his best to stop the bleeding from Crooked Foot's chest. "He got away," Matt said in answer to the question on Ike's face. "How bad is it?"

"It's bad," Ike said.

The sight of the wounded Indian boy only increased the feeling of urgency in Matt's brain. "I'm goin' after him," he stated.

"I can't leave him," Ike said. "He's bleedin' somethin' awful."

"You stay with him," Matt said. "I'll get back as soon as I can." He didn't wait to discuss it. In only a moment he was gone, disappearing into the night.

Chapter 16

Common sense told him that there was little chance of success in continuing the chase. Valuable time had been lost while he had crossed the ridge on foot to get back to his horse. The only thing he had to go on was the direction in which the shadowy figure had disappeared. But Matt was determined to find the remaining member of the gang. His determination had been for Ike until this night. Now it was for Crooked Foot. He had his mind set now to finish the job they had started.

Starting out from the point where he had taken a shot at Eli, he crossed over the creek, and made his way along the other bank, taking the easier route through the hills. With no light to follow a trail, he figured his best bet was to take the most direct path, counting on the idea that Eli would have done the same in his haste to escape. Holding Blue to a steady pace, he pushed on through the night until reaching a wide stream that bisected a narrow valley. Here, he was forced to pause. The man he trailed could have taken any of a number of directions. There was no choice but to wait until first light, and try to pick up the trail. Pushing his frustration aside, he settled where he was, and prepared to wait. It was not a sure bet that he was even on the outlaw's trail at this point. The thought that he may have been wasting time riding around in the dark was worrisome at the least.

With the first rays of light, he was scouting the edges of the stream, looking for some sign that his blind gamble had not been for naught. The sandy bank was smooth and undisturbed. No horse had passed this way. Matt stood looking first upstream, then downstream, feeling totally defeated, but still unwilling to admit it, even to himself. His only hope of catching Eli had been to follow his trail. He had only seen the man through a veil of darkness as Eli sped away in the night. Although he had been one of the men sitting at the poker table back in Springfield, Matt realized that he wouldn't be able to identify him if he saw him in a crowd.

With no options open to him, he climbed aboard Blue, and crossed to the other side of the stream. Within twenty feet of the point where he came out of the water, he saw the hoofprints. "Well, I'll be damned" he blurted, at first unable to believe his luck. He dismounted to take a closer look. Judging from the direction from which the tracks left the water, it appeared the outlaw had been riding down the stream, probably from a good distance back, in hopes of losing anyone pursuing him. "And I just happened to stumble on his tracks right where he came out," Matt murmured, still finding it hard to believe. With a trail to follow, he wasted no time getting back in the saddle.

Time was important. According to what Ike had told him, Topeka Landing and the Kansas River were not far from where he now was. He wanted to catch up to Eli before he reached the settlement and decreased the odds of finding him.

As the sun climbed to brighten the morning sky, Matt rode through a land of rolling hills and tree-covered slopes, following a trail that was becoming easier and easier to follow. That fact in itself should have served to give him concern, but his mind was on cutting the distance between himself and the man he pursued. Pushing Blue hard, pausing only now and then to study the tracks, he entered a long narrow ravine. In the next moment he was startled by a dull sound, like the sound of a fist hitting solid flesh. He saw the hole that suddenly appeared in Blue's neck an instant before the sound of the rifle penetrated the morning stillness. He immediately flattened himself against the confused horse's neck. Blue reared back in pain, and a second shot smacked into the blue roan's chest. The horse screamed in panic, and lunged forward as if to gallop, but took no more than three strides before its front legs folded and horse and rider went crashing to the ground.

Matt stayed with the horse, taking care to remove his foot from the stirrup to avoid being pinned beneath Blue's weight. Using the horse as cover, he pulled his rifle from the sling, and scanned the ridges that formed the ravine, searching for the source of the shots. In a few moments, two more shots rang out, the slugs thudding dully into Blue's belly, and Matt was able to spot his assailant. He brought his rifle to bear on a clump of juniper surrounding a large boulder

near the top of the ravine and opened fire, sending
three slugs glancing off the rock.

That son of a bitch, Eli thought as he ducked back
behind the boulder. He cursed for having missed
Matt with his first shot and hit the horse instead. And
then the big roan had reared up, causing him to miss
with his second shot. *One thing for sure, I sure as hell
stopped him from coming after me.* That thought brought
some satisfaction. However, Eli wanted the man he
knew as Shannon underground. So he moved to the
other side of the boulder, hoping to get a different
angle and a clear shot. His prey was almost totally
protected by the carcass of the horse. The only target
available to him was one moccasined foot left exposed at the rump of the dead horse. Eli rose up
slightly, took dead aim at the foot, and pulled the
trigger. He saw a little puff of dirt inches away from
the moccasin, but before he could fire again, he was
suddenly spun around by a slug slamming into his
left shoulder.

"Damn you!" Eli roared in anger as he clutched his
shoulder and ducked back down behind the rock. He
had been tricked into exposing himself. The shot that
found his shoulder had come from behind the dead
horse's neck. In all his years of raiding, murdering
and pillaging, he had never been shot before. At first,
his reaction was unbridled fury, and he moved to the
other side of the boulder and emptied his rifle into the
carcass of the horse. But as his sleeve became soaked
with blood, he was struck with the thought that he
had better do something to stop the bleeding. Several
scattered thoughts bombarded his brain as he looked
for something to stuff against the wound. It was

beginning to throb, and the blood would not stop. Topeka Landing was at least five miles away. Maybe he should get himself to a doctor. At the same time, he hated to leave while he had Shannon pinned down behind his horse. Another thought told him that Shannon could hold him off until dark, and then it might be a different game. In the end, he decided he was more concerned about the wound.

Lying low behind Blue's body, Matt figured he was in for a long siege before darkness gave him an opportunity to go on the offensive against his attacker. For that reason, he was surprised when he heard the sound of a horse galloping away from the ridge. Peering out from his fortress of horse flesh, he saw Eli riding down the side of the ravine on a buckskin horse, the sleeve of his shirt red with blood. *Lucky shot*, he thought, and got to his feet, watching until Eli disappeared past the north end of the long ravine. "Well, he won't be hard to identify now," he said before turning back to look at his horse. He and Blue had been partners since the war. It was hard to imagine that the big blue roan was gone. "I'm sorry I got you into this mess," he said, shaking his head sadly as he gazed at the bullet-riddled carcass. Now there was one more reason to finish the job. He picked up his moccasin and put it on, removed the cartridge bag from the saddle pack, and with some great effort, managed to pull his saddle from the horse. Then he set out on foot, following the direction Eli had taken. Near the end of the ravine, he found a dense thicket in which to hide his saddle. Once that was taken care of, he continued on his quest.

He wasn't sure how far he had walked when he

saw the buildings of Topeka, but it was now late in the afternoon. The place had evidently developed a great deal since Ike had been there, for now it appeared to be a town. Tired, but not weary, Matt walked with a deadly determination, bent upon one task only. He took no notice of the two men standing outside the stables as he passed by. They paused in their conversation to gawk in curiosity at the lone man in buckskins walking down the middle of the street, rifle in hand.

Matt's attention was suddenly captured by something at the end of the street. A small house stood alone beyond the general store and a saloon. A buckskin horse waited patiently at the hitching post in front of the house. Matt headed straight for the horse, certain that it was the same buckskin he had seen galloping down the ridge. When he walked up beside the horse, he paused for a moment to read the sign nailed to the fence beside the gate: JONATHAN P. MANNING, M.D. Matt cranked a cartridge into the chamber of the Henry rifle, and entered the doctor's office.

Inside, Matt found himself in a tiny waiting room. A short hallway led past several doors before ending at the back door of the cottage. He was there for only a second when an elderly woman came from one of the doors, carrying a basin filled with bloody water. She barely glanced at the tall, broad-shouldered young man in buckskins, but turned down the hallway toward the back door. "I'll be with you in a minute," she called back over her shoulder. "The doctor's busy at the moment." Pushing the back door open with her foot, she added, "A man was shot by robbers."

Matt went immediately to the room she had come from. Inside, he discovered the doctor bending over his patient, who was freshly bandaged and sitting on a couch against the wall. Both patient and doctor were momentarily stunned by the sudden appearance of the stranger in the treatment room. "Wait outside," Dr. Manning said. "I'll be with you in a moment."

There was no hesitation on Eli's part. He pulled the pistol from his belt, at the same time grabbing for the doctor with his wounded arm, attempting to use him as a shield. Matt, reacting equally as fast, dropped to one knee, and Eli's bullet passed over his head, imbedding in the plastered wall. The Henry spoke but once, leaving a small black hole neatly centered between Eli's eyes, about three quarters of an inch above his eyebrows.

The doctor, having been shoved off balance by Eli's attempt to shield himself, recovered his footing, but stood stone still, fearful that he might be next. He relaxed when Matt ejected the spent shell and lowered his rifle. They stood there staring at each other for what seemed a long time before either man moved. Finally deciding that the buckskin-clad executioner had only one victim in mind, Dr. Manning broke the leaden silence, even as his wife rushed into the room. "It's all right, Agnes," he said, to calm the alarmed woman. "It's all over." Then he looked at Matt. "It is, ain't it?"

Matt nodded and then replied, "It is." He paused for a moment, and then added, "That's the last of 'em."

A bit more confident now, the doctor complained. "I sure wasted a lot of time patching up that shoulder." He looked at Matt. "I wish you'd waited until he paid me."

Matt thought about it for a moment, then walked over to the body, and began emptying Eli's pockets. "How much does he owe you?"

"Ten dollars," the doctor replied, giving his wife a sideways glance. She remained expressionless.

"Ten dollars, huh?" Matt responded. "Here's fifty," he said, giving the doctor all the cash he found in Eli's pockets. "I figure he owes you somethin' for cleanin' up."

Mrs. Manning stood watching in disbelief during the exchange between her husband and the stranger. When it appeared that Matt was preparing to take his leave, she spoke up. "We'd better go get the sheriff."

"What for?" Her husband cut her off. "I mean, he shot in self-defense. The deceased fired the first shot. I saw it." He nodded toward Matt reassuringly. Then, seeing his wife's wide-eyed, questioning expression, he quickly said, "I mean, of course we've got to get the sheriff, but there's no hurry."

"I beg your pardon, ma'am, for this intrusion," Matt said to the bewildered woman, "but it was somethin' that had to be done." That said, he turned on his heel and strode down the short hallway and out the front door. The doctor and his wife followed Matt out to the porch, and stood watching as he untied the buckskin horse from the post. "He owes me a horse," Matt offered in explanation, then wheeled the powerful gelding, and rode out of town the same way he had walked in, leaving Dr. and Mrs. Manning to ponder what had just taken place.

In the short time it took to return to the thicket

where he had hidden his saddle, Matt decided that the man he had just killed had ridden a fine horse. The buckskin devoured the miles with seemingly no effort, his stride long and his gait smooth and constant. While deciding which saddle he would keep, Matt took a few moments to take a closer look at his newly acquired mount. After a brief inspection, he could not help but admire the animal—his broad chest, strong quarters, and depth of girth. And unlike his former master, there appeared to be no evidence of a deceitful nature. He almost felt guilty for admiring Blue's replacement so openly. As for the saddle, he decided to keep Eli's. It was no better than his own, but appeared to be a bit newer, and the buckskin was already accustomed to it. He transferred the rest of his belongings to the new rig, and after a final farewell to Blue's carcass, set out to find Ike and Crooked Foot.

Ike stood over the wounded Cherokee boy, staring at him in consternation, helpless to do anything to alleviate his pain. Ike had already done everything he could to stop the bleeding, but it looked as if it could start again at any moment. The bullet from Eli's rifle had crushed the boy's breastbone, caving it in and shattering his ribs. What amazed Ike most was the fact that the Indian boy was still alive. The bullet had somehow missed the heart, but it must have torn into his lungs, because Crooked Foot periodically coughed up blood. Ike feared the boy was choking to death, so he lifted him up to a sitting position against the side of the gully, hoping it would keep the blood from entering his throat. From time to time, Crooked Foot's eyes would flutter open, only to stare far off into the distance. Each time his eyes closed again, Ike wondered if it was for eternity. But the boy would not give in to the beckoning of the Great Spirit.

Turning away from the wounded boy for a few moments, Ike's thoughts turned toward his partner. At that moment, he wondered if he would ever see Matt Slaughter again. His young friend had been gone almost twenty-four hours now, and the sun was sinking low on another day. He looked back at Crooked Foot again. What to do? It was difficult to decide. The boy was dying, Ike was certain of that. How long should he remain here waiting for Matt?

In the next moment, his question was answered, for a rider suddenly appeared on the far bank of the creek, some five hundred yards away. Ike's eyes were not as keen as they used to be when he was young, so he picked up his rifle and moved to the side of the gully. Straining hard, he tried to focus on the man. It could be Matt, but this man was riding a buckskin, so Ike kept a steady aim on him. When the rider closed the distance to two hundred yards, Ike could say for sure that it was indeed his young friend. A great sense of relief swept over him.

"Hello the camp," Matt called out before crossing over the creek.

"Come on in, Matt," Ike returned, and put his rifle down.

Ike followed the gully down to the water where his horse and Crooked Foot's pony were hobbled. He waited there while Matt pulled up and dismounted. "He got Blue," Matt said, answering the question on Ike's face, "but I got him."

"Well, I reckon that about takes care of business," Ike said, after hearing Matt's accounting of the death of the last outlaw they hunted.

"How's Crooked Foot?" Matt inquired.

"You look," Ike replied abruptly. "He don't look good a'tall. Matter of fact, I thought he'd go under before you got back."

This was sorrowful news indeed to Matt. He had developed a fondness for the spunky Indian boy. He hobbled the buckskin, and followed Ike back up the gully, seeing at once that Crooked Foot was as badly wounded as Ike had said. The Cherokee boy gave no indication that he was even aware of Matt when he bent low to examine the wound. "Damn!" Matt uttered softly when he saw the extent of the damage. He stood up and turned to Ike. "We need to get him to a doctor."

"It's a long ways back to Springfield," Ike said. "He might be dead before we made it back there." Topeka was a lot closer, but after hearing the circumstances of Eli's execution, he assumed it would not be wise for Matt to return to that town.

Matt did not give the matter a second thought. "There's a doctor no more than six or seven miles from here. We'll take Crooked Foot to Topeka. The doctor's never seen you. You can take Crooked Foot in."

The boy was far too badly wounded to sit a horse, so Matt and Ike cut a couple of young saplings to use as poles for a travois. They fashioned a platform of tree limbs, and lashed them together with a coil of rope that was on Eli's saddle. It was a rough ambulance to say the least, but they figured it would serve to haul the wounded boy to Topeka Landing.

The trip was slow and extremely painful for the suffering patient. By the time they arrived on a hill overlooking the Kansas River, the boy appeared too weak to continue. "This looks like a good place to make camp," Matt said. "Maybe we'd better stop right now and bring the doctor here. I'm afraid we're gonna kill him if we go any farther." Ike agreed, and they lifted Crooked Foot from the travois, and laid him as gently as they could manage under a cottonwood tree. By the time they had him settled, it was beginning to get dark. "I expect you'd best go on into town and fetch the doctor," Matt said.

Boyd Jenkins glanced up when his eye caught sight of a rider approaching his stable. Pausing to see who it was, he became immediately alarmed, for it was another buckskin-clad stranger—the second one that day. When the first one had passed his stables earlier in the afternoon, a man was killed soon after. This one looked a lot bigger than the first one, and maybe even a bit wilder. Boyd didn't hesitate. He dropped the sack of oats he had been carrying, and ran out the back of the stable, figuring it best to alert the sheriff.

Cutting across behind the saloon and the general store, Boyd made good time reaching the jail, a small stone building just off the main street. Sheriff Sam Baldwin was still in his office, judging by the light in the window. Boyd hesitated at the doorstep to watch the stranger pass the general store, apparently headed for the doctor's office.

"What the hell's chasin' you, Boyd?" Sam Baldwin grunted when his office door was suddenly flung

open, and a panting Boyd Jenkins burst into the room.
The half-empty whiskey bottle on the desk was testimony to the melancholy fits the sheriff occasionally
suffered. Everybody in town knew of Sam's depend-
ence on alcohol. He needed it to bolster his courage to
face a complaining, domineering wife every night
when he went home. On some nights, when his melan-
cholia was more severe, he had been observed staggering a little when he locked up his office for the
night. Boyd took no notice of this in his excitement to
give the alert.

"Sam!" Boyd blurted. "There's another one of them
wild-lookin' fellers headed for Doc Manning's place!"

Sam did his best to think soberly when he responded. "What happened? Did he do somethin'?" He
had already had to deal with one man shot in the head
that day by a wild-looking stranger who just blatantly
walked into the doctor's office and blazed away.

"Well, not yet," Boyd answered, surprised by the
sheriff's apparent lack of excitement. "But this one
looks like that first feller, only this one's big as a bear
and looks a lot meaner."

"Well, it ain't against the law to go to the doctor's
office," Sam said, still trying to overcome the alcohol
in his brain.

Disappointed by Sam's reaction to his warning,
Boyd stood there shifting his weight from one foot to
the other for a few moments before speaking. "I just
thought you'd wanna know there was another gun-
man in town."

"Yeah," Sam said, his mind still spinning. "Yeah,
you done the right thing. 'Course I'd wanna know. I
ain't about to let no wild murderers think they can run

roughshod over my town." He pulled a rifle out of the rack on the wall, and proceeded to load the magazine. "Where'd you say he was headin'?"

"Doc Manning's place," Boyd replied, "just like the first one did."

"Right. We'll just see what's on his mind," he stated, his words still a little slurred.

The light had almost faded completely when Ike guided his horse up to the doctor's gate and stepped down from the saddle. He had no sooner tied his horse to the fence when he was surprised by the sheriff coming around the corner of the fence with a rifle aimed at his belly. "Hold on there, big'un," Sam demanded. "Just where do you think you're goin'?"

Ike paused to consider the rifle aimed at his midsection. His eyes fixed on the weapon, he paid little attention to Boyd Jenkins standing behind Sam. "I'm goin' to see the doctor," he finally stated.

"What for?" Sam demanded. "Are you sick?"

"I reckon that's me and the doctor's business," Ike replied without emotion.

"Is that so?" Sam blurted. "Well, I think we'll go down to the jail, and find out whose business it is."

By this time, Ike realized that the sheriff was half-drunk. "Is it against the law to go to the doctor in this town?" Ike had no time to waste on a drunken sheriff, but the rifle in Sam's hands had no sense of right or wrong. A bullet from a drunken sheriff was equally as deadly as one from a sober one.

"It's against the law to smart-mouth the sheriff," Sam said. "Now, you just untie them reins, and lead that horse down to my office."

By this time, Sam's loud voice had been heard inside, and Doctor Manning came to the door to investigate. Upon seeing Sam holding a rifle on the huge man in buckskins, he inquired, "What's the trouble, Sam?"

"Nothin' much, Doc," the sheriff replied confidently. "We've just got us another one of them wild ones in town—only this time I aim to see what he's up to before somebody else gets shot. One killin' a day is enough for this town."

"What's he doing on my front step?" Manning wanted to know.

Before Sam could reply, Ike answered him. "I was comin' to see you. I ain't done nothin', ain't committed no crime. I was just tryin' to see the doctor."

"Why? Are you ailing?"

"Well, it ain't that." Ike hesitated to give the reason for the need for a doctor. "I just need to talk to you, and it ain't none of the sheriff's business."

"I reckon I'm the one decides that," Sam snorted, and motioned with the rifle. "That way. Get movin'."

Dr. Manning could readily see that the sheriff had been nipping generously from the bottle. And he knew Sam well enough to know that he could be mighty belligerent when he'd had a few drinks. The big man did have a wild, even dangerous, look about him, but maybe he really was seeking medical advice. "Maybe it wouldn't hurt for me to talk to him, Sam."

Sam considered it for a moment, knowing that he held all the cards while he had his rifle on him, and the man looked capable of raising all kinds of hell. "We'll just go down to my office, and find out a few things about this feller. If I think he's not up to some-thin', I'll let him go." He turned to Ike. "All right, start walkin'."

Ike could see little choice but to do as he was told. Thoughts of Matt waiting back up in the hills with the wounded boy made him consider jumping the sheriff if the opportunity presented itself. But Sam was care-ful to keep an eye on his prisoner every step of the way. Once inside the jail, he directed Ike into one of the two cells, and locked the door. "You just cool your heels for a spell. I'm gonna check my notices first, and then you and I'll have us a little talk."

Ike at once berated himself for allowing the sheriff to lock him up. *I shouldn't have ever let him get me inside this building*, he thought. But it was too late now. He only hoped there was no old *Wanted* notice in the stack of papers Sam took from his desk drawer. It was bad luck to have been spotted riding into town. Maybe it should have occurred to him that the town was edgy after Matt had so brazenly executed a man in the doc-tor's office. If he had thought more about it before, he would have at least waited until darkness set fully in. It was bad luck all right, and he was about to find that it would only get worse.

"Well, lookee here," the sheriff sang out gleefully. He extracted one notice from the rest, and walked over to the cell door for a closer look. "This here's a dang good likeness." He chuckled to think of the catch he had just made. "Yessir, this description fits you like a glove, too. You'd be Mr. Ike Brister, wanted in Missouri for murder." He looked at Ike and grinned. "And you just come ridin' right in—mighty accommodatin', Mr. Brister, mighty accommodatin'. By God, this calls for a drink." He poured himself a drink from the bottle, now less than half full, saluted Ike with it, then tossed it back. "Yessir, wait till I tell the judge in the mornin'. We ain't never had a real famous outlaw in our jail before."

Ike remained a stoic witness to the sheriff's gleeful exhibition. He was angry, more so at himself than the sheriff, for not anticipating the presence of a *Wanted* poster in the jail. Even with a rifle pointed at him, he might have taken a chance at jumping the sheriff if he had given it more thought. His concern now was for Crooked Foot, maybe bleeding to death, waiting for his return with the doctor. There was nothing he could do about it at this point. It was just plain dumb, letting himself get caught like this. He had let the boy down.

"Well, Mr. Brister, I think I'll go get my supper. I hope you don't mind stayin' here by yourself for a little while." Sam's spirits could hardly get much higher. "Since you're such a famous man, I might even bring you a plate." He stood in the middle of the room, grinning broadly at his prisoner. When there was no response from Ike, he chuckled and turned to leave. Unable to resist one last taunt, he said, "The key to the cell door is right here in my desk drawer if you have to leave before I get back." Content with himself, he went out, closed the front door and padlocked it, feeling confident that nobody would be able to get in before he got back. That done, he headed for the hotel and supper.

"Oh Lordy," Ike moaned to himself. "Now what am I gonna do?" He went around the cell, checking the strength of the bars. They were all solidly in place.

There was no window in the cell, so there was little he could do but sit down and wait with images of a dying boy to torment his mind.

Matt paced back and forth across the brow of the hill, watching for sign of Ike's return with the doctor. It was now well past dark. Ike should have been back by now. Hearing a low moan from Crooked Foot, he moved quickly down to the cottonwood tree where the boy lay. The wounded boy mumbled a series of words barely above a whisper, speaking in the Cherokee tongue. Even though Matt spoke no Cherokee, he soon surmised that it was no more than senseless mumbling. Crooked Foot was still unconscious. He looked bad. Matt was at a loss as to what he could do to ease his pain. Crooked Foot suddenly cried out in pain, then appeared to sink back in sleep. Afraid that the boy had just passed, Matt bent close over him. Crooked Foot was still breathing. Matt got to his feet again. "Gawdammit!" He blurted in frustration. "Where the hell is Ike?" Climbing back up to the brow of the hill again, he watched the road below him for a few minutes longer before making his decision.

Something had happened. Ike wasn't coming back. Matt returned to the cottonwood once again, his mind made up. Crooked Foot uttered no protests when Matt picked him up and placed him on the travois once more. After making him as comfortable as possible, Matt climbed aboard the buckskin, and led Crooked Foot's pony down to the road into town. He could afford to wait no longer.

*   *   *

Only a few people noticed the silent procession that rode slowly down the middle of the darkened street, and these were mostly men talking outside the saloon. It was a curious sight, had anyone been sufficiently interested to take a close look—the somber and determined man on the buckskin, leading a body on a travois, a ghostly procession passing through the patches of light from the windows of the saloon. Though noticed, no one saw fit to make much of it, so Matt passed quietly by the hotel and the general store toward the doctor's office at the end of the street.

He saw no sign of Ike, and as he approached Dr. Manning's house, no sign of Ike's horse. That observation worried him, and he again feared that something bad may have happened to his friend. He was determined to find out, but his first priority was to get Crooked Foot to the doctor.

He pulled up to the fence in front of the little whitewashed cottage, and stepped down. Crooked Foot had not made one sound of protest during the ride down from the hill. Matt only glanced at him before going up to the front door and knocking. He held his rifle in his hand in case the doctor needed convincing to look at the boy.

"Oh . . . you . . ." Manning sputtered, at once alarmed to see the broad-shouldered young man at his door again.

"I brought you a patient," Matt said. "He's bad hurt."

Manning looked beyond him at the travois at the gate. "What happened to him?"

"Gunshot," Matt replied.

"Well, can you bring him inside? I can't see what I'm doing out there in the dark."

"I reckon," Matt responded.

"Put him on the couch there," Dr. Manning said when Matt returned carrying Crooked Foot in his arms. He stepped back to give Matt room.

"John?" A voice called from the back of the house.

"It's all right, Agnes," Manning answered, "it's just a patient." He bent over the couch to examine Crooked Foot. "My Lord," he gasped when he saw the wound in the boy's chest. He worked over the boy for a few minutes, then straightened up and looked at Matt. "I don't know what you want me to do. You bring a dead boy in here—there isn't anything I can do for him."

"Dead!" Matt was stunned. "Are you sure? Can't you do somethin' for him?" The doctor's verdict hit him hard. He couldn't help but feel that if he had not wasted so much time waiting for Ike, Crooked Foot might have been saved. "How long has he been dead?"

Manning shrugged. "I don't know—quite a while, I guess. Rigor mortis is already starting to set in." He could see the guilt in the young man's eyes. "I don't think there was much I could have done for him if you had brought him in any sooner—too much damage to the lungs and heart." He paused, then asked, "How'd it happen?"

Matt just shook his head sadly, and continued to stare down at the dead Cherokee boy for a few minutes. Finally, he looked up at Manning and said, "The man I shot in here, he did it." Only then did he remember to ask, "There was a man supposed to come fetch you before—a big man with a bushy beard—did he come here?"

"Was he a friend of yours? I should have known. He never got past my front gate. The sheriff arrested him, and took him to jail."

"Jail?" Matt asked, startled. "What for?"

"I don't know," Manning answered honestly. "When I came out to see what the fuss was about, your friend just said that he wanted to see me. Sheriff Baldwin said something about asking him some questions." He looked at Matt apologetically. "I think it was because he was dressed in animal skins like you."

"Where's the jailhouse?" Matt asked. When Manning told him, he said, "Much obliged," and picked Crooked Foot up from the couch.

"John?" Agnes Manning called out again when she heard the front door close and the bolt locked.

"I'm coming, Agnes." To himself, he muttered, "Wild men and wild times. It's a wonder any of us survive the day."

Still in a cheerful mood, and feeling a little more steady on his feet since he got some food in his belly, Sam Baldwin walked down the narrow side road to the jail. He carried a plate of beans and corn bread in one hand, and as he walked, he was thinking about the reward he was entitled to for capturing Ike Brister. *Not to mention the horse he was riding,* he thought. With ideas of his own for Ike's horse, he had purposely left it tied up by the jail instead of taking it to the stable. Now as he approached his office, he was surprised to see two additional horses tied up to the post beside Ike's and his own mare. One of them was pulling a travois. Curious, his attention was attracted to the horses, so he didn't notice the man standing in the shadows of the porch until he stepped up to the door.

"Damn!" Baldwin exclaimed. "You gave me a start. I didn't see you standin' there." He started to say more, but stopped short when he saw the Henry rifle pointing at him. Matt stepped into the light then, and Sam could guess at once that he was a friend of Ike's. "Now, wait a minute, mister, you don't wanna go makin' a big mistake here," Sam said.

"Open up," Matt replied.

"I brought your friend a plate of supper," Sam said, trying to sound as cordial as possible. "Hold it for me while I find my key."

Matt couldn't help but smile at the sheriff's feeble attempt. "Just set it down on the floor."

Sam did as he was told. "I just didn't want it to get no dirt in it," he muttered lamely. He worked the key in the padlock, and opened the door. Looking closely at Matt then, he asked, "You're the feller that shot that man in the doctor's office, ain't you?"

Matt didn't answer the question. He motioned toward the cell with his rifle. "Get him out of there."

"I figured it was just a matter of time," Ike said in way of greeting to his partner.

Sam hesitated. He knew he was going to take Ike's place in the cell, and was reluctant to do so. "I ain't got the key to the cells here. I left it home."

"It's in the desk drawer," Ike said. "What about Crooked Foot?"

"Dead," Matt replied, then frowning at Sam, he

warned the sheriff. "If you don't quit wastin' my time, I'm just gonna shoot you and be done with it."

From the look in Matt's eyes, Sam didn't doubt he meant what he said. He went to the desk, and pulled the drawer open. Matt could not see if there was anything else in the drawer or not, so to be safe, he brought his rifle up to his shoulder and took point-blank aim at the sheriff. It was more than enough to discourage any slight of hand by Sam if, indeed, there was a gun in the drawer.

"The boy went under?" Ike asked as he stepped out of the cell. Matt nodded. "I swear, that's a damn shame," Ike said, shaking his head sadly. "Maybe if I'da been able to get back with the doctor in time . . ." He didn't finish, knowing that things happened the way they were supposed to happen. Still, he needed some outlet for his frustration over the loss of the Cherokee boy. So he turned and administered a stout kick in the pants to the sheriff as Sam entered the cell.

"The doctor said Crooked Foot was too far gone to save, even if he had seen him earlier," Matt said.

"I reckon that's the way of things," Ike said, reconciling it in his mind. He reached down and locked the cell door, and held the key up for Sam to see. "Well, sheriff, if you have to leave before we get back, the key's in the desk drawer."

"There's a plate of supper outside the door," Sam replied. "How 'bout leavin' it here for me—there ain't no tellin' when somebody's gonna get me outta here."

"Why, shore," Ike said. "It's the least we can do to repay you for your hospitality."

Outside, they paused long enough to remove Crooked Foot's body from the travois. Then they dropped the travois poles, and tied the body across his pony's back. "It's a damn shame," Ike repeated when the body was secured.

Ready to depart Topeka for good and all, they stepped up in the saddle, and prepared to ride. "What about the plate of food?" Matt asked.

Ike grinned. "He said to leave it for him. We left it. You don't suppose he wanted us to slide it in the cell, do you?"

Chapter 17

They buried Crooked Foot under a walnut tree over-looking a winding turn in the river. The work was slow and tedious due to the lack of picks or shovels, most of it done with a short-handled mattock that Ike always carried on his saddle pack. They took turns digging and scooping until a suitable grave was exca-vated. Then the Cherokee boy was laid gently to rest, wrapped in his blanket, and the grave filled in. Ike laid some stones and a dead log across the grave to dis-courage predators, and that was that.

The burial complete, the two partners sat down beside the grave to decide what to do from that day forward. It was the end of the vengeance trail. They had done what they had set out to do. With the excep-tion of one man who had evidently ridden off on his own, they had run to ground every last member of the gang that had killed and plundered Old Bear's village. It was time for a new beginning—time to forget the sorrows of the past, and get on with the rest of their lives. There was a general sense of relief on Matt's part. His sorrow was not as great as Ike's. Ike had lost

his mate of many years, a woman he was truly de-
voted to, as well as a father-in-law and a boy who was
like a nephew to him. But Matt had developed a deep
fondness for the confident Cherokee boy in the short
time he had known him. He decided to keep Crooked
Foot's bow and quiver, determined to learn to use the
weapon, remembering the cartridges it had saved
them. Knowing the boy would want to be buried with
his weapons, they had laid the Springfield rifle in the
grave beside him. It was a difficult thing to do, because
it seemed too good a rifle to bury in the ground. There
was really no discussion about it, though. Neither man
wanted Crooked Foot's soul to enter the spirit world
without a weapon.

The two friends sat near the freshly dug grave for a
long time afterward, each man deep in his own
thoughts. Finally, Matt broached the subject on both
their minds. "Well, I reckon there's nothin' holdin' me
back from headin' to the big country," he said.
"There's a lot of land that I aim to see for myself."
There was another long pause while he waited for
Ike's response. When it did not come, he asked outright. "What are you aimin' to do? You goin' back to
the Cherokee Nation?"

"I've been studyin' on it," Ike drawled. He tilted his
head back and scratched thoughtfully under his bushy
gray beard. "There ain't nothin' to go back to in Old
Bear's village. Hell, I don't know if I could hack it with
Broken Reed gone." He pulled at his whiskers a moment more. "You'll most likely get lost, or freeze to
death if you start out across the high plains by yourself. And I'd hate to see that." Matt could see that the
grizzled old mountain man was hesitating to spit it

out, but he finally said it. "I expect I'd go along with you if you'd have me for a partner."

Matt's face broke out in a wide grin. "Why, hell, I thought we were already partners. I was hoping you'd wanna go with me."

His response brought an equally wide smile to the whiskered face of his friend. "Well, then, I reckon we'd best get started," Ike replied. "Tell you the truth, I was gettin' plumb stale holed up in that Cherokee village. Not that I'd take anything for the years I spent with Broken Reed," he quickly added. "We could follow the old Oregon Trail, but I expect it would be best to follow this river west, past the Big Blue, to the Republican. We can follow the Republican for a ways, then head straight north till we strike the Platte and the Oregon Trail again. I don't see why we can't make Fort Laramie before hard winter sets in."

Matt couldn't help but laugh. For someone who wasn't confident he would be invited along just moments before, Ike was quick to lay out a complete plan of travel. "Hell, let's get started then," Matt sang out, still chuckling at his oversized partner. With a final farewell to Crooked Foot, the two friends set out for new adventure in the vast untamed west, hoping to leave the label of *outlaw* behind them.

Every description of the plains Matt had heard in the past he soon discovered to be woefully inadequate. They rode from sunup to sunset with little change on the horizon, day after day. It seemed that when God was making the earth, He underestimated the number of trees He would need. And when He got around to shaping up the high plains, He discovered He had used up almost all of them in the hill country behind Him. The few that were left over, a handful of willows and cottonwoods, He had sprinkled along beside the banks of the creeks and streams, so the antelope and the buffalo could enjoy a little shade when they came in search of a drink.

Shade was not the issue, however, when Matt and Ike left the banks of the Republican, and headed due north. The days were already drawing up for winter, with chilly afternoons and cold nights. By the time they struck the Platte, and the old Oregon Trail, they had already seen the first snow flurry. Following the trail, another day's travel brought them to the settlement of Nebraska City and Fort Kearny. It was an uneasy army post on that cold afternoon in early October, for there had been several unconfirmed reports of Sioux raiding parties between Kearny and Fort Laramie. Fort Kearny had never been attacked by the Sioux, but the threat of trouble had been enough to cause the army to build a small stockade on the embankment of the river. Throughout the Indian wars that started some five years before, the fort had served as a major staging point for army troops, as well as a center for freighters traveling the Nebraska City Road, or the Oxbow Road, as Ike remembered it. The two travelers decided to stop over in Nebraska City for a few days to rest the horses, and maybe visit a saloon or two. As Ike so eloquently phrased it, "We owe it to them bastards we killed to take a drink in their honor, since it's their money that's buyin' the whiskey." Matt was not opposed to having a shot of whiskey, but he was more interested in finding a place to get something to eat other than wild game.

Jonah Batson glanced up to spot the two strangers when they were still fifty yards from the stable. He paused to lean on his pitchfork while he studied the pair. *Trappers or scouts, I expect,* he thought, judging by their animal-skin attire. He figured they might pass his establishment by on their way to the fort, but they continued to head straight for his stable. He propped the pitchfork against a stall and walked out to greet them. "How do," he said. "Lookin' to board them horses?"

"That's a fact," Ike answered, "if the price ain't too steep."

"Fifty cents a day with one portion of oats, paid in advance," Jonah said.

"How much do you charge for a man to sleep in the stall with his horse?"

"Same as the horse, fifty cents a day with no portion of oats."

"That seems a mite steep, don't it?" Ike complained. "Hell, all we're talkin' about is layin' down beside the horse."

"Hotel's half a block up the street," Jonah replied, unmoved. "It'll cost you more than fifty cents, though."

"We'll sleep with the horses," Matt chimed in. It was obvious to him that the man was not going to bargain with Ike.

"Still seems a mite steep to me," Ike mumbled, but dismounted and followed Jonah toward the back of the stable, leading his horse.

Matt paid for both of them, and pulled the saddle off the buckskin's back. "Where can we get a good supper?" he asked while he waited for Ike to unsaddle his horse.

"Well, you can get some supper in the saloon," Jonah answered. "But if you're talkin' 'bout home-style cookin', there's Libby's Kitchen, behind the hotel. That's where most of the teamsters eat."

Matt smiled. "That sounds like the place I'm lookin' for."

With the horses settled in, they walked out to look the town over. Considering the fact that the soldiers at the fort were uneasy about Sioux activity, no one in town appeared to give it any thought. "I expect I'm gonna need a shot before my supper," Ike said when they stopped in front of the saloon.

"You go ahead," Matt replied. "I think I wanna sample Miss Libby's cookin' while I'm sober. Maybe I'll join you later. If not, I'll see you back at the stable." He turned to leave, but then remembered the first time he met Ike. "Don't get in any card game. You're the worst poker player I've ever seen."

Ike grinned, not at all insulted by his friend's re-mark. "You just ain't ever seen me on a good night. I was drunk that night in Fort Smith."

Libby Donovan barely glanced up when the tall young man in buckskins opened the door and paused to look around the room. She had seen hundreds of roughshod men since she took over the hotel kitchen five years ago—trappers, soldiers, scouts, teamsters, saddle tramps. This one didn't look much different from the rest. Equally disinterested, most of the men gathered around the twelve-foot table wasted no more than a casual glance at the stranger, their attention fo-cused on the huge bowl of stew Libby was holding.

"Am I too late to get supper?" Matt asked.

"I reckon not," the belabored woman replied, brushing a wayward strand of hair from her face with the hand that held the serving spoon. A blob of stew dropped to the floor, and was immediately retrieved by a black-and-white mongrel dog that had been lying under the table. "Molly!" Libby yelled. "Bring out another plate." Turning back to Matt, she said, "Well, don't stand there with the door open. The food's gettin' cold. You can lay that rifle down on the table by the door."

"Yes, ma'am," Matt replied dutifully, and stepped inside. There was a table just inside the door where several weapons were parked. He propped the Henry carefully against the wall next to the table.

"Jake, slide over that way a little so's this feller can set down," Libby commanded. "Calvin there ain't gonna bite you. Are you, Calvin?"

The man called Calvin grinned and replied, "I don't know. If he gets his elbows in my way, I might."

"That would be a bite of some pretty rancid meat," one of the others remarked, causing the diners to laugh.

"Much obliged," Matt said to Jake as he wedged his wide shoulders in the gap created between the two men, and gave a brief nod to the others.

In a few minutes, a young girl came from the kitchen, carrying a plate, fork, and spoon. She gave the stranger a good looking over as she set them before him on the table. Matt barely noticed her. His eyes were following the bowl of stew in the older woman's hands, following its progress around the table toward him. Libby's portions were generous, and Matt feared that she might empty the bowl before she got to him.

She must have sensed it, because she sent Molly back to the kitchen to get another bowl. When she got to Matt, she said, "Don't fret, young feller, I ain't ever sent anybody away hungry."

She was as good as her word. Matt had never seen so much food in one place before. There was not a wide variety of dishes to be sure, but there were ample supplies of the few she served—stew, corn bread and biscuits, soup-beans, fried potatoes, and all the coffee you could drink. Like the other customers, Matt dug in with a vengeance. For a long period, until appetites had been sated, there was no talking beyond an occasional word, a grunt here, a belch there. After most bellies were tightened to discomfort, some casual conversation broke out around the table.

Matt sat back to finish his coffee and listen to the idle talk. His gaze shifted back and forth around the room until it settled for a moment on the young girl clearing the empty dishes from the table. She was looking at him, and did not look away when their eyes met. He smiled, causing her to blush and quickly avert her gaze.

"I ain't never seen you around here before," the man identified as Jake remarked.

Matt smiled. "I ain't ever been around here before," he replied.

"You figurin' on workin' for the army?" Jake asked. "From what I hear, the army's lookin' to hire more scouts."

"Hadn't figured on it," Matt said. "I don't know anything about this country out here. I'd be a poor scout right now."

"From what they say, a lot of the army's scouts

don't know much about this country. I reckon all they need to know is how to find their way back home and tell the soldiers if they see any Injuns."

A man across the table from them, who had been listening in on their conversation, joined in. "I hear they pay pretty good. Tell you the truth, I thought you looked like one of them army scouts when you walked in here—even thought you mighta been in the army."

There were beginning to be too many questions for his comfort, so Matt got up from the table. "I used to be in the army," he said, "but it was a different army." Turning to Libby, he said, "That was a mighty fine meal, ma'am. How much do I owe you?"

After he settled up with Libby, he picked up his rifle to leave. She followed him to the door. "If you're gonna be in town for a while," she said, "I serve breakfast and supper, six days a week."

"Yes, ma'am," he replied. "I expect you'll see me again." He glanced over her shoulder to discover Molly staring at him. Upon being discovered, she quickly turned and disappeared through the kitchen door. Outside, he breathed in deeply, embracing the cold night air. Then he went in search of Ike.

Ike was still in the saloon where the two had parted about an hour earlier. Much to Matt's relief, his huge partner had found a friendly game of cards and was only slightly drunk. When Matt walked in, Ike grinned wide, and introduced him to his friends. "Fellers, meet my partner, Shannon. He's come to make sure I get home all right." The three men all nodded and said howdy. Matt sat and watched for a while. It seemed like an honest game.

Later when they walked back to the stable, Ike

seemed content. He had a comfortable whiskey buzz on, and he had lost no more than five or ten dollars. And as he put it, "Where can you buy a better evening's pleasure for five dollars?" After settling down in the fresh hay Jonah had forked out for their beds, both men were leaning toward staying in Nebraska City for a few days more. Just before drifting off to sleep, Matt concentrated on the young girl at Libby's, trying to picture her face. No particular reason, he told himself. He was just curious.

Sheriff Sam Baldwin sat at the back corner table in the saloon with Boyd Jenkins across from him. It had been two days since Sam's deputy had come to work to find Lonnie Johnson's old hound dog cleaning up a plate of food on the front porch of the jail. The deputy usually unlocked the front door every morning and started a fire in the stove. But that morning he had been surprised to find the door unlocked. Inside, the sheriff was asleep on the rough bunk in a locked cell. The other cell was occupied by Lonnie Johnson, who had let himself in, being too drunk to find his way home. The deputy had laughingly told Boyd Jenkins that it was the first time the sheriff had slept off a drunk in the jailhouse, and one of the few times that Lonnie had enjoyed some company.

The incident was talked about in humorous conversation all over Topeka Landing, but not in the sheriff's presence. Sam was not prone to being the butt of any joke, and this incident was especially galling. On this day, having a drink with Boyd, Sam complained that there was nothing any man could have done to prevent Ike Brister's escape. "The son of a bitch had the drop on me," he explained, referring to Brister's partner. He tossed back the remains of his drink, and stared wistfully past Boyd, his mind on what might have been. "I had a five-hundred-dollar reward in my hands." His focus returned to the present then. "But a man don't argue with a Henry rifle aimed at him."

"You did as much as any man could, Sam," Boyd said in an attempt to placate the sheriff. "Well, I reckon I'd better get back to the stable." He prepared to get up from the table.

Sam's attention was distracted by someone at the door. "Who the hell's that?" he asked.

Boyd turned to see. "Don't know. I ain't ever seen him before."

Sam and Boyd were not the only ones noticing the man who stepped inside the saloon door, and stood surveying the room before entering. All conversation ceased for a moment as everyone gaped at the dark stranger. Dressed almost entirely in black, his shoulders protected from the afternoon chill by a wide black cloak that hung almost to the tops of his black leather boots, he stood motionless while deep-set eyes scanned the room from beneath heavy brows. A wide-brimmed, flat-crowned hat was pulled down to his eyebrows. His dark hair was shoulder-length and lay heavily upon his shoulders. He carried a Spencer carbine in one hand, and when he moved to approach the bar, he pushed the cloak back to reveal two revolvers worn in his belt, the butts of the handles forward.

"I swear," Boyd remarked quietly, "I believe the devil himself has come to call." Had he known more about Jesse Tyler, he would have realized how close to being accurate he was.

"What's your pleasure, mister?" The bartender asked.

"I'm lookin' for a man," Tyler replied. "He came this way—name's Shannon."

The bartender shook his head, then looked at a couple of other men standing at the bar. Like him, they shook their heads. "I don't recall meetin' anybody by that name," the bartender said.

Tyler scowled his displeasure. He had been tracking the man he knew as Shannon for weeks, and the trail had led to Topeka Landing. "Carries a fancy Henry rifle," he pressed. "He's riding with another man—a big man."

There was little doubt then. The bartender nodded vigorously. "You must be talkin' about the feller that walked right in Doc Manning's treatment room and shot some feller." The other men standing at the bar nodded in unison. "I don't rightly know what his name was, but the other'un, the big'un was locked up in the jail till that feller sprung 'im."

"Who was he?" Tyler demanded. "The man he shot, who was he?"

"I can't say, mister, didn't nobody know his name. Couple of the fellers toted him up to the cemetery and buried him. He weren't from around here. They said he was as bald as an onion, didn't look like he had no hair on him a'tall."

Eli! Tyler thought. The image of his former partner sprang immediately to mind. He gripped the Spencer tightly, the scowl deepening as he thought of Shannon leaving another dead man in his wake. One by one, Shannon had eliminated the entire gang that rode with Brance Burkett. Tyler had found Brance's body in a

gully north of Springfield—and now Eli here in this
town. His frustration had built to a blinding crusade to
kill this one man who tormented his soul so. Each mile
he trailed him intensified his hatred for the man who
had killed his brother. "Where is he now?" Tyler
demanded.

"Hell, mister, I told you. He busted his partner outta
jail and hightailed it." When the look on the stranger's
face hinted that he might hold him accountable for
Shannon's whereabouts, the bartender directed him
toward the table in the back corner. "There's the sheriff settin' over there. Maybe he can tell you more."

Tyler jerked his eyes over toward the table, squinting at the two men in the back corner. He had a natural aversion to lawmen in any form, but he wanted
Shannon, so he walked over to the table. Standing before them, he scowled at one and then the other, deciding which one was the sheriff, for neither wore a
badge. Baldwin broke the silence.

"I'm the sheriff here," Sam said. "What seems to be
the problem?"

"Shannon," Tyler replied. "I'm lookin' for him—
bartender says you let him bust his partner outta jail."

The comment caused Sam to redden a bit. "Was that
his name? I didn't have much choice," the sheriff
replied heatedly. "He got the drop on me with that repeatin' rifle."

"Which way did he go?" Tyler asked, unconcerned
with the sheriff's defense of his inability to hold his
prisoner.

"Who wants to know?" Sam responded, getting a
bit more hot under the collar from the stranger's tone.

Tyler didn't answer right away, his gaze like cold

steel as it locked onto Sam's. When he spoke, it came
as a growl. "Somebody who ain't got time to play
games with a two-bit lawman."

The two men glowered at each other for a long moment before Sam yielded, and shifted his gaze toward
Boyd, who was staring wide-eyed, waiting for Sam's
reaction. Just then aware of the deathly silence in the
previously noisy saloon, the sheriff realized that
everyone there was watching for his reaction. In an attempt to exhibit some authority, he started to get out of
his chair to face the sinister stranger.

"Set down," Tyler commanded softly, and brought
the Spencer up before him.

There was no bluff in the dark stranger's eyes. Sam
sank back down in the chair. He had faced some rough
and desperate men before—though not on many occa-
sions—but this was the first time he had ever faced
pure evil in its earthly form. He had no reason to believe the man would hesitate to shoot him, and his better judgment told him this was not the time to push his
luck. He tried to grin as he said, "There ain't no sense
in gettin' riled, is there?" Tyler continued to stare at
him. "It'd be a good thing if you did catch him. I got a
posse together, and we trailed him to the county line,
but they had too much of a start on us."

"Which way?" Tyler pressed impatiently.

"West," Sam sputtered. "They was following the
river. That's all I know. We had to turn back at the Big
Blue."

"When?" Tyler demanded.

"Three days ago," Sam replied.

Tyler paused to consider that. Three days. He was
getting closer to him. He could feel his blood heating

up. It was only a matter of time before the final reckoning. Satisfied then, he turned abruptly and walked toward the door, not willing to waste any more time.

Staring at the man's back, Sam could not resist making a move to save some of the respect he had no doubt lost as a result of his obvious backing down. He pushed his chair back, and drew his pistol as he stood up. "Now, mister, you can just hold up there a minute. I got a few questions I'd like to ask you."

Tyler stopped, and stood with his back toward Sam for a moment before slowly turning to face him. He didn't speak, but stood silently measuring his adversary. The gun in Sam's hand was trembling. Though slight, it did not go unnoticed by the sneering man in black as he made judgment upon the sheriff's courage.

"Drop the rifle," Sam ordered, his voice betraying a lack of conviction.

A thin smile appeared at the corners of Tyler's mouth, and the rifle dropped to the barroom floor with a loud clatter. Startled, Sam's eyes flicked toward the rifle, shifting back just in time to see a pistol come out from under the black cloak. The silence of the spell-bound saloon was shattered by three shots, two ripping into the sheriff's belly, the third from the sheriff's revolver, sending a slug into the floor. Tyler surveyed the spectators calmly before picking up his rifle, and unhurriedly taking his leave.

Chapter 18

Libby Donovan paused in the kitchen doorway for a moment, watching her daughter as the young girl slowly circled the table, stopping at each plate to dish out a heaping spoonful of corn pudding. *Poor Molly,* she thought, *not much of a life for a young girl.* It saddened her to know that her daughter had few prospects for a happy life, and she worried about what might become of the frail young girl if something should happen to her mother. It was a hard life for Molly. That fact in itself was not cause for despair. Most everyone Libby knew had a hard life. It was the fact that life was unfair when the cards were dealt, and every once in a while these thoughts came to trouble Libby's mind.

She had been a widow for twelve years now since God's hand had reached down to touch Robert Donovan in his prime. On stormy nights, even to this day, Libby imagined that she could still smell the faint sulfurous odor wafting up from the muddy ruts on the night lightning struck their wagon during the worst storm she had ever experienced. It had come upon them so suddenly that Libby sometimes felt that God had intentionally come for Robert. When the bolt struck the wagon, the flash of fire that jumped from the iron rim of the wheel was so bright that it blinded her for a few moments. When she could see again, Robert was lying dead in the mud beside the wagon, his skin burned black all over his body, the hair on his head singed off. He had been holding onto the wheel while he climbed down from the wagon carrying four-year-old Molly in his arms. When Libby looked around for the child, she found little Molly some yards away, still breathing, but unconscious.

In that horrible moment when God touched her life, Libby thought she had lost both husband and child. Little Molly lay sleeping for two days and three nights before she awakened, apparently without memory of the tragedy. She appeared to be normal except for one thing: the child never spoke another word from that day until this. And that was the in-equity of life, as Libby saw it. Molly was a bright and cheerful girl, though shy around other people. Because she was mute, most people assumed she was also slow-witted.

Libby could not help but sigh as she watched the girl serving her guests. She feared the day had arrived that she most dreaded. She had first noticed it when the tall young stranger in buckskins returned for breakfast the day before. And now it was even more obvious to her when Molly's eyes never left the young man as she ladled out the corn pudding on one plate after another. Libby felt the hurt that Molly was bound to experience.

Matt extracted his long legs from the bench, and

stood up, waiting for Ike to finish his last biscuit. When the big man finally called it quits, Matt retrieved his rifle from the table by the door, and stepped out on the porch. In a few moments, Ike followed him, and they stood filling their lungs with the crisp autumn air. "I could use a little shooter to settle my vittles," Ike announced.

"You go ahead," Matt said. "I want to check on my horse first. He was off his feed this mornin'. I'll catch up to you later." He knew Ike would most likely find a card game. There would be plenty of time to join him.

"All right, partner," Ike said cheerfully. "I'll save a snort for you."

Matt smiled as he watched the huge frame of his partner move toward the saloon up the street. There seemed to be an extra spring in the big man's step whenever he was headed toward a saloon and a card game. He breathed deep, taking in a lung full of the fresh air, then turned to leave the porch, almost running right over Libby. "Excuse me, ma'am!" Matt blurted. "I didn't hear you come out behind me."

She stood silent for a moment, still making up her mind to speak. The constant wisp of hair lay across her forehead, and the lantern light through the window traced shadows across her drawn face, making her look tired beyond her years. Matt wondered if she ever ate any of her own cooking, she was so thin.

"I heard the big fellow call you Matt," Libby finally broke her silence.

"Yes, ma'am," Matt replied. "My name's Matt Slaughter." Ike had slipped a couple of times since they had arrived in Nebraska City. Matt supposed it could do little harm. He doubted anyone was looking for him around these parts.

"You seem like a nice enough young man," Libby continued. "I saw you smile a couple of times at Molly, and I just hope you are as nice as you seem."

Her remarks served to confuse him, and he misunderstood her purpose. "Why, I'm sorry if I seemed too forward," he stammered. "I reckon I was just tryin' to be friendly. I assure you I don't have any notions about your daughter."

She smiled sadly then, confident that her first impression of the young man was the correct one. "I know you were just being friendly. I didn't mean to say you did anything wrong. You strike me as being a kind and sensible man, and I thought I could talk to you about Molly."

Still confused, Matt said, "Why, sure, ma'am, what do you want to tell me?"

Libby breathed a long sigh and began. "Molly's kind of special. She ain't been able to say a word since her and her daddy was struck by lightning twelve years ago. She can hear good enough. She just can't talk. So she's been pretty much right close to me all her life. She couldn't go to school, and she ain't ever had any friends—just worked with me in the kitchen ever since she was little."

Matt had suspected there was something unusual about the young girl, and now that he thought about it, he realized that she had never spoken when he greeted her. He had attributed it to shyness. "That's a real shame, ma'am. I'm truly sorry to hear it, but what does it have to do with me?"

"For whatever reason, she's taken a shine to you,"

Libby said. "I can tell. I can see it in the way she follows you around with her eyes."

"Oh, I don't think so," Matt stammered. "I doubt if she even—"

"There ain't no doubt about it," Libby interrupted. "I know her too well. And the reason I'm tellin' you about it is I don't wanna see her get hurt. She's like a child, and she could easily be hurt by a man that didn't care what he done." He started to assure her, but she interrupted again. "I'm tellin' you all this because I believe you're a decent man, and I'm hoping you'll do the right thing, and not take advantage of her."

Still astonished by the whole thing, Matt didn't know how to respond. After a few moments' silence, he sought to calm her fears. "Ma'am, I give you my word on it. I won't do anything to hurt your daughter. Me and my partner will be leavin' here in a day or two. You don't have to worry about me."

"I knew I had you figured right," Libby said, obviously relieved. "You have my thanks, for what it's worth." Having done all she felt she could do at that time to save her daughter's feelings, she abruptly turned and went back inside, leaving a bewildered and slightly amused young man.

He remained on the porch for a minute or two, digesting the rather unusual incident. He thought back, recalling the slight young girl's constant gaze upon him. At the time, he had thought nothing about it. Now, he shook his head and smiled, hardly believing the conversation that had just passed. *I don't know if I'll tell Ike about this or not*, he thought as he stepped off the porch and went in search of his friend.

*   *   *

Once he was sure he had picked up their trail, Tyler left Topeka Landing and pushed on westward, following the river. When he came to the Big Blue River, he saw the tracks where the posse had turned back and headed for home. Two sets of hoofprints continued on. He stayed doggedly on the trail until it led him to the Platte and the old Oregon Trail. From that point on, he would have to rely on luck and instinct, for it became impossible to distinguish one set of tracks from the many who had used the road.

Though it might take some searching, he knew he would find Shannon. *Shannon,* how the name burned in his thoughts, like a red-hot brand that seared his conscious mind. He had never seen the man he hunted, yet he felt he would know Shannon if he saw him. He had heard so many witnesses describe the tall, broad-shouldered man in buckskin clothes, carrying a Henry rifle, that he had formed a complete picture in his mind—complete except for the face. In his mental image, Shannon's face was blank. Every day that passed intensified Tyler's desire to look into that face, to study it, to know every feature, so that he would always remember it afterward. During the long hours in the saddle, he occupied his mind with the mental picture of Shannon's death by his hand. It sustained him through the cold October days, more so than food or drink.

Under cold gray clouds, Tyler rode into the settlement gathered close around Fort Kearny. With his heavy black cloak drawn up close around him, he presented a sinister image to the few people on the muddy street. The saloon being the logical place to inquire after the two men he searched for, he passed by the other stores and shops. As he slow-walked his horse by the hotel, something caught his eye that triggered his reactions. He immediately jerked his horse to a stop. Pulling hard on the reins, he backed the horse until he was abreast of three horses tied up before the hotel—a pack horse and two saddled horses. It was the buckskin gelding that had caught his attention. It looked a lot like the horse Eli used to brag about.

Tyler dismounted, and tied his horse at the rail. Then he proceeded to take a closer look at the buckskin. *By God*, he thought with grim excitement, *that's Eli's saddle all right*. A cruel smile touched his lips, and the muscles in his shoulders twitched in anticipation of the final reckoning.

"Ike tells me you're leavin'."

Matt looked up to see Libby standing behind him with the coffeepot. "Yes ma'am," he replied and held up his cup for a refill. "It's time we were on our way. We thought we'd get one more good meal under our belts before we go back to eatin' nothin' but wild game."

Libby glanced at Molly at the other end of the table. She thought she detected a faint look of despair in her daughter's eye, and figured she had overheard. She bent close to Matt's ear, and whispered. "I'm beholding to you for not taking advantage of an inexperienced young girl."

Matt was at a loss as to how he should respond. He still found it difficult to believe the depth of infatuation Molly had developed after such a short time. He was beginning to think that the whole situation was only in her mother's mind, and the daughter felt no emotion toward him beyond innocent curiosity. Not knowing what to say, he merely nodded his head, and smiled at Libby. She returned his smile, and moved on to the next customer. She had barely filled the cup when the door was suddenly flung open to reveal an ominous figure dressed almost entirely in black.

He stood there, the Spencer carbine in his hand, his heavy dark cloak pushed back on both sides to clear the two pistols he wore. For a long moment, there followed a void in the noisy conversation around the table as everyone there sensed an evil presence had invaded the room. Matt glanced over at Ike. Ike shook his head to indicate that he did not recognize the man. Figuring it had nothing to do with him, Matt turned his attention back to his plate. The dark stranger scanned the faces of the boarders seated at the table. His gaze stopped on Matt, then shifted to Ike, then settled back on Matt. Matt continued to eat, not realizing he had been singled out.

"If you're coming in here to eat," Libby told him, "you're gonna have to deposit them guns on the table there."

Tyler did not react beyond glancing at the weapons by the door. Then he looked back at Libby with eyes as dead as charcoal. "Move," he said. When she did not, he reached out and shoved her aside. Most of the men reacted then, seeing Libby almost lose her footing. "Set down," Tyler warned, training the Spencer on the breakfast table. There was little anyone could do, with all the weapons stacked up on the table by the door. "Shannon!" he called out, his eyes riveted upon Matt.

Ike tensed and started to get up, but Matt signaled

him to remain seated. He turned to face Tyler and the weapon aimed at him. "Are you lookin' for me?" he asked, his voice calm and even.

A smirk spread slowly across Tyler's face. "Yeah, I'm lookin' for you."

Matt waited, but Tyler offered no explanation, the smirk still in place. The man was obviously enjoying the moment. Matt became impatient. "Well, you found me. Now, what the hell do you want?" As he said it, the thought came to him that the man might be a bounty hunter. Then another thought struck him, maybe there *had* been one of Brance Burkett's gang that had never been accounted for after they left Old Bear's village. It was his guess now that this man was the one who was missing. With this thought, the situation took on new meaning—one with eminent danger. He was caught with no chance to defend himself against execution.

"Get up," Tyler ordered. Then to the others in the room, he warned, "Just set right where you are, and you won't get hurt. But one of you makes a move, and you'll get it before he does. That goes double for you, big boy." He directed the last remark at Ike. Turning back to Matt, who was now on his feet, he said, "Back up to that wall there." With no other choice, Matt did as he was told. "You don't know who I am, do you?" Tyler asked.

"No, I don't," Matt replied calmly. "Should I?"

Tyler was beginning to get a little irritated by his victim's apparent indifference to the danger he was in. After searching for so long for his brother's killer, he craved some show of fear. "My name's Tyler," he said. "I had a brother named Wesley, and you killed him back in West Virginia. It took me a while to find you, but I'da tracked you all the way to hell if I'd had to. Now, you son of a bitch, you're gonna pay for killin' my brother."

Tyler. So much had happened since Matt won the Henry rifle at that turkey shoot, that he had all but put the showdown with Tyler out of his mind. *So this is the way it's going to end,* Matt thought. *Well, I'm not going to make it easy for him.* "Your sorry brother bushwhacked me. He got what he deserved," Matt said, matter-of-factly. "And you'd better make your shot count, because I'm takin' you to hell with me."

"Is that so?" Tyler grinned, pleased with the prospect of Matt making a desperate effort to reach him before he was stopped cold.

The room was stifled by the heavy silence as the stunned spectators were afraid to breathe for fear of instant retaliation. One voice broke the silence. "You're gonna have to take us both," Ike stated soberly.

Tyler almost chuckled. "Let's see how fast you can move with a bullet in your brain," he replied to Ike.

Matt tensed, preparing to charge his adversary. Tyler, anticipating as much, took dead aim on Matt's forehead. The sharp crack of a rifle suddenly shattered the heavy silence. Stunned by the bullet that ripped through his cloak, just missing his side, Tyler spun around to see Molly holding Matt's rifle. Seething with anger, he raised his rifle to fire at the terrified girl, but Matt was upon him before he could pull the trigger. The two crashed to the floor, grappling for control of the Spencer. As they rolled over and over on the rough plank floor, Matt managed to get his hand on one of the revolvers Tyler wore. Snatching it free of the holster, he buried the muzzle against Tyler's stomach and pulled the trigger. Tyler was mortally wounded, his face twisted in pain, but—determined to kill Matt—he drew the other pistol from his belt. Before he could bring it to bear, Ike trapped his wrist in a viselike grip. He held him fast until the life drained from Tyler's body, and his sightless eyes stared into eternity. Ike, his body still pumping adrenaline at a gallop, lifted the lifeless form and flung it against the wall, then stood staring at it for a moment.

"Thanks, partner," Matt said calmly. "I reckon that's definitely the last one."

"You all right?" Ike said after a moment more when he began to calm down.

It occurred to Matt then that it mattered a great deal to Ike. "Yeah, I'm all right." He got up then and turned toward the corner and the table where Libby was holding Molly in her arms. The terrified young girl was still shivering with fright. Matt's rifle lay on the floor at her feet. He walked over to them. Libby, seeing Matt approach, released her daughter and stepped aside. Matt put his arm around the trembling girl. "That was a brave thing you did," he said. "You saved my life, and I'll never forget it." She looked up at him, then quickly averted her eyes again, her slender body pressing close against him. He held her for a moment longer before releasing her, wishing he could do something to repay her. "Here," he said, reaching up to remove the silver St. Christopher medal that he always wore. "I want you to have this. It's always taken good care of me. I hope it takes care of you." He glanced at Libby before putting it around the girl's neck. She smiled and nodded her approval, so he fastened the catch and smiled down into the young girl's face. The radiant face that returned his gaze required no words to convey the message in her eyes. Matt felt deeply touched, and he knew he would see that face in his mind long after he had departed Nebraska City.

The big gray metal coffeepot bubbled up to a boil on Libby's stove, and she folded a cloth to take hold of the hot handle. Dragging the heavy pot over to the corner of the stove where it would stay warm, she looked over at Molly and nodded. Molly didn't have to be told; she knew what Libby wanted. The girl took the cloth from her mother, and poured a large cup almost to the brim. Taking the cup then, she went through the door to the hotel on her way to the front desk.

"Ah, there's my girl," the desk clerk greeted her. "Good morning to you, darlin'."

Molly smiled and nodded. Mr. Glover always gave her a cordial greeting every morning when she brought his coffee. He was a nice old man, and it pleased her that he seemed to appreciate this small kindness so much. Turning to go back to the kitchen, she glanced out the front window of the hotel. The first rays of the morning sun broke through to reveal two early riders moving down the main street. Molly went to the window to watch them. Two figures in buckskins rocked easily in the saddle, the morning sun at their backs. She reached up to feel the silver medal attached to the chain around her neck. She rubbed it softly between her fingers as her gaze lingered on the younger of the two riders. A tear threatened as she followed him with her eyes, and she knew that someday, somehow, she must see him again. It seemed impossible that someone could touch her heart so fatally, then ride out of her life forever. She glanced quickly back at the desk to make sure Mr. Glover was not watching. Then she brought the medal to her lips and kissed it. *Matt Slaughter: the name shall forever dwell in my heart.* She drew her shoulders back, turned and went back to help her mother start breakfast.

Read on for a preview of the next Western
adventure featuring Matt Slaughter

THE HOSTILE TRAIL

by Charles G. West

Ike Brister took a cautious step forward in the knee-deep snow, his gaze unwavering as he watched for the first indication that the confused bull elk was about to charge. His rifle ready, he hoped he wouldn't have to use it. The elk eyed him suspiciously, tossing his head back and forth and pawing the snow in warning. Moving deliberately, Ike took one more step and stopped. He was as close to the huge animal as he dared. He glanced toward the clump of pines on the slope to his left. *Hurry up, dammit,* he thought. *This son of a bitch is fixing to jump into my lap.* The agitated bull elk had exhausted his patience with the strange creature seeming to challenge him. He lowered his head and shook his huge antlers back and forth violently as he pawed the snow. Ike raised his rifle and aimed at the massive head, just in case the elk was preparing to charge. He waited, his finger on the trigger. A figure rose silently in the pines, and a second later, the elk bolted sideways, an arrow imbedded deep in his lung. Enraged and confused, the bull tried to sidestep away from the pain in his side, only to feel the lethal sting of a second

arrow a few inches from the first. Ike kept his rifle
sighted on the crazed animal in case it still had a notion
to charge him. A bull elk sometimes took a little time
dying, and he might take a notion to take Ike with him.
If at all possible, Ike wanted to avoid firing his rifle in
this part of the mountains. The shot would echo
through the canyons for miles and might bring a Sioux
hunting party down on them. There had been several
Sioux hunting parties working this side of the
Bighorns within the past week.

Much to Ike's relief, the elk did not charge. Confused,
it tried to retreat, bounding up the slope, still trying to
sidestep away from the pain in its side. But before reaching the top, its legs became wobbly, and it went down on
its knees in the snow. There it remained, waiting for the
two white men to finish the kill.

"What in hell was you waitin' for?" Ike asked when
he caught up to his younger friend. "I thought me and
that damn elk was fixin' to have us a dance."

Already preparing to skin his kill, Matt Slaughter
grinned up at his friend. "I'd have paid money to see
that," he teased. "Seein' as how you two are about the
same size, you'da made a handsome couple."

"Huh," the big man snorted. "Next time you can be
the bait, and I'll do the killin'." They both knew that
was just idle talk, because Ike couldn't hit the side of a
barn with a bow. Ike would say that he had just never
had any use for a bow as long as he had his Spencer
rifle. Although he would never mention it, Matt knew
there were other reasons—reasons that Ike didn't care
to acknowledge. Sometimes a man aged faster when
forced to live by his wits most of his life. Lately, Matt
could see signs of his partner's aging—a hand not as

steady as before, an eye that was not as keen as when he was a young man. Still, the old man was not quite ready to return to the settlements just yet. And before he reached that stage, Matt promised himself that he would take care of him.

As far as the bow was concerned, Matt took to it like he was born with one in his hand. This particular bow was special. It held sentimental value for both men. It had belonged to a young Cherokee boy who had been killed only a few months before by a white bush-whacker. Crooked Foot had been held in high regard by Matt and Ike, and Matt had kept the boy's bow. He had spent a good deal of time practicing with the weapon, and it had proven to be time well spent. Making a winter camp in the Bighorn Mountains, the two partners found the bow essential. It was not only a silent weapon, it saved on the consumption of precious .44 cartridges.

The need for silence and secrecy was especially important now that there had been an increase in Indian activity between the Bighorns and South Pass. It was a dangerous time for two lone white men in the Powder River country, even in the dead of winter. The Sioux and Cheyenne had raided all summer along the Bozeman Trail, attacking any parties traveling that route to the Montana gold fields. It had not helped matters when the army built Fort Reno on the Powder River just that past August. The fort, originally called Camp Connor, had not been garrisoned as yet, but Chief High Backbone and Red Cloud knew there would be soldiers there soon. It was fairly obvious to the Sioux leaders that the purpose of the fort was to protect travelers on the Bozeman Trail.

At the beginning of winter, the partners had planned to wait out the cold weather at Fort Laramie. After a couple of idle weeks, however, they decided there was nothing of any nature for them to do for employment. The army would not be hiring any more scouts until spring. And it was painfully obvious that what cash they had would soon disappear if they spent their days hanging around the post trader's store. At the beginning of their third week at Fort Laramie, Ike announced, "Hell, I'd rather head for the hills and live like an Injun than set around here till spring."

Matt wasn't sure the bushy-faced old trapper was serious, but the idea suited him just fine. He wasn't comfortable in crowded places, and Fort Laramie was beginning to close in on him. Ike's remark was all it took. They set out for the Powder River country the next day. Even a blizzard on the second day out failed to dull their determination as they made their way northwest with the Laramie Mountains to the west of their trail.

After seemingly endless travel from one snowy camp to another, they found themselves in the Bighorn Mountains, and decided to make their base camp there. In a narrow canyon, protected from the winter winds by steep rocky walls, they built a shelter for the horses, using young pine trees. Game was not that plentiful where they made their camp, but they agreed that it was better to ride some distance from their base to hunt so as not to draw any curious Sioux. Firewood was also a problem. The canyon was convenient to abundant pine, but green pine burned with far too much smoke, causing them to travel considerable distances to find suitable wood for the fire. If they had allowed themselves to consider the difficulty of their situation and the hardship it created, they might have headed back to the settlement.

"I'da heap druther you was a nice young cow," Ike commented to the elk as he worked to force his knife through the tough flesh. "This ol' boy was gettin' on in years. I'll bet he was as old as I am."

"I hope to hell he'll be better eatin' than you'd be," Matt teased as he packed snow into the chest cavity to soak up the blood. They had been so long without fresh meat that they did not have the luxury of being picky. Old and tough, this elk was the first game they had found in almost a week. And to make matters worse, they had come across recent sign of Indian hunting parties close to their camp. Sioux or Cheyenne, they couldn't tell which, but as Ike had commented, two white men in their country were not welcomed by either tribe.

"I reckon the Great Spirit took pity on us, and sent this old bull wanderin' up here before we got so hungry we started eyeballin' each other," Ike said with a chuckle. "He musta got run off by some younger bull and lost his ladies." He sat back on his heels, and threw off his bearskin robe to give himself more room to work. "Well, it was just a matter of time before he got took down by a pack of wolves. He'll serve a better purpose feedin' the likes of us." Ike rambled on as he worked steadily away at quartering the elk until he realized that Matt wasn't listening. He looked up to see his partner signaling him to be silent.

Matt listened for a few moments, his ear turned to the wind. He turned then to look at the horses. His buckskin's ears were twitching, and a moment later Ike's horse neighed softly. "Best get that meat loaded on the horses," he called back over his shoulder as he got to his feet and scrambled up to the top of the ridge.

Detecting a sense of urgency in his partner's tone, Ike dropped his skinning knife on the elk hide beside the half-butchered carcass, and hurried after Matt. "Damn," he exclaimed softly as he flattened himself beside him in the snow. They were still over a half a mile away in the valley below the two white men. Riding single file in the narrow gulch, a hunting party of a dozen Sioux made their way at a leisurely pace toward the ridge. "We ain't cut meat in a week, and when we finally find one ol' tough elk, along comes a huntin' party," Ike complained.

"I don't know if they've been trackin' the same elk," Matt said, "but if they have, he's gonna lead them right to us when they reach the snow line." A couple hundred yards more and the hunting party would reach the snow line, and a clear trail with not only the elk's tracks, but also those of three horses. It would lead them right up the slope. "I expect we'd better get busy," Matt said, his voice devoid of any sign of excitement.

They withdrew from the crest of the ridge, and wasted no time getting back to the business at hand. The safest action would be to flee immediately, but neither Matt nor Ike had any intention of leaving the entire supply of fresh meat to the Indians. Working feverishly over the carcass, both men chopped at the bones and sliced the flesh into quarters. While Ike started loading the meat on the pack horse, Matt ran back up to the top of the ridge to check on the progress of the hunting party. There was no time to linger. The Indians were already closer than he had anticipated, and had just discovered the tracks in the snow. He could hear bits of excited words carried on the wind as the Lakota hunters talked among themselves. Matt didn't wait any longer.

"Tie down what you've got!" he sang out as he hurried down the hill. "We don't have time to take the rest." Ike did as he was told, and Matt grabbed one of the remaining sections of meat and tied it with the loose end of a strap while the big man ran for his horse. The pack secure, Matt stepped up in the saddle and held the buckskin back while he grabbed the pack horse's lead rope. Ike, his huge bulk plowing through the knee-deep snow like a buffalo bull, took a giant leap for the saddle, only to miss the stirrup with his foot. The resulting collision between man and horse caused the bay to sidestep and kick its hind legs in the air.

"Damn you!" Ike roared. "Hold still!" The bay, however, was leery of further contact with the big trapper, and continued to pull away until Matt drove the buckskin up to block it. "Damn fool horse," Ike grumbled as he stuck his foot in the stirrup, embarrassed even in the face of imminent danger. It didn't help when he looked up to see Matt's wide grin. "Let's get the hell outta here," he said, and gave the bay a sharp kick with his heels. Matt followed, and the two white men charged down the slope, driving their horses as hard as they dared through the snow.

Ready to find
your next great read?

Let us help.

Visit prh.com/nextread

Penguin
Random
House